THE RISING OF 12 THE SHIELD HERO

Aneko Yusagi

Table of Contents

Prologue: The Shield Hero's Morning............................6

Chapter One: Instant Awakening....................................22

Chapter Two: The Alchemist...31

Chapter Three: Filolials and Dragons.............................58

Chapter Four: Stardust Blade.......................................93

Chapter Five: Knock and Run......................................106

Chapter Six: Level Drain..119

Chapter Seven: Plagued Earth.....................................145

Chapter Eight: Demon Dragon.....................................169

Chapter Nine: Forced Power-Up...................................187

Chapter Ten: Purification...217

Chapter Eleven: Perfect Hidden Justice.........................234

Chapter Twelve: Justice vs. Justice..............................251

Chapter Thirteen: Atonement......................................292

Chapter Fourteen: Secret Base....................................307

Chapter Fifteen: Form is Emptiness..............................338

Prologue: The Shield Hero's Morning

This is out of left field, but my mornings usually started early. I was up and out of bed before the slaves even woke up. Well, maybe not when I'd been up all night compounding medicines or taking care of odds and ends, but still . . .

My name is Naofumi Iwatani. I was originally a university student in present-day Japan. One day I was in the library reading some book called *The Records of the Four Holy Weapons*, and that's when I had the misfortune to be summoned to another world to serve as the Shield Hero. A phenomenon they called "waves" threatened to destroy the world I was summoned to. I found out later that the phenomenon was a result of separate worlds beginning to fuse together, and my mission as a hero was to stop that from happening.

In the beginning, the thought of being summoned to another world was like a dream come true. But then I got caught up in an awful conspiracy, which ended up with me being framed and thrown out on the streets without a penny to my name. That's probably why I developed a warped personality—a distrust of others so severe that even I recognized it was absurd. But I did eventually manage to expose the conspiracy and have those who orchestrated it held responsible, so it's gotten somewhat better.

After that, it was just one incident after another. I tried establishing friendly relations with the other heroes and failed, and then there was the whole Spirit Tortoise mess. But resolving the Spirit Tortoise ordeal ended up buying us a big chunk of time before the arrival of the next wave. I've been using that extra time to build my own private army to face the waves. That was an idea I got from observing Kizuna Kazayama and her companions. They were heroes from another world we visited while dealing with the Spirit Tortoise mess.

In order to do that, I started rebuilding the village that Raphtalia was from. Raphtalia was my most trusted companion, and I was kind of like a surrogate father to her. Her fellow villagers had ended up becoming slaves, but we brought them back to the village and began training them. Of course, that came with its own set of problems too. But we had taken care of those for the most part, and the reconstruction of the village had been going smoothly.

"Now then . . ."

It was still dim out, but . . . I looked out the window at the rising sun.

"Ho! Ha! To!"

Ren was diligently practicing swinging his sword. Oh yeah, I'd almost forgotten that he was already staying here in the village.

Ren was the Sword Hero, and he had been summoned

from a different Japan. One with VRMMOs, a technology that let people travel into online worlds. When we were first summoned here, he had been preoccupied with projecting an image of imperturbable "cool." But now he was showing a sincere willingness to take things more seriously. I probably would have gone and given him an earful if he'd still been in bed, but it seemed like he was serious when he mentioned having a change of heart the other day. I headed outside to talk with him.

"Already training this early?"

"Oh hey, Naofumi. Morning. Yeah, I'm going to do what it takes to get stronger."

There were four holy heroes, including myself. I managed to get the other three to safety after they were defeated by the Spirit Tortoise, but then they ran off and disappeared.

I'd initially tried to take the Spear Hero—Motoyasu—into custody, with the cooperation of his former companion Elena, but that ended in failure. Afterward, on the way back to the village, I ran into Ren and tried to take him into custody, but . . . he fled too, after being seduced by Witch's sly tongue. Witch was the root of all evil and the one who had originally framed me. On the upside, Motoyasu agreed to come with me after having finally realized the true nature of Witch.

That was all well and good, but then Filo tried to cheer up Motoyasu, since he'd gotten depressed. As a result, Motoyasu started acting really strange and ultimately ended up stalking Filo. Even just thinking about what had happened made me start to feel confused. Just suffice it to say that Motoyasu had gone a bit bonkers. After that, we used my portal to run from Motoyasu and returned to the village safely.

I enjoyed a string of mostly problem-free days for a short period afterward, but then some bandits started stirring up trouble in my territory. Naturally, I headed out to suppress them, but it turned out to be complicated. Ren had been deceived by Witch, consumed by a curse, and was wreaking havoc as the bandit boss. After that (I really just wanted to forget this part), I ended up using Motoyasu, who like Ren was off-kilter, to lure him out for Filo and me.

At first, Ren seemed intent on resisting. I started to think that taking him into custody wasn't going to be possible, but Eclair managed to successfully get through to him via a dialog of swords. After that, Ren embraced his newfound mission to save the world and has been training under her guidance, while staying in my territory.

The only thing was, Motoyasu ended up getting away again. As far as I could tell, he had managed to implement the power-up methods that I'd told him about, so I wanted to think he'd be fine to some degree. But I was sure that our coming battles were only going to get tougher.

With that in mind, I figured I should learn the Hengen

Muso style that had given Eclair the skill to defeat Ren. I decided to study under the master that had taught her. The master was an old lady who had recovered from a grave illness and ended up becoming exceedingly feisty after I administered her medicine while out peddling my wares. The old lady told me she had the perfect training method for me, so I was training separately from Ren and the others.

"You're using a different training method than me and Eclair, aren't you?"

"Yeah."

"You do your best too, Naofumi."

"Why the hell do I have to do my best? And why me too? Never mind. Sorry."

When I was trying to capture Ren, he used skills from the greed curse series. It required him to pay a price. The price for greed was decreased luck and an inability to amass any kind of wealth. That apparently included equipment, and the cheap armor that he had been wearing was ragged and completely unusable.

The consequences for me using Blood Sacrifice had included suffering a massive amount of damage and reduced stats. Similarly, Ren was suffering from his own set of consequences and persistent curse effects. I was pretty sure the price he had to pay for using the Gold Rebellion curse skill was the forfeiture of his riches. The persistent curse effects caused a reduction in quality of anything he touched, and also reduced the quality of any drop items he obtained. I'd finally managed to capture Ren, but he'd joined the team at a time when he was in a really problematic condition.

It became clear right away what the consequence was for the gluttony curse that surfaced while Ren was fighting Eclair. He had apparently been level 95 before losing to Eclair, but that had now dropped down to 85. So the price for triggering the curse had been his levels, or so it seemed. Even though he seemed to want to help out now, I'd have to think long and hard about letting him fight in the condition he was in.

"Later, then."

"Later."

Ren returned to swinging his sword. I waved to him and walked away. After that, I dropped by the monster stable. I grabbed the feed bucket and began feeding the monsters. Then I got in a bit of light exercise with them. I played with them, in other words. The village slaves were in charge of looking after the monsters, but I took it upon myself to tend to them in the mornings.

"Alright then, you guys. What should we do this fine morning?"

The monsters all cried out excitedly in unison. Sometimes I would throw a stick and have them fetch it, and other times we'd chase each other around, kind of like playing tag.

The slaves also looked forward to participating in these games. They woke up early so that they could get ready and be waiting by the time we started. Of course, that only included slaves or monsters that weren't out hawking our wares. The earthworm-looking monsters, called dunes, were in charge of working the land, so they got to join in every time. The dunes got along really well with the lumo slaves.

"Bark! Bark! Again, bubba!"

Keel came running back with the stick I'd just thrown hanging out of her mouth. Yeah, she was pretty much just a dog now. Literally.

Keel had originally been a demi-human slave that lost her parents just like Raphtalia. She'd apparently shown potential for being able to use a therianthrope form, so Sadeena taught her how. Now she spent most of her time running around in therianthrope form—an animal form, basically. Hers looked like a Siberian Husky pup. But recently, I couldn't help but feel like Keel was quickly turning into an actual dog.

Other than that, I made breakfast when I felt like it. All of the prep had already been taken care of today, so I just helped the cooking division slaves do the cooking, and then I served the villagers.

That reminded me. We had some new slave children in the village. One of the slave trader's assistants stopped by while I was out and dropped off some slaves. They weren't originally from this village, but I had a serious lack of manpower, considering what was coming. We'd established a basic framework for how things operated in the village and development had really started to take off. Now was the time to start thinking about beefing up our offensive capabilities in preparation for the coming waves, so I needed to gather up more heads without being too picky.

After applying their slave curses, I left it up to Keel and the others to deal with the new slaves. I didn't need to manage them directly anymore. The veteran slaves would see to it that they learned all of the rules and whatnot. Raphtalia was in command. Keel and the first round of slaves I'd overseen assisted her. They took care of pretty much everything, including the scolding, which made things a lot easier on me.

"Good morning, Mr. Naofumi."

"Rafu!"

"Oh hey, Raphtalia and Raph-chan! Morning."

Raphtalia had brought the slaves to eat breakfast. Raphtalia was my trusted sidekick. She had originally been a slave, but she became a hero after being chosen by the katana vassal weapon in another world. She was the first person to believe in me in this world. I was like a surrogate father to her. Whenever I made mistakes, she was always careful to point them out. It was just how you'd expect a parent and child to act.

"Rafu!"

Raph-chan was a shikigami, or what they called a familiar

in this world. I'd made her from a lock of Raphtalia's hair when preparing to search for Raphtalia after she'd gone missing in another world. Raph-chan was a cute little thing that looked kind of like a tanuki or a racoon. She was really good about playing along with the situation. I enjoyed doting on her, but Raphtalia always got upset if I gave her too much attention. Raphtalia said it made her feel awkward, for whatever reason.

"Good morning, Mr. Naofumi."

Atla came strolling up. I'd purchased some new slaves recently in Zeltoble, and one of those was Atla's older brother. The brother had been the actual product, and his sickly younger sister, Atla, basically got thrown in as part of the package—a bonus, I guess you could say.

The siblings were demi-humans, like Raphtalia. Specifically, they were a type of demi-human called hakuko. Hakuko were supposed to be one of the highest-ranking types of demi-humans. They were pretty much famous in Siltvelt, which was the country that worshipped the Shield Hero.

Despite being one of those hakuko demi-humans, Atla had been suffering from a congenital disease and was basically on the verge of death. But when I gave her some of the Elixir of Yggdrasil that I'd gotten hold of, her condition began to improve instantly. Before long, she was walking for the first time in her life.

She'd been covered in sores and wrapped in bandages

from head to toe, but the medicine took care of the sores too. Now she was one of the village's most beautiful, young girls. She'd been blind, unable to walk, and on the verge of death, yet she managed to make a near-complete recovery. It was truly impressive.

"Oh hey, Atla. Where's Sadeena?"

Sadeena was a killer whale woman with a penchant for drinking. She had the ability to transform, and she usually ran around in her therianthrope form. She played the role of the dependable big sister to the village children. She also had tons of combat experience, and we really struggled when we fought against her in the coliseum tournament.

Sadeena apparently had a thing for men that could outdrink her. Since I was physically unable to get drunk, she sexually harassed me every chance she got. Atla and Sadeena both liked me, so they tended to hang around together a lot.

"I haven't the slightest idea. Come now, Brother. Let go of my hand. Off you go to find Sadeena."

"No, Atla! If I let go of your hand, you'll just run to him, right?!"

That was Fohl holding on to Atla's hand to make sure she didn't come to me. Fohl was Atla's big brother. He was the reason I'd originally bought the siblings, seeing as how I'd needed offensive capabilities. He had a sister complex and the spirit of the Alps . . . No, never mind that. His little sister meant everything to him, but he was completely at her mercy too. He was one of the older slaves in the village.

"Brother, take a look at the sky over there."

"Huh?"

Out of nowhere, Atla used a completely hackneyed line to divert Fohl's attention. Immediately after, she jabbed her finger into her big brother's stomach.

"Aiya!"

"Guh!"

Taken by surprise, Fohl hugged his stomach tightly and fell over, writhing in agony. Between the two of them, it seemed like Atla actually had the most combat potential. I was pretty sure that wasn't just my imagination. According to the old Hengen Muso lady, being blind made Atla more sensitive to things like the surrounding life forces, flows of magic, and sounds, which gave her the ability to identify opponents' weak spots precisely. As a result, she had become a poking specialist.

"I'm still . . . not going to let go!"

"Don't be so stubborn, Brother!"

They were a strange pair of siblings in more ways than one.

"You two, stop messing around. Finish eating and get out of here. Atla, sparring isn't until after you've finished breakfast."

"I'm looking forward to it!"

"Yeah, good for you. Fohl, you better get out there and start leveling. Otherwise, your little sister is going to pass you up."

"Ugh . . . I know that!"

Fohl glared at me and nodded.

Just recently, the two of them—well, just Fohl actually—had been affected by a skill Motoyasu used and started attacking Atla. The scene was still fresh in my mind. I say "attack," but he was really just hugging her and wouldn't let go. Either way, it was clear that Fohl's feelings for Atla went beyond brotherly love.

". . ."

And then there was Filo. She had run off to play with Melty and still hadn't returned. Filo had become my second ever companion, after Raphtalia. She was a bird-type monster called a filolial that could also transform into a human. In her human form, she was a young girl with blonde hair, blue eyes, and a pair of wings on her back.

Filolials loved nothing more than pulling carriages, and they exhibited a special type of development when raised by a hero. Filo had great fighting instincts, and she'd helped me make it out of tight spots time and time again. She had a childlike innocence and an insatiable appetite.

Filo tried to cheer up Motoyasu not too long ago and ended up becoming the sole target of his romantic pursuits. As if that weren't bad enough, she'd also had her precious carriage stolen away from her, so she was a bit on edge lately.

"Alright, everyone, once you finish eating, get started on

your tasks for the day. That will be all."

As I was giving my orders, a single sleepy-eyed girl came strolling up along with her two . . . companions.

"N————"

Her name was S'yne. She was a vassal weapon holder who wasn't from this world or even Glass's world. Her vassal weapon was a sewing kit, or something like that. She fought with scissors and a ball of thread. And for whatever reason, I'd ended up looking after her here in the village.

She had silver hair and appeared to be around 15 years old at first glance. She was on the short side. I guess she probably would have been considered cute, but I didn't really look at her that way. Her home world had been destroyed, and now the people who had destroyed it were here in this world, trying to kill the holy heroes. She was basically acting like my bodyguard now.

"Good morning, Mr. Iwatani."

One of the stuffed dolls that S'yne had with her spoke on her behalf. I wondered if the reason S'yne looked so tired was because she'd been up all night making the doll. Apparently, she could use stuffed dolls as familiars.

Perhaps it was because sewing was her specialty, but there were some real issues with the designs of the stuffed dolls she made. First of all, for whatever insane reason, she had made a stuffed doll that looked like Raph-chan and gave it the ability to talk. Raph-chan squeaking "rafu!"—and nothing else—is exactly what made her so cute. When the stuffed doll started speaking human language fluidly, it immediately lost half of its allure. S'yne made it stop talking when I pointed that out, and now it's sitting on my bed beside my pillow.

The newly designed stuffed doll was based on Keel's therianthrope form. I'd call it Keel #2 for now.

"Good mo————"

The translation functionality of the vassal weapon that S'yne was using was damaged as a result of her world having been destroyed. Half of what she said just ended up turning into static.

"Morning. You know, your stuffed doll sure is speaking a lot more clearly now," I said.

"Please, allow me to explain."

The Keel #2 stuffed doll responded and pointed at an accessory hanging off of its collar.

"This accessory has the ability to translate. My master used it on me after taking it off of the dead body of her arch-enemy's companion, who you defeated."

Like I mentioned earlier, there were invaders from another world who were trying to kill the four holy heroes. Just recently, a couple of them had attacked us. They apparently got all kinds of benefits from destroying other worlds, and they had no interest in settling things amicably, like we had done with Glass and Kizuna.

Those benefits included what was usually referred to as "resurrection" in games. They had the ability to return from the dead. The enemies had been quite skilled at combat, as well, and it had been a tough battle. Luckily for us, the circumstances at the time had prevented them from resurrecting long enough for us to finish them off for good.

So the equipment was something that S'yne had scavenged off of the corpse of one of those enemies.

"That's probably something we should be trying to study," I said.

"You can have it, if that's what you would like."

It's not like I wanted to monopolize the technology, but I wouldn't be able to communicate effectively with S'yne without it. If the familiar used it to act as an intermediary like this, it would make talking with S'yne a lot easier. And we were still focused on analyzing the accessories we had gotten in Kizuna's world. I'm sure it would have been convenient if we figured out how the translation functionality worked, of course. But my shield already translated for me, so the only person that really needed the technology was S'yne. Studying it would be low on the list of priorities.

"I'll ask for it when I need it, so just hold on to it until then."

"Understood. I will continue using it, in that case."

"Can S'yne not use it directly?"

"Her vassal weapon interferes with it. We're lucky that I can even use it."

Ugh . . . So S'yne couldn't use the technology herself. It certainly seemed convenient, but I guess it wasn't so easy to exploit. I probably wouldn't be able to use it either.

"I see. Oh well. Are you going to eat, S'yne?"

S'yne responded with a quick nod and held her plate out. I put some food on her plate and she sat down at a table and started eating in silence.

Things were never boring in the village.

Chapter One: Instant Awakening

Once they finished eating, the slaves each got started on their own tasks for the day. Some of them trained, others were getting started studying magic, a number of them headed out to hawk our goods, and others helped with the reconstruction.

My work varied from day to day too, but I was supposed to spar with Atla after finishing breakfast. Fohl had gone out to hunt and level up. Atla had been on guard duty, but Raphtalia was filling in for her. As for why I was sparring with Atla, well, it was complicated. It all started when I called the old Hengen Muso lady to the village to talk.

"Hey, old lady. I want to start training too," I told the old lady.

Rishia and Eclair had been making clear progress, so I figured I needed to get serious about training too. I asked for the old lady's help. Starting a conversation by calling someone "old lady" like that probably sounded pretty rude, but that had become her nickname, so that's just the way it was.

"Duly noted. However, you can't start training until you learn how to sense life force."

"Hmm . . . I thought that might be the case."

"I'm starting to get a feeling for it," Raphtalia interjected.

"Oh? It seems you're starting to understand, young grasshopper," replied the old lady.

The old lady looked at Raphtalia and seemed to be able to verify her claim.

"In that case, I'll have you work on something a bit more difficult later, young grasshopper!"

"Am I supposed to do more sitting meditation in the mountains, then? Or is my only option to use life force water or something?" I asked.

I was fully aware that there were no shortcuts and I would need to put in the work, but still, it had just been one problem after another lately. I wanted to learn the style quickly. But I guess that was just wishful thinking.

"Well, it's a slightly rough approach, but I do have a method in mind that might work well for you, Saint," the old lady replied.

"Then spit it out already. I don't mind if I have to suffer a bit."

Getting stronger quickly was all that really mattered.

"There is someone that can see life force even better than I. If you were to spar with this person, then I am sure you would be able to get a feeling for it as well, Saint."

"Oh yeah, I heard you had said something about Atla having an aptitude for the art."

Eclair had mentioned the old lady saying Atla didn't even need to study the style.

"That's right."

Fohl was standing there with us. The old lady looked at him, and he cautiously looked at Atla.

"Huh? What is it?" Atla asked.

"I believe that sparring with this girl will help you understand life force, Saint."

"Well, she did seem stronger than Fohl last time we went out hunting," I said.

"Say what?! It goes without saying that I'm stronger than her!" Fohl cried out.

"Brother, please refrain from belittling me in front of Mr. Naofumi."

Atla poked Fohl in the side sharply.

"Guh!"

Fohl nearly fell over backward when she did.

"Ugh . . ."

"There you have it, Fohl. Right now, you're weaker than Atla. If you want to redeem yourself, go train with this old lady here," I told him.

"Brother, thank you for everything you've done for me."

After everything Fohl had done to help raise Atla, I couldn't believe she was content with expressing her gratitude in nothing more than a few words.

"A . . . Atla?! Ugh . . . Fine! I'll get stronger, no matter what!"

His determination to grow stronger was evident in his expression. Atla was spurring his growth. In that sense, I guess her attitude actually wasn't all that bad.

"And I will train with Mr. Naofumi!"

Atla wrapped her arm around mine. I didn't really like the idea of her hanging on me, but if she was going to be my sparring partner, then I guess I would have to give her a little leeway.

"That settles that. Raphtalia, you go ahead and go with the old lady to—"

"No, thank you!"

Raphtalia objected for some reason. I wondered why. She had seemed motivated to train up until that point.

"Hmm . . . I suppose Raphtalia joining in for a bit of healthy competition could make for effective training. Rivalry gives birth to ambition!"

Now the old lady was compromising too. Was rivalry really going to help? I guess I had read a manga where something like that happened before.

"In that case, Saint, please procure some life force water. Also, if you're truly serious about training, then we will have to go into the mountains at some point. Please consider making time to allow for that in the near future."

Studying the Hengen Muso style would normally require going off deep into the mountains. But since learning about life force water, we had been able to train in the village, and even in the more urban area of the town. Thanks to that, Eclair and Rishia had been able to train much more consistently.

Ren was apparently planning on studying under the old lady with Eclair too, so I wasn't sure how much life force water we would need. The old lady originally intended to have Ren train with me. But Ren didn't seem interested in taking any shortcuts to getting stronger, so she said it would probably be good to have him and Eclair train together and push each other to improve.

And that's how Raphtalia and I ended up sparring with Atla. We needed to develop the ability to see life force with our own eyes before we could progress any further.

"Alright, Atla. I want you to use that same attack I asked for before, but this time make it powerful and swift," I said.

"Understood!"

I blocked Atla's jab, and a loud twang rang out. I felt something travel into my body and burst. It felt exactly like the technique that the old lady had used on me before. I was glad that I had used a weak shield for our training. If I'd been using one of my more powered-up shields, that attack would have done some real damage.

"Ugh . . ."

I used my own inner flow of magic to forcefully expel the foreign energy from my body. But I remembered the old lady mentioning that was the wrong way of doing it.

"Ugh . . . I managed to expel it, but this is tough. Alright, let's do some sparring then."

"Okay! Here I come! Aiyah! Aiyaya!"

The old lady had given me a bunch of pointers. She told me that I needed to do more than just block. Apparently, sparring with Atla as if it were a real fight would be more effective. She told Raphtalia to do the same.

"Mr. Naofumi . . ." Raphtalia said worriedly.

"The old lady says that if I continue to take Atla's attacks I should start to see life force. I just have to stick with it."

I continued to take the attacks until I was too exhausted to keep standing. I flumped down and took a break.

"You're next, Raphtalia!" Atla shouted.

She beckoned Raphtalia over with several flicks of her wrist.

Why was she always so provocative? Raphtalia responded as expected. She readied herself with a dead-serious expression on her face, regardless of the fact that she was using a wooden practice sword.

"I hope you're ready!" said Atla.

"I'm ready to see you try!" Raphtalia responded.

The two edged closer . . . and closer . . . The tension between these two when they sparred was enough to make anyone watching think it was a real battle. Did they not realize they were only supposed to be sparring? Or maybe I needed to

be taking the sessions that serious too.

"Hiya!"

Raphtalia closed in on Atla rapidly and swung her wooden sword down. Atla dodged the attack by a hair's breadth and jabbed at Raphtalia sharply. Raphtalia bent backward and dodged the jab as she followed through with her swing, swiping sideways. Atla crouched down and thrust at an opening in Raphtalia's guard, but Raphtalia swiftly blocked the jab with her wooden sword. A loud thud echoed out.

"Here I go!" taunted Atla.

Atla gave another sharp jab, which Raphtalia redirected to the side with her arm. Then she countered by swinging her wooden sword down once again.

"Tsk! You don't give up!" Atla snapped.

Atla did a backflip to put some distance between them.

"As soon as one of my attacks lands, this match will be over. Of course, I will see to Mr. Naofumi's training afterward. You can spend that time recovering quietly," she said.

"That's not going to happen! You're the one who's going to experience the impact of my blade, Atla! Then you can watch me and Mr. Naofumi train!"

Raphtalia placed her hand on the back of the wooden sword's blade. I was guessing she was channeling something into it. I still couldn't see life force, so I wasn't sure.

"It looks like you can't afford to hold back," said Atla.

"I could say the same about you!"

The two exchanged glances and then swiftly charged forward. They clashed, and sparks flew. Were they really just pretending to be serious? They were putting on a real performance considering they were only sparring.

"Impressive, as usual," said Atla.

"Still not as impressive as you," Raphtalia responded.

Their matches were always unusually spirited like this. The old lady mentioned that observing them fight was also part of my training. My mind wandered and I gazed on as the two continued to battle it out.

Eventually midday rolled around, and I made lunch. It would have been nice if I had the time to just train all day long, but that wasn't the case.

"Your cooking is delicious as always, Bubba Shield!"

Keel got so excited that she turned into a dog and started wagging her tail. Did my cooking really make the little loincloth pup that happy? Whatever. If it motivated her, that was a good thing.

"Alright, we've had lunch. I guess we should go give the old guy a visit at his weapon shop."

"Agreed," responded Raphtalia.

"Understood!" Atla replied.

We wrapped up our training and used my portal skill to teleport to the castle town.

Chapter Two: The Alchemist

I walked into the weapon shop. Imiya's uncle was standing behind the counter.

"Oh hello, Shield Hero."

"Hey. How's it going?"

"The weapons are selling as fast as I can make them. I'm setting aside a portion of the profits for your equipment, of course."

Oh! I liked hearing that! With everything I had going on, it seemed like I was always broke lately. I still didn't have enough financial leeway to be spending money on equipment. If Imiya's uncle working meant a reduction in equipment costs, that was a good thing.

"Thanks. Imiya and the rest of you handy bunch are a real help."

"Don't mention it! We can't thank you enough for giving us such fulfilling work."

Imiya's uncle was a type of therianthrope called a lumo. They looked like moles. Imiya was the first lumo that I had bought from the slave trader. She was good with her hands, so I decided to buy more lumo slaves. When I did, it turned out that one of them was her uncle, so I just referred to him as Imiya's uncle in my head. He had a name, but . . . what was it, again? These lumos all seemed to have really long names.

I asked the old guy to take on an apprentice so that I would have someone to make equipment back at the village. So I brought Imiya's uncle to the shop and introduced him to the old guy, and it turned out the two already knew each other. Imiya's uncle had studied blacksmithing together with the old guy a long time ago, and the two of them had been close.

"We're still trying to work out the peculiarities of that mountain of materials. We spend all of our time arguing about that lately. It even turned into a bit of fisticuffs just last night."

"That's something I didn't expect to hear."

He had gotten into an argument with the old guy that ended up getting physical, and yet here he was, acting completely normal and tending to the shop. I got the feeling those two really trusted each other.

"What's going on?"

The old guy came strolling out from the back of the shop. He was holding a hammer in one hand. It looked like he had been in the middle of working on it.

"Oh? It's you, kid! How have things been lately?"

"Not bad. Been doing a bit of training lately, among other things. How about you? How is that equipment coming along?"

"A few days isn't really enough time to make much progress with that stuff. Is that all you're here for today?"

The old guy responded cheerfully, so I mulled over whether there was anything else I needed for a moment. Then I slowly looked over toward Raphtalia and Atla, who I'd brought along with me.

"Well . . ."

I didn't really have any money to spend, but I figured that Imiya's uncle working there was kind of like having a line of credit. In that case, there was something I'd been considering asking the old guy to do for me.

"It's about that Siderite Shield you showed me before."

"Hmm? What about it? Do you need it to get stronger or something?"

"No, nothing like that. Shooting Star Shield is already a lifesaver as it is."

Honestly, I had been using Shooting Star Shield in battles pretty much nonstop since I learned it. It was a versatile skill that would remain useful for a long time to come. My battles had made that clear. Plus, it would probably be even more effective if I used an accessory on that shield.

"I was wondering if the Siderite Shield had some kind of special meaning for you and that's why you were keeping it tucked away like that."

"Hmm . . . I just didn't want to sell it because the material is so rare, so I've been keeping it in storage. Why?"

"Oh, really? In that case, maybe it wouldn't hurt to ask."

"What is it? Spit it out already, kid."

I shifted my gaze toward Raphtalia and told the old guy what I had in mind.

"Do you think you could melt the Siderite Shield down and make a katana? A Siderite Katana?"

The old guy and Raphtalia both nodded simultaneously, as if my suggestion made total sense.

"I'd been wondering about that for a while now. I'm guessing the little miss's weapon is similar to your shield."

Ah, that's right. I still hadn't told the old guy about Raphtalia's katana. It was a vassal weapon from another world, which made it something like a seven star weapon. Raphtalia pulled her katana out and showed it to the old guy.

"It's from the other world. They called it a vassal weapon, which is most likely equivalent to what we call the seven star weapons here in this world," I explained.

"I see. In other words, you're thinking that if I rework the Siderite Shield into a katana, the little miss will be able to gain some kind of powerful skill."

"Exactly. Do you think you could do that?"

"Mr. Naofumi is ordering a weapon for you. I'm jealous! I want a weapon too."

I ignored Atla. She could fight just fine with her bare hands. She didn't need a weapon.

"I suppose it's possible," said the old guy.

"Will you do it for me?"

"Sure. It's really just a collector's item that's taking up space anyway. I'm happy to do it if it will help you and the little miss out, kid."

"Should I move it to the forge later?" asked Imiya's uncle.

The old guy nodded.

"But a katana . . ."

The old guy looked off into the distance. He seemed to be lost in thought.

"What is it?" I asked.

The old guy and Imiya's uncle both seemed to be reminiscing now.

"Shield Hero, katanas were our master's specialty," replied Imiya's uncle.

"Yeah, the master was a swordsmith by trade, although he was still skilled at making other weapons too," added the old guy.

"I see."

I remembered having heard something about blacksmiths specializing in certain kinds of weapons. In Europe a really long time ago, back in my world, all of those details were decided by permits and stuff. Of course, this was a different world and things seemed to work differently here. The old guy seemed to be able to handle just about anything, so I made all kinds of requests. But it might have just been that the old guy and Imiya's uncle were unusually well-rounded.

"In the end, the master certified me in everything. Even so, I honestly don't think I've come anywhere close to surpassing the master's skill yet."

"I see."

I remembered them mentioning recently that their master was a womanizing troublemaker. He was the kind of craftsman that had impressive skills in spite of having a problematic personality. And his specialty was katanas.

"I already have all of the materials, so it shouldn't take long. Come check back again in two or three days."

"Got it. As for payment . . ."

"It's not like you're going to buy it off of me, right? It'll be good practice for me too. You don't need to pay me for the little miss to just hold it."

That's what I loved about the old guy. His generosity really made things easy on me.

"Thanks. I'll give you plenty of business when I order equipment for all of the villagers one of these days."

"Righto!"

That's why I wanted to pay the old guy back in whatever way I could.

"And don't hesitate to let me know if you're looking for some rare ore or something. Alright, later then."

"Goodbye," added Raphtalia.

"Until next time," said Atla.

"Righto. It seems like things are getting livelier for you, kid. Even I can't help but get excited."

We parted with the old guy and made haste back to the village.

"Master! Big sis! Welcome baaack!"

Oh? Filo was back at the village. She came trotting up to me in her filolial form.

"Oh hey, Shield Hero. Welcome back."

One of the slaves that took a special interest in the monsters welcomed me back. That was unusual.

"Shield Hero, we have a really stubborn visitor that we don't know how to deal with," the slave said.

"Huh?"

Eclair and Ren showed up a few moments after the monster-enthusiast slave. Eclair seemed a bit perturbed. I wondered just what was going on.

"Hold on, surely it can wait. She's being watched," said Eclair.

"But she's almost gotten away several times already!" snapped Ren.

"What's going on?" I asked.

I looked at Ren.

"I don't really know. Someone is here to see you, Naofumi."

"Surely you can deal with the visitor, Ren."

"Well . . . yeah, you'd think so, but . . ."

Ren was acting oddly too.

"This one is a bit of an oddball. She says she wants to see you immediately, Mr. Iwatani," said Eclair.

I sighed.

"Who the hell is she?"

"She's some alchemist that supposedly caused all kinds of problems in Faubrey," answered Eclair.

Say what? Faubrey was the superpower that worshipped the four holy heroes. Why would an alchemist from Faubrey be here?

"I received word from the queen several days ago. It appears as if the alchemist was deemed a heretic and thrown out of Faubrey. And then she showed up in Melromarc," Eclair explained.

Just what kind of alchemist was this?

"If she's that suspicious, then throw her the hell out, no questions asked!"

"Well, the queen said something about poison becoming medicine in the right hands. So I figured we should ask you first, Naofumi," said Ren.

Hmm, he did have a point, I guess.

"When she saw the monsters that you've been keeping, she started talking about wanting to inspect them and—"

"Oh . . . So this is the infamous bird god!"

An unfamiliar woman appeared from out of nowhere and started poking and prodding Filo.

"Wh-wh-whaaat?!"

"Whoa!"

"When did she get here?! I didn't even notice!" cried Raphtalia.

"Impressive speed! Her approach rivals even that of my brother when he's gone mad," Atla commentated.

"M . . . Maaasteeerrr!"

Filo screamed out. Her response reminded me of when Motoyasu had grabbed her.

"Oh, it seems to understand human language too. This must be the filolial queen variant that the legends speak of!"

The woman had long, silvery blonde hair and dark brown skin. She appeared to be human. Probably in her mid-twenties. She had curves in all of the right places and she was wearing a lab coat. She seemed to fit the "hot older sister" role that was common back in my world. But any big sister role just made me think of Sadeena.

"These feathers go really deep. I wonder if it has any unusual organs."

The alchemist (?) forcefully pried Filo's mouth open and grabbed her tongue. Filo tried to struggle but was easily subdued. The alchemist seemed to be able to hold her down as effortlessly as if she were taking candy from a baby.

"Mmmrrghhhh!"

The alchemist stuck her head deep into Filo's mouth, but Filo flapped her wings violently and spit the alchemist's head out.

"How am I supposed to inspect you if you struggle like that? Settle down."

Just before Filo could toss her away, the alchemist (?) pulled out a syringe and thrust it at Filo. Unable to dodge in time, the needle stabbed Filo right in the mouth.

"Wha . . ."

Filo flumped down onto the ground with a thud.

"I . . . feel so weak . . ."

"Umm, lady . . ." I said.

"Wait just a moment. I'm right in the middle of inspecting this monster."

"Well, that monster is mine, and I can't have you just doing whatever you want with her."

"Oh?"

When she heard what I said, the alchemist (?) seemed to lose interest in Filo momentarily.

"Does that mean you're the Shield Hero?"

"Umm, yeah . . . and who are you?"

"Me? I'm Ratotille Anthreya. My friends call me Rat."

"Umm, I see. I'm Naofumi Iwatani. Just call me Naofumi."

"Nice to meet you, Naofumi."

Rat's eyes were fixed on Filo, who was still slumped down on the ground.

"So do you mind if I inspect this monster of yours?"

"M . . . Master! Nooo!"

Hmm . . . I had a feeling that the mystery that was Filo would be unraveled if I agreed, but I also couldn't help but feel like there would be significant consequences for Filo.

I sighed.

"I'm going to have to refuse for now."

"Aww, that's too bad."

Filo must have started to recover, because she stood up slowly.

"Oh my, it looks like I'd need to use a stronger sedative to inspect her, anyway."

"Nooo! Save me! Mel-chaaaan!"

Filo ran away and disappeared into the distance. I had a feeling she wouldn't be coming back for a while.

"So I guess you're the person who wanted to see me. What do you want?"

"That's right. I took the liberty of checking out the monsters in this village and a *certain* plant."

"Okay . . . ?"

"And I'm intrigued. I'd love to tinker around with things a bit, if you don't mind."

"You say tinker . . ."

What in the world did this lady plan on doing? It seemed like she already knew about the bioplant, so she must have done her homework before showing up.

"You're the alchemist that stirred up some trouble in Faubrey, right?"

"Trouble? That wasn't trouble. Those idiots don't want to admit their own ignorance. They simply couldn't understand my research."

She was clearly one of those mad-scientist types.

"Those idiots referred to my research as 'godless deeds,' of all things. And then they exiled me. Their 'gods' are the four holy heroes and the seven star heroes, right?"

"So what? You want one of those four holy heroes to acknowledge your work and that's why you came here?"

I glanced over at Ren, but he shook his head.

"That's not it," replied Rat.

"Then why did you come here?"

"I originally came to investigate the Spirit Tortoise. But my interests have already begun to shift."

Rat reached out to grab my hand with a look of passion in her eyes. I pulled my hand away.

"Don't touch me. I can't stand women like you."

"Oh? Then I won't touch you, but I'd still like to tinker with your monsters."

My monsters, huh? I didn't think I really had that many yet.

"Every one of them exhibits development like I've never seen before. I'd love to observe them."

I couldn't deny that all of my monsters had begun to exhibit abnormal development. They were around level 25 on average, but I'd been told they were all bigger than usual.

I looked over at the three caterpillands, which were caterpillar-like monsters. They were helping the slaves clear away stalks of the overgrown bioplant. Wait . . . three? I had only purchased two caterpillands. One . . . two . . . three . . . I counted them several times, and there was definitely one too many! What the hell?! There were only two this morning!

"Who the hell got a new caterpilland without asking?!"

"Uh oh!"

The slave that had just been standing near us tried to hide one of the caterpillands in a hurry.

"It's too late!" I shouted.

The slave must have been one of the culprits. And the caterpilland she hid was the biggest one too. Since I hadn't seen it this morning, it was safe to assume they had been hiding it somewhere and raising it in secret. We had expanded the bioplant field. It was starting to look like a forest. Maybe that's where they had been hiding it. On top of that, I could check its stats, which meant that it was registered to me!

The monster-enthusiast slave was using her whole body to try to hide the caterpilland, but it wasn't enough. And behind them was the bioplant. Something about the scene felt vaguely familiar. The fact that I was seeing it in a sepia tone was just my imagination, I'm sure.

"I feel like I've seen this before . . . in an old anime . . ." said Ren.

I guess they had something similar in his world too. But whatever. That was beside the point.

"There's no new caterpilland! There's no new caterpilland here!"

"It's huge! I can still see it!"

Was she seriously going to try to pretend it wasn't there? What valley did this princess come from?! The caterpilland behind her was huge and looked just like one of those bugs!

"I want you all to think about what you've done!"

The slaves cast their eyes downward. And then Atla stepped forward, for whatever reason.

"It's time for your punishment. Each one of you will be severely punished, by order of Mr. Naofumi. We'll start with—"

"Umm . . . Atla, you stay out of this. I want them to tell me what's going on."

What had Atla been planning on doing to them? I could easily imagine her choosing a punishment far worse than anything I would have done.

"Alright, I want to know how this happened."

"Listen, it's not like anyone wanted to upset you, bubba."

Keel stepped forward and spoke in defense of the monster enthusiast.

"And how the hell did you manage to get it registered to me, anyway?!"

"The man that sells slaves secretly did it for us."

"That damned slave trader!"

When the hell did he do that?!

"Why is the slave trader dealing with my slaves?!"

"It was the first egg we all found together!"

"Huh?"

The slaves explained. They had taken an egg from a monster nest that they had found when they went out to level. Bringing it back to the village had been easy enough, but they had no idea how they would manage to raise it.

"Did Raphtalia know about this?" I asked.

"I did not!"

"If we'd told Raphtalia, she would have told you, right?" said Keel.

"Of course I would have! What were you thinking, Keel?!" Raphtalia snapped.

Keel continued her explanation. Even the slaves recognized that hatching a monster egg without registering someone as the monster's owner would be dangerous. They were trying to figure out what to do when the slave trader showed up.

I had been giving them some spending money when they

went out to peddle our wares. They all put together what they had left of that money and paid the slave trader to take care of the registration. Rather than registering it to one of them, the slave trader mentioned that registering it to me would make it stronger and more impressive, and the rest was history.

Hmm . . . I had intentionally adjusted the caterpillands' levels to keep them from getting too big, and yet this one was still huge. It was fifty percent bigger than the other caterpillands. I wasn't sure what I should do.

"Don't kill it!"

"Shut up, valley girl!"

"What in the world is 'valley' supposed to mean, bubba?" asked Keel.

"I'm guessing there's a character from a story in Naofumi's world that did something similar," said Ren.

He had seriously gone and just calmly explained my wisecrack. Oh well. I didn't want to explain it, anyway, so whatever. But damn it, these brats just did whatever they wanted. The slave that kept spouting off valley princess lines was doing her best to stand up for the caterpilland.

"Listen, if you just do whatever you want, you're not only making trouble for others, you're making trouble for me too! If you wanted to raise the monster so badly, you should have talked to me!"

I already had my own transactions with the slave trader, so

if they did things on their own it would most likely just double the effort involved.

"And you better look after that thing properly. If I see you pushing the responsibility off on others, I'll sell it off without a second thought."

"I . . . I will!"

Sheesh . . . These brats just caused one problem after another.

"It's like you're running a daycare, Naofumi," Ren said.

"What the hell?!"

That bastard! What was he thinking saying that?! A daycare?! He couldn't have been more wrong! I glared at Ren and was about to give him a piece of my mind, but Keel started shouting.

"See, I told you! I told you bubba would forgive you!"

"But you said Bubba Shield would sell it if he found out, Keel. You told me I had to keep it a secret. Because he'd sell it without hesitation, since he's a money-grubber."

"I said penny-pincher, not money-grubber!"

"You guys . . ."

What a bunch of . . . Wait, did that brat not say it was the *first* egg they found?

"Was this the only egg?" I asked.

"Nope."

"What?!"

The slaves were shaking their heads. They must have been really good at finding monster nests, because they started pulling out tons of eggs that they'd hidden away at their residences.

"The slave trader is going to process them for us once we save up enough money."

"That's a lot of eggs! What were you planning to do after hatching all of those without even asking?!"

That would have been a complete disaster. Then again, I guess it would have been easy enough to dispose of a bunch of baby monsters.

"We didn't plan that far . . ."

I'd never really thought about there being monster eggs in the wild. We could always use the extras to make food. I had a feeling they'd get mad at me if I said that though.

"Are those all caterpillands?"

"Who knows? We got them from lots of different places, so I have no idea."

Rat plopped her hand down on my shoulder.

"What is it? I'm busy right now. We'll talk later," I told her.

"I'll analyze and take care of the eggs for free if you'll let me do my research here."

Hmm . . . I was all about cost-benefit analysis, so "free" always got my attention. Then again, they say there's no such thing as a free lunch too. I couldn't make up my mind.

"We decline!"

The monster-enthusiast slave, a.k.a. valley girl, refused before I could even respond. The little brat seemed to become unusually aggressive whenever it came to anything dealing with the monsters.

"Hold on now. Let me think about this," I said.

Keeping Rat around might not be a bad idea. She was an expert on monsters, after all. There were plenty of ways I could make use of her. I might have been expecting too much, but they did call her an alchemist. Maybe she could take over modifying the bioplant and monsters for me. That said, something about the timing of it all seemed just too perfect.

"Is this some kind of conspiracy? Some kind of performance to get me to agree?"

"It's not!" shouted Keel.

"Naofumi, I agree that it all seems a little bit too convenient, but I don't think that's the case," said Ren.

Hmm . . . So it wasn't just me that thought it seemed convenient. But just saying so wasn't going to accomplish anything. In that case, I'd try a different approach.

"Rat, what is it that you hope to achieve? Depending on your answer, I might consider letting you stay."

"Achieve? I want to create a powerful monster."

"Oh?"

So she wanted to create a powerful monster. That was really simple and straightforward. I knew of games that had monster fusion and mixing systems, so it wasn't like I couldn't understand where she was coming from. But I guess if someone was actually trying to do something like that with real, living creatures, it was only natural that it would repulse some, just like it had in Faubrey.

"In order to do that, I need to analyze monsters and combine various alchemical techniques with magic. But those fools called my research evil and said it was beyond the forgiveness of the gods. They destroyed my lab and killed my research subjects. It was a real mess."

"Umm . . . So in other words, you're basically a monster tamer that was researching how to make monsters stronger using alchemy."

"That's more or less accurate."

Heh. I'd said that assuming that she would argue, but I guess she was fine with being considered a monster tamer. I'd figured she was just loony, but she seemed to be able to look at things objectively too. Add a sense of purpose to the mix and the result is recklessness.

"Let's look at this from a basic common-sense perspective. Eclair, I want to know what you think."

"Huh? What I think?"

Eclair's wary expression turned to one of confusion as she responded.

"Do you think the research she's doing crosses any lines?"

"I don't really know enough to say one way or the other, personally. However, having seen Filo in action, I do believe that monsters should be considered part of our offensive capabilities."

It was an honest reply. But it didn't answer the question. There was a high likelihood that the research wouldn't be openly accepted. But I still wasn't sure what to do.

"Rat, would your research include something like making Spirit Tortoise clones and using them to fight?"

"That does seem like something I would come up with. Shield Hero. What was your title of nobility again?"

"Mr. Iwatani is a Count," replied Eclair.

"Well then, Count. It's an interesting idea. Is that something you're considering doing?"

"Let me continue. I'm guessing you heard rumors about us having gone to another world, right?"

"I did. I heard that you went chasing after the enemy and then returned after successfully defeating him."

"In that other world, there was an alchemist that had created clones of a certain beast that was at least as powerful as the Spirit Tortoise."

If someone was trying to do the same kind of thing here in this world, I couldn't trust them. I was putting the idea out there to see how she responded. If she went for it, she was out.

"Well, that's boring. I'm not interested in research that someone else has already done."

Rat ran her hands through her hair. Her reply sounded like she was being completely honest.

"It was an intriguing idea at first. But if it's already been done, it's nothing more than reference material."

Hmm . . . I thought she might just be a whacko, but she seemed to have her own personal philosophy. She wasn't interested in mimicking others.

"I don't really get it. Are we talking about monster taming, like in games?"

Ren tried to put it into game terms as he asked me and Rat.

"To be more specific, one of my objectives is filolials."

Normal filolials weren't really all that strong. She was probably referring to Fitoria or something. Fitoria was ridiculously strong, after all. She's the one that had held the Spirit Tortoise back when things got tough. She had been considered a legend before that, but her involvement in the fight had proven her existence to the world.

"This is only what I've managed to figure out on my own, but there's a theory that the heroes created the legendary filolial. The same bird god that is supposed to be as powerful as the infamous dragon emperor. I want to create a monster like that. One that will be remembered for generations to come. One that will fight for the people."

That made sense. She wanted to create a legendary monster herself, in other words.

"We use filolials as transportation, so they can be found living in most regions. I want to create a monster that will benefit the people."

"I can understand where you're coming from," I said.

I'd played my share of monster tamer games. I'd actually been wondering lately if there were some way I could upgrade Raph-chan to make her even more powerful. Raphtalia didn't know that, of course. But if I gave Rat some freedom to do her thing and it turned out I could trust her, it might be worth asking for her help.

"I can't stand liars. I'll agree if you're willing to become my slave so that I can ensure you can't lie. Are you still interested?"

"Slave? That's typical of you, Naofumi," said Ren.

"It is indeed," added Eclair.

"Sure. If that's all it takes, I'm happy to have you take away my dignity," Rat replied.

She'd breezily accepted my offer without batting an eye. But I didn't like the way she said it. Regardless, I felt like I could trust her to some extent. As long as she was a slave, it would be easy to punish her if she lied.

"Hmm . . ."

So basically, if I brought her into the village, that meant she would be able to help power up all of the monsters. Having her on the team might not be a bad thing. If I had a slave curse put on her, I could always just force her to do my bidding if she started causing problems later.

There were also plenty of things she could help with in addition to taking care of the eggs that Keel and the others had brought back. That could work out nicely. Rat could make progress with her research, and our offensive capabilities would be bolstered to better handle the coming waves.

"I work my monsters hard. Does that bother you? I work them like slaves, literally. I'll do the same with you too."

"Human or demi-human, slaves are slaves. Treating them specially because you feel sorry for them is just another form of discrimination."

Oh? Special treatment is discrimination, huh? She had some interesting ideas. That reminded me. Back in my world, I remembered hearing about women outside of Japan demanding equality and not wanting to be treated specially. In the bigger cities in Japan, they had cars on the trains reserved for women. People that wanted true equality disliked those. What Rat was saying was similar to that, I guess.

"I can't stand the idea of protecting certain living creatures while just ignoring the rest."

"Oh?"

"I refuse to believe the theory that monsters are a result of the waves. Monsters can fight against the waves just like the heroes, after all!"

Valley girl glared at Rat angrily. She obviously realized that they were different regardless of both having a thing for monsters.

"I think I understand what you want to do. You believe the monsters can make a big contribution to our fight against the waves."

"I do!"

"Then how about this . . ."

I showed Rat one of the bioplant seeds.

"This is a plant. It can be turned into something like a monster, depending on how it's modified. But altering it could also make it produce beneficial medicinal herbs. What do you think about that?"

"Something like that would be a piece of cake for me!"

Hmm . . . Her line of thinking seemed to match up pretty closely with what I wanted to do.

"Mr. Naofumi, are you really thinking of taking her in?"

Raphtalia was clearly skeptical. I couldn't argue that Rat seemed suspicious. But that suspiciousness and her willingness to use whatever means necessary to gain my trust had earned her points in my book.

"We'll start with a temporary trial period and see how it goes. That should be fine."

We needed more specialists in the village. S'yne had been a similar case. It wouldn't be fair to have accepted S'yne, but not give Rat a chance.

I shook Rat's hand.

"I'm looking forward to working with you," Rat said.

Eclair suddenly spoke up.

"Pardon me, but if that settles the matter, there's something else I'd like you to look at," she told me.

"What now? There's something else? Was this not what you wanted me to deal with?"

"Oh! That's right, Bubba Shield! We have another problem!"

Valley girl jumped in and started trying to tell me something. Why was she still here?

"We found something while you were out, Naofumi," added Ren.

Was there no end to it? I left the slaves behind and followed Eclair out of the village. Rat seemed curious and tagged along. Valley girl followed us too, without asking, of course.

Chapter Three: Filolials and Dragons

Outside of the village, there was a mountain of wooden crates. What the hell? Those weren't there yesterday.

"Take a look inside," said Eclair.

I opened several of the crates and looked inside. There were a variety of weapons and other supplies, as well as some monster eggs.

"What is this? Did you guys just decide to buy a bunch of stuff with the money I gave you? And someone just left it all here? Or is this all the stuff that you stole, Ren?"

Ren had been a bandit chief until just recently, after all. I looked over at Ren, but he was shaking his head.

"No. I don't remember getting any of this stuff," he replied.

So Ren had no idea what it was either. Maybe it was from Motoyasu. He could have left it here as a present for Filo. That seemed like something he would do.

"Read this," said Eclair.

"What?"

I looked at the lid of the crate I currently had open. Upon closer inspection, the same thing seemed to be written on all of the crates. The writing was really messy. In large letters the following was written: "To the Shield Hero: Please give these gifts to the disadvantaged slaves."

"What the hell?"

"The supplies appear to be some kind of donation. There are some fairly expensive items among the equipment. The supplies include quite a bit of rare medicinal herbs, ores, and wood too," Eclair explained.

"Who in the world would do something like this?" I asked.

"Most likely Siltvelt or Shieldfreeden is responsible. Based on the way the characters are written and the type of ink used, I would say there's no doubt about it," she continued.

"Can we accept it?" I asked.

"It's practically impossible to determine the original owner of any of it. They went to great lengths to carefully remove any type of identifying markings. Even if we found the person or persons responsible, it would be difficult to take any action against them," she replied.

I suspected it might have been the people in Siltvelt who I sold the slave hunters to. There had been people doing similar things at the Zeltoble slave market. In other words, it was a donation to earn them brownie points, I guess. I sure hope they didn't expect anything in return.

"Any riffraff causing trouble for Mr. Naofumi deserves certain death. Let us go execute them immediately!" Atla exclaimed.

"That's going a bit far. It's not like they're really causing me any trouble."

I figured I would just look the other way and accept the gifts.

"Having to deal with it is a hassle though," said Ren.

"I guess so. What about the eggs? Rat, can you tell what they are?" I asked.

"Seems to be eggs from everything from usapils to some rarer breeds. Then there's this . . ."

Oh? So she could tell with a single glance.

"This one could be a problem."

Rat pointed at an egg in the crate that was larger than the others. What was it? Maybe it was the egg of some beast as powerful as the Spirit Tortoise or something.

"What is it?"

"It's a dragon egg. A rather expensive and powerful one. Rare, I'm sure."

Well, then . . . I guess they had left something troublesome, after all.

"A dragon, huh? That's pretty cool," Ren said.

"Yeah! I . . ."

Valley girl yelped in agreement, but then her voice trailed off and she looked away with a frown on her face. What was that? But she began smiling again soon after. Rat, on the other hand, didn't look happy. Maybe she didn't like dragons.

"Having a dragon here in the village would be lovely!" valley girl exclaimed.

"I guess valley girl likes dragons, unlike Rat," I said.

"Valley girl?!"

"That's another one of Mr. Naofumi's fabulous nicknames. I'm jealous," replied Atla.

She sounded like a complete ditz. I decided to just ignore her. Actually, hadn't I told her to shut up? That hadn't lasted long. Valley girl glared at me when I called her that.

"What is with that name?" she asked.

"Well, I don't know your real name," I replied.

"I'm sure he got the nickname from some anime or something," said Ren.

"Bingo," I replied.

I'd chosen that name because she kept insisting the caterpillar wasn't there earlier. She should have been thanking me, as far as I was concerned.

"If you don't tell him your real name, Mr. Naofumi will almost certainly continue to think of you as 'valley girl' until the end of time. Hurry up and introduce yourself!" said Raphtalia.

She seemed to be in a rush to explain that to valley girl for some reason.

"I'm Wyndia."

"I see. You're fine with 'valley girl,' right?"

"No!"

"That's just mean, Naofumi. Think of the poor girl," Ren said.

He rolled his eyes. Ren was sticking up for valley girl, a.k.a. Wyndia, but now she was glaring at him.

"Oh, fine. Whatever," I replied.

"We need to have everyone introduce themselves. Otherwise, you never know what Mr. Naofumi will end up calling them," said Raphtalia.

"Is it really that big of a deal?" I asked.

Surely there was nothing wrong with giving people nicknames.

"We're off topic. Back to the dragon egg," I said.

"Everyone be careful. But you're right. What should we do about that?" Raphtalia asked with a troubled look on her face.

A dragon, huh? I had a feeling Filo wouldn't like that. It wasn't like it was a special gift from someone I knew. Accepting it could end up causing a big fuss. Being given something so expensive just gave me more to worry about. Still, if there was no way to return it, I guess I would just have to accept it without complaining. Throwing it away would be a waste, after all.

"I guess we'll keep it for now. If anyone makes an issue out of it, we'll just feign ignorance. How do monster seals work with dragons, anyway?"

"You'll have to apply a high-level monster seal. It looks like they were nice enough to leave all of the equipment required for the ceremony. I can take care of that if you'd like, Count," Rat replied.

"Yeah, let's do that. By the way, why do you seem to dislike dragons so much?"

Rat seemed a bit annoyed when I asked her.

"The upper class of dragons lose all sense of integrity once they go into heat."

"Huh?"

"You didn't know that? Regions where lots of dragons live are always dirty. They're dangerous for all sorts of reasons."

"Really?"

I thought about the regions I knew of where dragons lived. There was the village in the east where Ren defeated a dragon, and then the mountainous area where we had gone bandit hunting. There had been dragon corpses teeming with pathogenic germs in both areas. Describing the regions as dirty wouldn't have been strange at all.

"Dragons have no integrity, so those areas end up full of half-dragon creatures in no time."

"That sounds dangerous."

If it were a fantasy game, there would probably be a bunch of half-dragon or part-dragon subspecies coming out of the regions. I wondered if that was an actual problem here.

"Well, they have their territories and they stay within them. But they mess the ecosystems up without a second thought, so I don't like them. And the dragons that people use are just half-breed dragons mixed with weaker monsters, really."

Hmm . . . So it was like when an invasive foreign species messed with the ecosystem back in Japan. Native species had been pushed to the brink of extinction due to black bass being released in lakes there. There would be problems similar to that. Or issues with crossbreeding leading to native species being driven out or becoming extinct, I guess.

"The real problem is the pureblood dragons that refer to themselves as dragon emperors. Those dragons have zero regard for race. They'll even try to mate with humans."

They did sound like troublesome creatures.

Hmm? Wyndia seemed upset.

"They have manners!" she shouted.

Why was she talking like she knew about dragons? And seriously, she was really annoying when it came to monsters.

"There are even races of demi-human mixes, already. The aotatsu demi-humans are a well-known example," Rat explained.

Aotatsu? "Ao" was "blue" in Japanese. "Tatsu" could mean "dragon," so I guess "aotatsu" was supposed to be referring to the azure dragon. The white tiger race was called "hakuko," so it made sense. I'm sure one of the past heroes must have chosen this name too.

"Although, the pureblood dragons do have manners and are well-behaved as long as they don't go into heat."

"And the reason you looked disgusted is because this egg is one of those vile dragons?"

"Pretty much. The high-level monster seal for dragons allows you to restrict reproductive activities, so make sure you check that box. Otherwise, all of the village monsters are going to be violated."

It didn't really make sense to me. I spent all of my time hunting dragon couples in the monster hunter game I'd played. It seemed strange that the dragons didn't wipe out the humans and demi-humans if they reproduced so aggressively.

"The Dragon Emperor would never allow that!" shouted Wyndia angrily.

Dragon Emperor, huh? I kept hearing that name. Fitoria had mentioned it. They'd talked about it in Kizuna's world too.

"Oh yes, the legendary king of the dragons that supposedly fought the queen of the filolials, right?" Rat replied.

"I heard about that thing in the other world. Is there one here too?" I asked.

"It's just a legend. It's questionable whether either creature actually exists. Oh, wait . . . I think I heard the queen of the filolials is the one that held the Spirit Tortoise off, right?"

So basically, there must have been some legend about the dragon threatening the existence of humans and demi-humans. And then the queen of the filolials showed up to kill it, I guess.

"But despite supposedly being so promiscuous, I've hardly run into any dragons. The Tyrant Dragon Rex is about it, I think," I said.

"That thing was fearsome. We fought a dragon once in the coliseum too," Raphtalia added.

Oh yeah. We'd instantly killed that one, so I'd completely forgotten about it.

"Dragons are generally only found in regions that people don't visit. Have you ever been in dragon territory, Count?" asked Rat.

The roads I'd traveled were pretty much limited to where I'd gone peddling wares. Now that I thought about it, I'd hardly ever gone up into the mountains or into any caves. We'd gone hunting in the mountains just before catching Ren, but that was about it. I did remember fighting some part-dragon monsters then.

"Ren's fought a dragon. Right, Ren?"

"Yeah. I went and defeated it based on what I knew from a game and ended up causing a huge mess. I don't know how I'll ever make up for that."

I guess he legitimately regretted it, because he started looking really depressed. Ren had an excessively strong sense of responsibility.

"If you're sincere about doing your best to save the world, I'm sure that's enough," I told him.

"Yeah, I guess so, but still . . ."

"You know that you can't make up for it by dying, right?"

If any of the other holy heroes died, it would make my job

harder when the waves struck again. Fitoria had told me that, and the reality of it had become clear in Kizuna's world to a certain extent too. I couldn't let Ren die.

"..."

Wyndia had been glaring at Ren for a while now.

"Well, they have their territories and they don't leave them, so you won't run into any unless you purposely head there to find them," Rat continued.

"I see. Either way, I don't believe in wasting resources, so let's hatch it and raise a dragon."

"The more the reconstruction progresses, the less the village feels like the Lurolona I remember!" Raphtalia exclaimed.

Rat would be tending to the monsters and plants. I imagined the village being a farm, and now I couldn't think of Rat as anything but a farmer. She would be the farmer, and we could harvest some herbs or something using the bioplant. We could make a profit using the monsters too. It was exactly like one of those relaxing farming games we had back in my world.

"Raising a dragon is a hassle. You'll get a taste of what dragon knights have to deal with," said Rat.

"Oh yeah. I remember seeing some of them when we fought the Spirit Tortoise. They weren't very strong."

I recalled seeing them screaming and falling out of the air after being attacked by the Spirit Tortoise familiars.

"Who knows what will happen when you raise one though.

It might develop differently, like the filolials," she replied.

"Hmm . . . You have a point. I'll be careful."

And so I decided to hatch the dragon egg. That said, it would be a while after performing the monster seal ceremony before the egg actually hatched. I had to be the one to do the hatching, apparently. Rat looked like she was in a bad mood as she went about taking care of the preparations. And then . . .

"Why the hell do I have to carry the egg on my back?!"

I had to carry the dragon egg around on my back to keep it warm.

"Can't Ren do this?!"

I glared at Ren.

"No . . . It would probably rot if I touched it," he replied.

Ren was still suffering from the effects of his curses. It wasn't like I had forgotten that. One of the consequences for using his curse skills was that the quality of anything he touched deteriorated. Because of that, he was being careful not to touch anything.

"No! Definitely not the Sword Hero! Even the Shield Hero is a better choice than him!"

Wyndia insisted that it be anyone but Ren. I kind of wanted to ask her why she was being so hostile toward Ren, but . . . whatever. I'd just think of carrying the egg around as one of the hardships of raising an expensive dragon.

"Where is Raph-chan?!" I asked.

"Why are you bringing up Raph-chan now?" Raphtalia responded.

"I need to pet her to destress!"

Nothing could beat Raph-chan at times like these. Why wasn't she here?! I found out later on that she'd been taking a nap back at the village, by the way.

"Hahaha! You're so silly, bubba!"

Keel was pointing at me and cracking up.

"You bastard! Damn it! I can't do this, after all! All I really need to do is register it to me, right?!"

"You can't register yourself as the parent if you don't carry the egg. This is part of laying the groundwork for a successful registration. If you don't do this, it will end up ignoring your commands all the time, so just deal with it!"

Rat sounded annoyed when she replied. Were dragons really that much of a hassle? I almost wanted to just get rid of it right away.

"They'll really ignore commands?" I asked.

"Yes! I'm a monster researcher, so you better believe it!"

"The fact that you're saying it is exactly why I can't believe it . . ."

"What was that?!"

"Okay, okay. Fine. I get it."

Damn it. What a hassle. And then Filo returned with Melty in tow. Her timing was terrible. It was like when that one really annoying classmate sees you make a fool of yourself.

"Ahahahaha! Naofumi! What is that?!"

"Shut the hell up, second princess!"

"You promised you wouldn't call me the second princess!"

"Then don't laugh at me, you idiot!"

"Idiot?! Did you just call me an idiot?!"

"Umm . . ."

Raphtalia didn't know what to say to all this. The strange look on her face just made it worse. Then Atla butted in.

"I don't know what it looks like, but if it makes Mr. Naofumi uncomfortable then we should dispose of it."

"Buying one would be expensive, so no!" I shouted.

Sheesh . . . Why did things have to turn out like this?

"Okay, Count. What do you want to do about the dragon's gender?" Rat asked.

"Huh?"

"We can influence the gender by adjusting how warm we keep the egg. You can choose whichever gender you prefer."

I think I'd heard about egg temperatures determining the gender of certain reptiles. I guess the same was true for dragons.

"You'd probably prefer a . . . female, right? It might be able to use a human form like your filolial variant, after all," Rat continued.

"And what are you basing that on? Keel said something similar before. Is it because I'm surrounded by females?"

I slowly looked over toward Filo.

"Whaaat?"

Assuming it did exhibit a special pattern of development due to me raising it, which gender would be best? If it ended up being able to use a human form like Filo, I could imagine things getting really messy if it went into heat. With that in mind, I'd want to choose the gender that would spare me from becoming a victim.

"Male it is."

"I want to know why you decided that after looking at Filo," Melty said with an uncomfortable look on her face.

Wasn't it obvious? I'd be more likely to make it out unscathed if it were a male.

"Okay then. I'll make sure it ends up a male. You just relax and keep the egg on your back. You should only have to carry it around for two or three days before it hatches," said Rat.

"Yeah, whatever. Damn it! This isn't funny!"

"Once again, I look forward to working with you, Count."

And so the village ended up with its own resident alchemist.

That wasn't quite how the average day went though. I would usually go out hunting later in the day, if I had some spare time. That day I'd made an appearance in the castle town and dealt with Rat and the mountain of gifts, so there hadn't really been time for hunting. Once evening rolled around, I made dinner and fed the villagers.

"Bubba! I want seconds, bubba!"

"Sure, if there's any left."

"Of course there won't be any left! Make another batch!"

Making enough food to satisfy Keel and all of those other growing pigs was real manual labor. After all was said and done, it was pitch dark outside by the time we finished eating dinner.

"Stop it, Brother! Let go of me!"

"No!"

"Alright, Fohl, I'm counting on you to look after Atla. Don't let her get away tonight."

"I . . . I won't . . ."

I passed Atla off to Fohl after he got back from training.

"Mr. Naofumi! There's no way you'll stop me from getting away, Brother!"

"There's no way I'll let you get away!"

I could never decide if those siblings got along well, or terribly. Just as Atla and Fohl left, Sadeena showed up with Raph-chan on her shoulder.

"Little Naofumi! Let's have some fun!"

"The drunkard has arrived."

"Good evening, Sadeena," said Raphtalia.

"Oh? Isn't it about bedtime, little Raphtalia?"

"You're right. The children should be getting to bed," I replied.

"Stop treating me like a child!" Raphtalia shouted.

I had a feeling we repeated this same exchange every night. Some of the slaves were afraid of going to sleep and it was Raphtalia and Sadeena's job to go stay with them until they managed to.

"Alright, we'll make sure the children go to sleep. After that, let's have some fun, little Naofumi!"

"Hell no!"

"You know you want to!"

Sadeena started to pull her vest off, but Raphtalia grabbed her shoulder. She was emanating murderous intent.

"Sadeena?" she said.

"Oh my!"

Sadeena giggled like it was all a game, but I really wished she would stop already.

"That's too bad. I'm game any time you are though!" she said.

"Go to bed already!"

Sheesh . . . Speaking of Sadeena, she had continued to level here and there after her reset and was already level 62. I couldn't help but think her method of fighting might have been more effective than Filo's power-leveling. Fohl had reset his level on the same day and he was still only level 39.

"Alright, Sadeena. Let's go," Raphtalia said.

"Yes, ma'am! See you later, little Naofumi."

"Yeah, whatever."

The morning had started off early with taking care of the monsters, and it ended up being a long, busy day. I didn't have time to go level at all. I wondered if maybe I should go level with Sadeena. That would probably be kind of like making a bargain with the devil though. Ren couldn't swim, but maybe I should try sending him as a sacrifice next time.

I was just thinking maybe I should go to sleep when I heard a knock on the door.

"Naofumi, are you there?" asked Ren.

He'd shown up just moments after Raphtalia and Sadeena left.

"What's up?" I asked.

"Umm . . . After what happened this afternoon, I went out with Eclair and the slaves. I figured out what the consequences for using the gluttony curse were."

"Oh? What is it?"

Checking his stats hadn't been enough for Ren to tell what the consequences of the gluttony curse had been. He'd been testing likely effects one by one, so figuring it out had taken time.

"It looks like I can't gain experience until the effects of the gluttony curse wear off."

"Ugh . . ."

He had sacrificed experience points to use the skill, so I'd suspected that he might not able to gain experience for a while as a consequence.

"And you're sure it wasn't because you were fighting near me?" I asked.

"Yeah."

Way back when I was in Kizuna's world, we'd done some testing to figure out more about the penalties for holy heroes fighting together. One of the penalties was not being able to gain experience when fighting near another hero. It turned out that "near" meant a radius of around one kilometer. It was a distance that felt rather close, and yet far at the same time.

If we fought within a kilometer of each other, we wouldn't be able to gain experience. If he had been further away than that and still wasn't able to gain experience, then it was likely that was due to the effects of the curse. Damn. Ren had it at least as bad as me. All of the curse effects he was suffering from affected his development. We'd have to wait for the effects to start wearing off before we could really work on getting him stronger. He was as good as useless with the way things were now.

"And you came to tell me that?"

"Yes. I also wanted to ask if you would check my writing practice for me."

Keeping Ren's future in mind, I'd been teaching him the written language of this world. I wanted him to be able to read magical tomes so that he could learn magic. The problem was that only I could check his quizzes, since no one else understood

Japanese. Maybe I could teach Rishia Japanese. She'd managed to learn the languages of the other world pretty quickly.

"I have to get up early tomorrow, so I was about to go to bed. You mind if I give you the graded quiz back tomorrow?"

"That's fine. I'm sure you're worn out. Get some rest."

"Yeah."

Maybe I should've seriously considered having someone take Ren to the hot springs on the Cal Mira islands. They were supposed to be effective against curses. The curse that Raphtalia, Filo, and I were suffering from couldn't be fully healed that way, it seemed, but Ren's cursed weapon hadn't been powered up. It would probably work for him.

I could make some scheduling adjustments and send him to the islands with Eclair. The activation was probably over, so using a portal skill shouldn't be a problem. Even if it was, I could just have Raphtalia bind to the hourglass in the underwater temple and then she could use Return Dragon Vein to take them close to the islands.

"You should go with Eclair or the old lady sometime soon and focus on healing," I told Ren.

The trip only took one day by boat. If he went with Eclair or the old lady, he wouldn't have to worry about wasting any time. They could get some training in on the way. It wasn't like he couldn't spare a day off from studying writing and magic. I was teaching him, after all. If everything went as planned, he should be able to learn it more quickly than I had.

"Okay. If you say I should, then I'll go."

"You'll be able to put up a good fight once you implement the power-up methods."

Ren was training now, but he was also working on implementing the power-up methods I'd told him about. The effects of the curses didn't directly affect his combat, so he shouldn't lose, even if he did happen to run into any of those creeps that were trying to kill the heroes. Probably. Just to be extra safe, I'd send Eclair or the old lady to protect him. That should be plenty.

"Alright, I'll send someone with you tomorrow, so be expecting that."

"Later, Naofumi."

After Ren left, I got in bed and went to sleep. And that was a typical day of mine at the village. The things I had to do varied from day to day, but that's how my days went, more or less. I was always busy. Ugh . . . I really needed to go level up sometime soon.

This egg on my back sure made it hard to sleep.

It was afternoon, two or three days later.

"Mr. Naofumi."

Raphtalia glanced at me with a slightly bitter look in her eyes. Even I felt like we might have gone a bit too far.

"I'd say things turned out pretty good," I said.

"Yup. We did all of this in just two days. I really am a genius," Rat replied.

Rat and I had modified the bioplant. The results had been truly impressive. Getting an expert involved really made a big difference after all.

We'd registered Rat as one of my slaves. I made sure that she hadn't been lying to me about anything. The slave curse we used on her was a powerful one too. There was no way I was going to let her get away. Betrayal would mean death. I wasn't planning on lowering my guard, but Rat was absorbed in her research and seemed to be content with her current treatment.

On to what we'd done. I'd asked her to focus her research on developing a bioplant variant that could be used to create simple housing. I figured I would be getting more slaves eventually, so I wanted to build more dwellings. I'd thought maybe our interesting little plant could take care of that.

The experiment had been a success. Rat developed a convenient bioplant that would take on the form of a house when instructed to do so. She named it "camping plant." I was really tempted to make a wisecrack or two about that one, but the name did describe the plant's purpose perfectly, so I couldn't really argue with it.

The plant used photosynthesis to convert sunlight into magic power during the daytime. At night, that magic power could be used to make the plant's flowers give off light. The slaves were as adaptable as ever, and they had no problems getting settled in the camping plant houses, despite the fact that the whole idea seemed a bit dangerous at first. The nice thing about the houses was that we could just use weed killer to get rid of them when they were no longer needed. To sum it all up, we had successfully developed an extremely convenient and simple dwelling environment.

And now the village was covered in green plant-houses, which was why Raphtalia was criticizing me.

"Sorry," I told Raphtalia.

"About what?" she asked.

"You're upset because I'm turning your village into a mysterious fantasy world where people don't belong, right?" I answered.

"Well . . . I guess there's no avoiding it. I understand the merits."

Raphtalia aside, Rat had been really ecstatic about the modifications we'd made to the bioplant. She called it a "revolutionary" use of the plant.

I wasn't sure about "revolutionary." I'd just used the shield's abilities to modify it. The shield had a strong effect on the outcome. I made the rough modifications, and then Rat tweaked the details. My next request was for her to develop a bioplant variation that could create medicinal herbs. I would have been happy with a bioplant that could make medicine, but she'd told me that would be too difficult.

We'd had several failures before arriving at the current

camping plant, of course. The first prototype had been a man-eating house, for example. Rat told us it was dangerous and repeatedly said not to go inside, but Wyndia and Filo ignored her and excitedly ran in. The plant ate them. But Raphtalia and I destroyed the plant and managed to get them out safely. The faces of the villagers were full of mixed emotions when that happened.

Other than that, I'd had Rat take a look at the monster eggs. She noticed right away that my monsters exhibited extraordinary development. She came and asked me about it. When I told her about the maturation adjustment on my Monster User Shield, she got really excited and spent a while looking the shield over.

"Wow. I'd heard that monsters raised by heroes would be more advanced. I guess that explains why," she said.

"Yeah, probably. Do the other heroes have something similar?" I asked.

Since Ren was at the village, I'd had him test it out before. He'd gotten a similar weapon.

"The hero I know never mentioned anything like that to me," she replied.

"I see."

Then again, she didn't get along with Faubrey's seven star hero very well, apparently. She'd mentioned the hero being really uptight. The hero really disliked unconventional research like monster modification or alchemy, which was her specialty. It seemed like she didn't really want to go into the details, so

I hadn't asked her about what kind of person the hero was. Besides, I'd already requested that the hero get in touch with me so that we could talk. I really should have heard back long ago.

Anyway, research into using a bioplant variant to produce food was well underway too. The flavor of the food was already more than adequate, so I'd leave the rest up to Rat. She could work on creating some variation in the types of food produced. I had the slaves taking care of raising the monsters, so we would probably be able to really get serious about our peddling operations before long.

"This seed made building a laboratory for myself simple too. It's done nothing but good for us," said Rat.

Rat's lab was a huge building that she'd built using the camping plant. She'd brought a massive test tube from who knows where and set it up in the lab. It was filled with bubbling liquid, and some kind of monster was floating in the liquid. It reminded me of some kind of mutant beast in a science-fiction film. When I first saw it, I couldn't help but wonder if taking her in might have been a mistake.

All of this had happened over the past two days. That was a lot of change for two days. Too much, maybe. A huge laboratory had been added to the village in only two days . . .

Wyndia and Rat had become rivals when it came to the monsters, by the way. Wyndia thought it would be best to strengthen the monsters by having them fight. That clashed with Rat's assertion that modifying them was the best way to make them stronger. They were both looking for ways to make the monsters stronger, so regardless, they couldn't hate each other. The two of them were always busy discussing something or other. That said, Wyndia was obviously far less educated than Rat, so it seemed like Rat was just toying with her more often than not.

"Alright, I'm going to focus my research on the bioplant until I get tired of it. Let me know when you can provide some funding for other research."

"I will. I want to start working on modifying the monsters directly too," I told her.

The offensive capabilities of my subordinates were of paramount importance to me. There was no way around it. It had become clear from the fight with the Spirit Tortoise that I could never have too many allies. And having stronger monsters could only make things better.

Crack! Crack!

I heard cracking sounds coming from my back. I guess the egg was about to hatch.

"I can feel signs of new life," said Atla.

"Yeah. You can sense that, huh?" I replied.

I took the egg off of my back and looked it over.

"Is the egg hatching?" asked Raphtalia.

"Looks that way."

The egg was a lot bigger than Filo's had been. A crack formed on its surface, and a baby dragon slowly began to emerge.

"What do dragons eat, anyway?" I asked.

"I'm guessing meat," said Raphtalia.

"Do we even have any meat?" I wondered out loud.

We'd had some smoked meat and some dried meat in the village storehouse, but I wasn't sure if there was any left.

"It depends on the type of dragon, but this one is an omnivore," said Rat.

Thank goodness. We could feed him fruit from the bioplant. We had been harvesting more than we needed lately, and it was slowly becoming a key product of our peddling operations.

"Kwaaaa!"

The baby dragon peeked his head out of the egg and squeaked at us. Hatching a monster sure brought back memories. It was just like when Filo . . . No, she'd been a lot more energetic. The baby dragon was about as big as my head. He was definitely bigger than Filo had been when she hatched.

"The thing sure is shaped weird," I said.

The baby dragon looked like a fat little gourd with pathetically tiny wings on its back. He had a fat tail and two horns, but still didn't have scales yet. I scooped him up into my arms. His body was warm.

"Kwa!"

The dragon blinked several times and then looked me in the eyes.

"Kwaaa!"

He raised one of his hands when he squeaked, as if he were saying hello. That reminded me. I figured I should absorb a piece of the egg shell into my shield. I picked a piece up and held it up to the shield.

Zap!

What was that? The shield sparked. I recalled something similar happening while we were in Kizuna's world. It had been the Demon Dragon Shield that time, I think. It had reacted similarly then.

"Tee hee . . . He sure is cute. It reminds me of when Filo was just a chick," said Raphtalia.

She was poking at the baby dragon with her finger. The dragon was biting at her finger playfully. Was this creature really supposed to turn into a sex fiend?

"So this is a dragon. I can feel an incredibly warm life force stirring," said Atla.

She gave the baby dragon a warm welcome too. Based on what I knew about dragons, I imagined they wouldn't get along with white tigers. But that didn't seem to be the case here.

"Alright, I should do a quick checkup," said Rat.

She looked the baby dragon over carefully, poking him lightly here and there.

"Good. No major problems. Healthy, overall. Looks like a male. Everything went as planned," she said.

"That's good," I said.

A male meant it shouldn't be a problem even if it displayed an abnormal development pattern and ended up being able to use a human form like Filo. Then again, just being able to use a human form would be a problem in and of itself, but whatever.

When Rat let go of the baby dragon, it flew over to me and started climbing up my leg. What a little rascal.

"I guess you have a good idea of how to raise him, right?" Rat asked.

"Think so?"

"I recommend you start taking him out to hunt from early on. The amount of food growing dragons eat is just scary," she said.

"You're telling me?"

"Ah, that's right. You're surrounded by a bunch of kids that might even be able to out eat a dragon, aren't you?" she replied.

Rat took my wisecrack in earnest and nodded. She'd stole the punch line, and hearing it come from her mouth just made me depressed.

"What kind of dragon is he?" I asked.

"It's a wyr. They value devotion highly and are one of the most loyal types of dragons. They are a mix between purebloods and tyrellas."

"Tyrellas?"

"A tyrella is a big lizard-type monster. They can't fly, but they make for excellent transportation. They're rare though."

"I see."

I had no idea what she was talking about. I'd never seen one. Then again, I hadn't actually seen that many different kinds of dragons either.

"They aren't found in Melromarc, so you might not be familiar with them. They're not kept as pets around here either."

"Oh really?"

"It's a monster you're more likely to see in Faubrey, Shieldfreeden, or Siltvelt."

"I see."

"Is this the dragon from that egg?!"

Wyndia came over and approached the hatched dragon excitedly.

"Kwa!"

The baby dragon wasn't shy at all. It was acting cute to get as much attention as possible.

"Alright, I guess we'll take him out to hunt later," I said.

"Yeah! I don't think Filo will be happy though."

Wyndia nodded in agreement. She was playing with the baby dragon. All said and done, Wyndia was good about doing as she was told. She didn't try to complain about killing poor monsters or anything like that. On the contrary, she usually got really excited about going hunting. She seemed to be all about the strong preying on the weak. I didn't understand her at all. But she was probably right about Filo not being happy. Dragons and filolials were natural enemies, so there was nothing we could do about that.

"Your name is Gaelion," she said.

"Who said you could name him?!"

"Mr. Naofumi, the village children all chose the name together," said Raphtalia.

"Oh, really? In that case, I guess it's okay."

Coming up with a name was a hassle, anyway. I probably would have named it something lame like Dran. Considering that, Gaelion didn't seem bad at all.

"I'm going to go show him to everyone!"

And so Wyndia took charge of Gaelion and we took him out to level with the other villagers. I hoped he would grow up and become a strong fighter quickly.

"I miss Raph-chan," I said.

Raph-chan had been sitting on Filo's head a lot the past couple of days. She seemed to really like it there and wouldn't come to me when I called out to her. That made me kind of sad.

"Oh yeah, I wanted to ask you about that. Where did you find that monster?" asked Rat.

I glanced over at Raphtalia. She had a really bitter look on her face. I wondered what I should do. Giving a detailed

explanation would probably just end up causing trouble. But Raph-chan was my favorite. I wanted to make her stronger so that she could help out even more than she already did. I decided to explain, after all.

"Raph-chan is a shikigami that I made in the other world. Shikigamis are the equivalent to what we call familiars in this world. I used a lock of Raphtalia's hair as the base material and out came Raph-chan."

"Mr. Naofumi! That's your answer after pausing to think for so long?!" Raphtalia snapped.

Well, of course.

"I can use my shield's abilities to enhance her various attributes, just like with the bioplant. Doing so seems to require different materials and consumes energy though."

I was always tinkering around with Raph-chan's attributes. Enhancing them required materials, so I was making progress slowly but steadily. On a fundamental level, it worked a lot like powering up my shield.

"I didn't know there were familiars like that. I thought it was a new type of monster," said Rat.

"Making a new type of monster like her is my goal," I replied.

"That's news to me! What are you thinking, Mr. Naofumi?!" exclaimed Raphtalia.

Oh, damn. I'd accidentally revealed my aspirations to Raphtalia.

"And I guess you've been secretly planning to do this for some time," she said.

"Hmph. I won't change my mind about this one, Raphtalia. I can't let Raph-chan be the last of her kind."

"I don't understand why you're so passionate about her."

No matter how much two people trusted each other, there would always be things they couldn't understand about each other. But I didn't think that was necessarily a bad thing. It wasn't just because Raph-chan looked like Raphtalia. I really liked how she always played along with me too.

"What are you upset about, Raphtalia? If that's what Mr. Naofumi desires, then it's your duty to accept it as his retainer," said Atla.

"I'm upset because it's exactly the kind of thing I shouldn't accept! Think about it, Atla. Would you want someone to make a monster out of your hair?"

"If it were a monster that Mr. Naofumi would adore, then I would happily offer a lock of my hair!"

I thought about making a shikigami or familiar from a lock of Atla's hair. I pictured a little white tiger. If such a thing existed, I was sure it would be cute. But it was hard to imagine it being as cute as Raph-chan.

"Mr. Naofumi, I can tell what you're thinking just by looking at your face. I don't know why you like Raph-chan so much."

Ugh . . . Raphtalia had read my mind again.

"I couldn't tell what he was thinking this time. But I won't let you win like that again," said Atla.

What was she getting worked up about? Did Atla really want to read my face? Had she forgotten she was blind?

"In that case, Count, why not try raising the mutability of the familiar's attributes?"

"After what happened with the bioplant, I really wanted to avoid doing that."

"It's not like mutation can't produce favorable results too, you know. If you trust the familiar, then surely increasing the mutability just slightly is an option."

Hmm . . . She had a point.

"The legends say that the heroes created the filolials. Since you like her so much, maybe a monster based on her could end up becoming the next filolial," Rat continued.

What a glorious thought. And it wasn't unrelated to Rat's goal of creating a useful monster like the filolials. It would be killing two birds with one stone. I would get to make Raph-chan stronger. Rat would get to create the next filolial. That settled it. I'd try raising Raph-chan's mutability just a bit. I'd turn my familiar into a monster.

"Please don't do that, Mr. Naofumi," Raphtalia pleaded.

"I won't let anyone take away Raph-chan's future. Not even you, Raphtalia."

"Oh, jeez . . ."

She must have sensed my strong sense of determination,

because Raphtalia didn't push the issue any further.

"Anyway . . . Enough about that. We still need to go visit the old guy at the weapon shop today."

I decided to change the subject and avoid any more argument. The old guy was probably finishing up the katana I'd asked him to make right about now.

"Understood. Let's go then."

Raphtalia always let me run away from arguments in the end. That's what I liked about her. And so we left Rat behind and used my portal to make our way to the old guy's weapon shop.

Chapter Four: Stardust Blade

"There you are, kid."

When I arrived at the weapon shop, the old guy came out to greet me like he had been waiting on me. Business seemed to be booming. The shelves appeared to be rather bare inside the shop. Surely it wasn't just my imagination.

That reminded me. The supplies that had been left at the village two days earlier ended up taking care of a lot of my equipment needs. But getting rid of the equipment just to give the old guy work would have been a waste. If nothing else, I'd just have him reforge it.

"If you need help getting more materials, just let me know. The villagers will give you a hand if I tell them to."

"That's Tolly's family at your village, right? I'd feel bad."

"All the work I give them is really detailed. Digging holes might be a good way for them to destress."

Imiya and most of the other lumos tended to be really quiet and submissive. I figured they were the type that would accumulate a lot of stress. They would need a way to blow off some steam. They always looked like they were having fun when they were digging in the dirt, so I was pretty sure they would consider mining to be a fulfilling task.

"If we had the queen set us up with a mine, I'm sure they would clean it out for you."

"Thank you for your thoughtfulness, Shield Hero," said Imiya's uncle.

He bowed his head to me. I guess I was right about mining being a good way to destress for them. They would probably see it as an exciting event or something.

"Really? Well, if you two say so, then I might just take you up on that," said the old guy.

"Going by our stock of supplies, you should probably take him up on it soon," Imiya's uncle replied.

So they were running low, after all. I'd make the arrangements and send them out mining later.

"I'll get them on it and have the supplies delivered," I said.

I'd have Filo or her Underling #1 deliver the supplies to the old guy's shop.

"Thanks, kid. I'll make a list of the ores I need for you."

"It's nothing. I've asked my fair share of favors too."

"That's right. I finished that last one up for you already."

The old guy disappeared into the back of the shop and then returned with a single katana in hand. The design looked rather crude. The base of the blade near the guard still looked like a chunk of unprocessed siderite. I wondered if he'd shaped it that way on purpose. The old guy noticed where I was looking and started to explain.

"This is to guide the power of the siderite up into the blade. I know it looks strange, but there's nothing I can really do about that."

"I thought that might be the case."

It just looked like a poorly made katana to me.

"It'd been a long time since I last made a katana. Just like I suspected, I'm still far from the master's level."

"It looks like a pretty impressive blade to me," Raphtalia whispered.

She was squinting at the blade. Did it really look impressive? I tried using my appraisal skill.

Siderite Katana: quality: excellent

The quality was higher than it had been for the shield.

"I'm sure our master would have been able to make something much more impressive," said the old guy.

Oh? Regardless, I never felt like the old guy's work was lacking, so it was hard to imagine that being true.

"I'm not interested in wasting time wishing for the impossible. And even if your master were here, I still would have come to you."

"Thanks, kid. You're right. Crafting a variety of things is good for me."

"I'm not going to let you leave me behind, so I guess I

should get to work too. I'm getting some good ideas here," Imiya's uncle interjected.

"Oh? I won't let you catch up!"

The old guy and Imiya's uncle started glaring at each other. I'm sure I was only imagining the backdrop of flames that appeared behind them. They were good friends, but they were obviously rivals too.

"Can you sense anything about this katana, Atla?"

Being blind made Atla sensitive to life force, which allowed her to sense the presence of people. I had been curious whether she could sense other things as well, so I decided to ask what she thought.

"You mean that blade, I assume. I can feel power emanating from it. It seems to be slightly different than the usual equipment."

It seemed like she could sense something. Then again, she always made her way around the village effortlessly, so I figured that might be the case.

"It seems to be an excellent piece of equipment. Giving it to Raphtalia would be a waste," she added.

"You're really something," Raphtalia replied.

She seemed to realize that saying anything more than that would just cause trouble and decided not to engage Atla.

"Alright, let's have Raphtalia try holding it, then," I said.

"Righto! But don't be firing off any skills in my shop!"

"Yeah, yeah."

He was referring to the time I used Shooting Star Shield in the shop. I'd just wanted to show it to the old guy, but it ended up making a bit of a mess. I guess he was still upset about that.

Raphtalia held the katana and her weapon copy activated.

"It worked. I was able to copy the weapon."

"Oh yeah? Did you get any new skills?" I asked.

"I did. Let's see. The skill is called . . ."

It was probably Shooting Star Katana. Ren was the Sword Hero and he got his Shooting Star Sword skill when he copied the Siderite Sword. The other heroes and I had also gotten skills that were a combination of "Shooting Star" and our weapon names.

"Stardust Blade."

"Huh?"

It was "Stardust" instead of "Shooting Star." They both had to do with stars, but that still wasn't quite the same thing. I guess if a shooting star fell to the earth, it could be considered stardust. The weapon had come from siderite, so it wasn't a completely unrelated concept.

Also, the name wasn't being translated into Japanese by my shield. It was giving me a transliteration of the English instead. That reminded me that Raphtalia's vassal weapon had come from Kizuna's world. That must have meant that different rules applied, and it would give different skills too. That was kind of disappointing.

"The skill name is a bit different," she said.

Now that I thought about it, I had no idea how skill names were even decided. The skills that Kizuna, Glass, and L'Arc used had all been translated into Japanese by my shield. And yet, here in this world, Raphtalia's katana had given her a skill that sounded foreign.

"I thought it would be named 'Shooting Star.' That's disappointing," I said.

"Why is that disappointing?" she asked.

I thought I would be able to say she had joined the shooting star idiots. And that we were shooting star buddies.

"You're always letting Mr. Naofumi down, aren't you?" said Atla.

"Why are you blaming it on me?! The katana chose the name on its own!"

"Atla, you're overdoing it with comments like that. Watch yourself," I said.

"Understood!"

Did she really understand? Raphtalia gave the Siderite Katana back to the old guy, since she had finished copying it.

"Crafting this was good practice, anyway. Let me know if you need anything else," he said.

"Will do. And you give me a call if you get stuck too. There could be some kind of trick to working with those Spirit Tortoise materials that I could help figure out."

"Yeah, that's a possibility. Got it. I'm sure you want to try that new weapon out, right? Go give it a swing or two."

"Yeah. Alright, we'll be back. I'll bring some of that ore you wanted next time."

"I'll look forward to that."

And so we hurried back to the village. As for Stardust Blade, the name of the skill might have been different, but it was basically the same as Ren's Shooting Star Sword skill. The required SP and the cool down time were both reasonable, and Raphtalia said it should be quite useful.

Around a week passed, and things were strangely peaceful. I continued my Hengen Muso style training by sparring with Atla daily. When I had a bit of spare time, I took the lumos out to the mines and had them mine ore, which I delivered to the old guy afterward. Just as I had expected, the lumos really seemed to enjoy their time digging in the mines. They looked exactly like moles when they were digging around in the dirt with their claws. The look of joy on the old guy's face when he got the ore was unforgettable.

Wyndia and Rat had been keeping a regular growth log for the baby dragon, Gaelion. He had been growing really quickly since he'd been going out and leveling with the slaves. Sadeena had helped out, and he'd reached level 38 in just one week. He looked much bigger too.

It was morning, and I was already sighing. This again?

Atla had made a habit of showing up in my bed lately. Her advances had been overt to start out with, but recently she was bordering on outright aggressive. The fact that she was able to sneak into my bed without me noticing meant that she had some real skill. I wondered if she'd been practicing moving around silently or something. Maybe that was her way of dealing with my tendency to be sensitive to the presence of others.

I had a talk with Fohl every time it happened, but Atla still always managed to get away from him. In the beginning, Fohl had mistakenly assumed she was sleeping. Last night, he had apparently gotten sleepy and conked out. Atla had made him a snack before that, and I was guessing that she had mixed some kind of sleeping drug in it. Maybe she'd gotten her hands on something from Gaelion. I'd heard that he'd gained an ability called Sleep Breath.

Before that, she'd put Fohl to sleep . . . physically. I wondered what had happened this time.

"Sorry, Mr. Naofumi! I fell asleep with the children last night, which is why I didn't come back."

The door swung open suddenly, and Raphtalia, of all people, came barging in with the worst possible timing. Her expression changed to one of puzzlement.

"Umm . . . Nothing happened between you two, right?"

"What the hell would happen?"

Atla showing up in my bed like this sure was troublesome. Being puritanical, Raphtalia was probably upset now. But come on, did she really think I would do something like that? Sadeena was the one that actually scared me. She showed up every now and then too. She'd get drunk and come to "hang out." I woke up early, so I was always tired at night. Didn't she know that?

Raphtalia sighed.

"You're right. You're not that kind of person," she said.

"What's that supposed to mean? Anyway, get Fohl over here. He's the one we should really be worried about."

This time he'd been on the floor, wrapped up in a bamboo mat. He'd been back at the house lying on his stomach and struggling, unable to move.

"Mr. Naofumi? Why don't you stop her?" asked Raphtalia.

"I told her to leave and chased her out once. She ended up sleeping outside in front of the house. Before that, I set her slave curse to punish her if she got into my bed and she still showed up."

"Is she some kind of monster?!"

I chased her out and she went and slept in front of my house. I tried to use the slave curse to punish her, but apparently it was ineffective. She had gotten used to being in pain from head to toe when she was sick. She just kept sleeping like nothing had happened. So this is what it meant to make good on one's word. Fohl had gotten really pissed off, but what was I supposed to do?

"That's right. You're not that kind of person."

"That's the second time you've said that today, so I'm going to repeat myself too. What's that supposed to mean?"

"Hmm? What's the matter, Mr. Naofumi?"

Atla woke up. She was acting like she was completely innocent. Did she not realize we were trying to figure out what to do about her?

"Do you really not know?" I asked.

"Does sleeping together really bother you that much?"

"Honestly, it's a problem. I'm sure you're in pain too."

"Rather than feel any pain, it makes me feel warm inside. Why can't we sleep together?"

"Your brother will make a fuss about it."

"Atla! Why do you keep trying to go sleep with a jerk like that?!"

"See what I mean?"

"Don't worry about it, Brother. I'm simply fond of Mr. Naofumi is all."

Well, damn it. I guess Atla was just going to be a troublemaker. Her personality was completely different than when she had been sick. I could only think of one possibility.

"Raphtalia. Fohl."

"Yes?"

"What?!"

"I think this might be a side effect of the Elixir of Yggdrasil."

"Huh?"

Yeah. I couldn't imagine it being anything else.

"Look at the old lady. She calls me 'Saint' and acts fond of me too. The Elixir of Yggdrasil must make the recipient infatuated with whoever gives it to them. Maybe that's why even the slave curse can't stop Atla."

It was the single weakness of the otherwise almighty medicine. That had to be it. The side effect must have been stronger in Atla's case since the medicine had been so effective for her. Setting the slave curse settings to be any more restrictive could be dangerous. Worst case, Atla could die.

"We'll just have to be extra careful until the side effects wear off," I said.

"I see. Understood!"

"Huh?!"

Raphtalia seemed to be persuaded by my theory, but Fohl sounded unconvinced.

"Is something wrong?" I asked him.

"Oh, uh, no! You're right! It has to be a side effect! The medicine was powerful enough to completely heal Atla, after all. There's no doubt it's just a side effect!"

"You're wrong, Mr. Naofumi! I am truly fond of you, Mr. Naofumi!" Atla argued.

"Come on, Atla! We're going leveling again, today!" shouted Fohl.

"But, Mr. Naofumi!" Atla called out.

Fohl dragged Atla out of the house. Then again, I'd be training with her after breakfast, but whatever. I closed the door. As soon as I did, I heard a knock.

"Yes?"

Raphtalia responded and opened the door. But there was no one there.

"Huh?"

Raphtalia looked all around. Confused, she closed the door.

"There was no one there," she said.

"Yeah. Over the past few days, someone in the village has been playing pranks, it seems."

Morning and night, one of the slaves had been knocking on my door and then running away whenever I was at home. It had been happening especially often whenever I was the only one there. The fact that it had happened while Raphtalia was there was unexpected.

"I thought that maybe the door was just making noises at first, but that doesn't seem to be the case."

I had one of the soldiers who fixed up the houses take a look at it, but he told me that it wasn't crooked or anything. I tried standing by the door and waiting for whoever it was the other day. I opened the door the instant there was a knock. It had been Keel. I tried the same thing once early in the morning, and it had been Atla showing up at her usual time. When it was

Keel, she had shown up with some of the other slaves to ask what we were having for breakfast, so I was pretty sure she wasn't the culprit.

"Maybe I'll try interrogating the villagers at breakfast time."

"Do you really think any of the children would do something like that to you?"

"One of them is doing it, whether I think so or not."

"I guess so . . ."

Raphtalia wanted to believe in the villagers. I could understand how she felt. But it was a fact that one of them was misbehaving, and that meant that whoever it was needed to be punished.

"But whatever. It's about time for me to make my usual visit to the monster stable. You want to come with me?"

"Umm, sure."

And so I went about finishing up my usual morning routine before making preparations for breakfast.

Chapter Five: Knock and Run

At breakfast, once all of the slaves had gathered, I made a quick adjustment to the slave seal settings and then addressed them.

"I want whoever has been causing mischief lately, when I'm at home, to come forward now."

Nobody responded. On top of that, none of the slave seals activated. Did that mean it wasn't one of the slaves? In that case . . . I glared at Ren and the soldiers that were stationed at the village. They all shook their heads in denial. Who the hell was it, then?

"Hmm . . ."

"What's wrooong, Master?"

"Rafu?"

Filo was eating breakfast with us today. Raph-chan was sitting on top of her head, like usual. What was so great about her head, anyway?

"Someone has been knocking on my door and then running away whenever I'm at home alone."

Whoever it was would be gone by the time I could open the door, which meant that the person had to be really fast. That was true even if they were hiding somewhere. I could try having Atla or Raphtalia keep watch, but the culprit seemed to have really sharp intuition and didn't show up when someone was standing guard. The worst part was that they came in the middle of the night too.

"Oh? Should I stand guard?" asked Filo.

"Rafu?"

"The person doesn't come when someone is standing guard. I'll just have to lure them out. I'm going to catch them no matter what."

Filo didn't give a reaction to my show of determination, which meant that she wasn't the culprit either.

"Okaaay!"

"Listen up, Raphtalia and Atla. I'm going to catch the culprit this afternoon, so I want you to stay away from my place after lunch."

"Understood. I've been wanting to ask the master about using life force, so I'll go do that," said Raphtalia.

"But, Mr. Naofumi, I want to be with you," Atla replied.

"Didn't you just hear me say I was going to lure the culprit out? That goes for all of you. Don't come knocking on my door today, no matter what."

"Okay!" shouted the slaves.

Of course, if the culprit didn't show up, that would make all of them suspects. Either way, after I finished my late morning training, I headed back to my house to lure the culprit out and waited for a knock.

Knock, knock.

I warned everyone to stay away from my place that morning. That had to be the culprit. I wasn't going to let them get away today. Even if it wasn't the culprit, I was going to catch whoever just knocked!

"Shield Prison!"

I trapped whoever had knocked on the door in a cage of shields and then opened the door to see who the prankster was. The prison was shaking as someone crashed around inside. The trap had been a success.

"What's going on, Count?"

"Oh hey, Rat. What are you doing here at a time like this?"

"I'm just taking a walk for a change of pace. What's going on here?"

"I mentioned that some prankster had been knocking on my door and running away this morning, right?"

"I guess you did. So the prankster is in there? I wonder who it is."

We waited for the prison's effect to wear off so that we could see who was inside.

"Kwaaaa!"

I'm pretty sure Rat and I both had the same look of bewilderment on our faces. I guess it did make sense to suspect the monsters if the culprit wasn't a slave. But I never imagined that one of the monsters would be doing something like knocking on doors and running away. Gaelion the Knock and Run Dragon flew away as soon as he was free from the cage of shields. Without hesitation, I brought up the monster seal settings and delivered him a punishing jolt.

"Kwaaaaaa?!"

Gaelion fell out of the sky and writhed about on the ground.

Including his tail, Gaelion was around two meters in length now. He looked pretty much like what someone might expect a dragon to look like. I guess his tail was a bit on the fat side though. He had big eyes and still looked cute. He seemed a bit overweight too. His growth had finally started to level off to a certain extent. He hadn't gotten as big as I imagined he would.

Wyndia heard Gaelion squealing and came running over.

"What's wrong with Gaelion?!"

"He's the prankster I mentioned this morning. I caught him in the act."

"Huh? Gaelion was the culprit?!"

Wyndia looked at me and seemed to be contemplating whether or not to try and protect Gaelion. I guess even she knew better.

"Don't try to stick up for him. Wrongdoing must be punished."

"Fine. Bad Gaelion! Causing mischief is not okay!"

"Kwaa . . ."

"What's going on, Master?"

Filo and Raph-chan heard the ruckus and came over. I guess Filo wasn't off playing with Melty today. Or maybe she had gotten curious after this morning and stuck around the village.

"Ohhh! He's getting scoooolded!"

Filo started dancing around happily when she noticed Gaelion was being scolded.

"Gaelion is getting scoooolded! Take thaaaat, dragon! Maaasteeer's only gonna ride Fiiiloooo!"

"Kwaaaaa!"

Gaelion clearly became upset when Filo mocked him.

"Rafu! Rafu rafu!"

Raph-chan was smacking Filo lightly with her hands and tail as if trying to scold her for behaving in such a way, but Filo went on dancing completely unfazed. I decided to punish Filo too.

"Akyaaaa! Wh . . . why meee?"

"Don't laugh at others' misfortune."

"B . . . buuuut Master does!"

Hmm . . . She had a point there. I immediately deactivated the monster seal.

"Did you just let her win the argument?!" Rat snapped.

"I do laugh at the misfortune of others. So I have no room to talk."

"Rafu!"

Raph-chan's squeak was timed perfectly. That's right. I had no room to talk. I'd take pride in that.

"Really?"

Rat held her head in her hands. She had a look of bewilderment on her face. I'd laughed at the misfortunes of Witch and Trash, and I'd laughed at Glass when she got scolded by Kizuna. Even if there was merit to my objection, my words would hold no weight.

"Umm . . . Just because you two are rivals doesn't mean that you can treat him like that," said Wyndia.

"Boo!"

"You know what will happen if you make me mad, right?" I taunted.

"Nooo!"

What was this farce?

"Sheesh . . . Why would you do such a mischievous thing anyway?" Wyndia asked Gaelion.

She stroked his face gently. Gaelion squeaked meekly.

"He says he wanted the Shield Hero to play with him," she said.

"Huh?"

"You haven't spent much time playing with him, have you? But you spend plenty of time with that bird," she went on.

"Hmph!"

Filo and Wyndia glared at each other.

"Hold on, now. Are you saying that Gaelion is going to cause problems like this if I don't play with him?"

"Kwa!"

He nodded! Was he a little attention-seeker? Sheesh . . . I looked over at Rat.

"Physical contact and spending time with your monsters is important. That's true for both of them," she said.

Oh, really? What a hassle! Raph-chan never acted selfish like that.

"Alright then. Filo. Gaelion. I'll make a little bit of time to play with each of you on alternating days. But if either of you interfere with the other's time, you lose your play time."

"Hmph!"

"Kwa!"

The two of them glared at each other and made complaining noises.

"Okay, fine. Neither of you get play time."

"F . . . fine!"

"Kwa! Kwa!"

They both gave in and agreed to my plan. Raph-chan would get more play time than either of them, of course. I'd play with her all day long if she wanted me to.

"Alright, today is Gaelion's day."

"Kwaaa!"

"Whaaat?"

"You're older than him."

"Hmph . . . Fine. I'll be back later, theeen. Come on, Wyndia. Let's gooo!"

"Okay."

Filo took Wyndia with her and went out to level.

"Alright, Gaelion. What do you want to do? I'll play with you until the end of lunch break."

"Kwa!"

Gaelion wagged his tail happily like a dog. He had good reaction times, so I figured we could spend some time playing with my Frisbee Shield. I transformed my shield into a frisbee and threw it. Gaelion flapped his wings and dashed off after the shield gaily.

It didn't make much sense getting caught up on how things worked in a fantasy world, but the little guy sure could fly. I chucked the frisbee and when he caught it, it disappeared for a brief moment and then reappeared in my hand. Gaelion was in good spirits. He flew back over to me and licked me all over my face. Unlike a certain bird that never shut up, his innocence sure was refreshing.

I continued to play with Gaelion for a bit, and after a while, Raphtalia and Atla showed up.

"Mr. Naofumi, did you catch the culprit?" asked Raphtalia.

"Yeah, it was this little fella."

"Kwa!"

"Huh? Gaelion was the culprit?"

I nodded to Raphtalia.

"He was sad because I hadn't been playing with him."

"Well, I guess you had left him completely to Wyndia and Rat."

"I can sympathize!" Atla interjected.

"Kwa!"

Atla and Gaelion shook hands firmly. Why the hell were they getting along so well now?

"Since Raphtalia and Atla are here, that means break time is over."

"Kwa . . ."

Gaelion sounded incredibly sad when he squeaked. But that wasn't going to make me keep playing with him. Raphtalia rubbed him on the head and made a suggestion.

"I know he can't participate in our training, but surely you could let him watch."

"I don't want to spoil him."

"That's too bad, isn't it? Off you go," Atla snapped.

"Kwa?!"

Gaelion looked at Atla like he had been betrayed. Wasn't she shaking his hand just a few moments earlier?

"Why do you always have to be so extreme?"

Raphtalia was staring at Atla in amazement. I felt the same way. After thinking for a few moments, Raphtalia looked at Gaelion and spoke to him gently.

"How about this? You can watch us train, but you have to do your best to level quickly in return."

"Kwa!"

Gaelion nodded enthusiastically. Hmm . . . He couldn't speak human language, but he seemed to be pretty intelligent. Raph-chan was still cuter than him, but I'd have to give Gaelion props for being humble.

"Well, leveling up and getting stronger is his job, so I guess if watching us will motivate him, then that can't be a bad thing."

"There you have it," said Atla.

"What is that supposed to mean, Atla? You were ready to turn your back on him without a second thought just a moment ago," Raphtalia responded.

"Seriously."

"Kwa! Kwa!"

And so Gaelion ended up watching our afternoon training nearby. I wasn't playing with him, so it wasn't like I'd breached the agreement with Filo. But eventually night fell, and Gaelion still hadn't left my side.

"It's nighttime already, you know."

Gaelion had forced his way into my house. He was rather large, so that was a problem. I was trying to be tolerant, since I'd mostly just left him on his own since he had hatched. But I was starting to run out of patience.

"You know, Gaelion might be just what you need, actually," said Raphtalia.

"What I need?"

"To deal with the Atla issue. You could have Gaelion run her off before she gets in bed with you."

She was suggesting I use Gaelion as a guard dog, in other words. I was pretty sure I could have Filo do the same thing. But that sure was a bold suggestion for Raphtalia.

"Little Naofumi! I'm here to pick up little Raphtalia!"

Sadeena called out and then stuck her head in the door.

"Oh hey, Sadeena."

"Oh? What's this? Why is little Gaelion in your house?"

"The little guy won't leave my side. And now Raphtalia is suggesting that I use him as a guard dog to keep Atla out."

"I see. Well, the children who were most traumatized by their experience as slaves have started to get much better lately. Before long, Raphtalia should be able to start sleeping here again. It might not be a bad idea to have him deal with Atla until then."

Sadeena seemed to agree with Raphtalia's idea.

"Can't we just talk Atla into stopping?" I asked.

"I already tried that. Sadeena did too."

"Yeah, we did. And then little Atla said she wanted to marry you. That one surprised me," added Sadeena.

I sighed. Atla sure was brazen. Or something like that. She was just a bit confused after having been healed. It would pass. Either way, I wasn't the kind of sicko that would marry a little girl like that.

"I tried to make it clear to her. I told her you were a loser that wasn't interested in anything like doing the dirty with a girl," said Sadeena.

"A los—you wench!"

What was she thinking calling me a loser, of all things?!

"Atla's reply was even worse than Sadeena's remark. She said, 'It's okay. Mr. Naofumi will lie with me when he is ready.'"

I didn't need Atla believing in me like that! Oh, hell! What a mess! I wanted to just run away from it all.

"It would be best if you just outright rejected her, little Naofumi."

"I turned her away, of course."

That wasn't enough to make Atla give up. She had an iron will. She added a lot to our offensive capabilities and she followed orders without complaining. Her excessive fondness for me was her only problem. I'd just leave it at that.

"I guess all I can do is hope that Fohl will hurry up and grow stronger than her so that he can finally stop her from coming over here."

I had even considered selling her off to get rid of her. But she was stubborn enough to ignore the slave curse's punishment, so it was plenty likely that she would just escape and end up right back here. Besides, I didn't really want to go that far. We'd just have to come to some kind of agreement.

While Raphtalia, Sadeena, and I were talking about dealing

with Atla, Gaelion started digging around in my stuff that was lying around the room. Did he find something stinky? I could hear him sniffing at something. He had his head stuck in a bag that was full of materials meant to be used for new weapons and equipment.

"Hey! Don't mess around with that stuff!"

Gaelion was a curious little guy. Filo did the same kind of thing every now and then. I was used to dealing with it. Or that's what I thought, anyway. Never in my wildest dreams did I imagine that something in that bag would trigger the incident that was about to happen.

Chapter Six: Level Drain

"Kwa!"

The bag fell over and everything came tumbling out. First Gaelion was knocking on my door and running away, and now he was rummaging through my bags. I guess Filo still did that kind of thing too, though. She would also rummage through my garbage. She called it "treasure hunting." I guess Gaelion was no different. Actually, I wouldn't be surprised if they were in the middle of some kind of jurisdictional dispute over who should get to rummage through my garbage or something.

"Oh, come on. Have some consideration for the person who has to clean that up."

A bunch of monster bones, some ore, and the dragon emperor core that had been part of my Barbaroi Armor all came tumbling out of the bag. The dragon emperor core must have caught Gaelion's attention, because his eyes were glued to it as it rolled across the floor. He started to bat it around, like a cat probably would have done.

I guess Filo and Gaelion both liked shiny objects. I seemed to remember Filo being mesmerized by the dragon core I'd been using before this one. That brought back fond memories of Romina working with the cores back in Kizuna's world.

"Kwa?!"

Seeing Gaelion bat the core around playfully did make me feel a bit warm and fuzzy inside, but this wasn't play time. I decided to give him a little scolding and then clean up.

"Is that a dragon emperor core?! Little Naofumi, hurry up and take that away from Gaelion!"

"Huh?"

Sadeena suddenly started shouting at me. There was a look of urgency in her eyes. Gaelion bit at the dragon emperor core and held it in his mouth.

"Hey! That doesn't belong to you. Give it to me!"

Gaelion completely ignored my reprimand and let the core slide deep into his mouth before . . . Gulp! He swallowed it whole.

"Hey! Spit that out!"

I grabbed Gaelion by the shoulders and shook him. Did the monster seal have some kind of punishment that could make him spit it out? I pulled up the settings and started poking around.

And that's when it happened.

"Kwa?!"

Gaelion opened his eyes wide and starting convulsing, like he was having a seizure.

"Kw . . . Gya . . . Gyuuu . . ."

He broke into a cold sweat. His eyes were squeezed shut

tightly and he was moaning, as if he were trying to resist something. I could hear a faint creaking sound resonating from his whole body.

"H . . . hey . . ."

"Umm . . . There's an incredibly sinister life force flooding out of Gaelion! There's so much of it!" Raphtalia shouted while looking at Gaelion.

"Sinister life force?"

"Yes! Be careful!"

I turned around to look at Gaelion, and some blackish, purplish . . . magic power or something was flooding out of his body. It was visible to the naked eye. I'd seen this color before. It looked like the aura that surrounded Filo whenever I used the Shield of Wrath.

"Little Naofumi, stand back!"

Sadeena faced Gaelion and readied her harpoon. She thrust it at him and tried to catch his tail with it, but Gaelion curled his tail up quickly and jumped sideways.

"Gyaaoooo!"

Gaelion looked up at the ceiling with bloodshot eyes and howled. When he did, a cloud of magical breath shot out of his mouth and instantly blew the ceiling right off the house.

"Gya!"

With a loud swish, Gaelion spread his wings out wide and took flight. Alright! I had the monster seal settings open already, so I'd just use the punishment setting to drop him out of the sky. I activated the monster seal. But the screen just flickered, and nothing else happened.

"You blew my damned roof off! Settle down!"

If the seal wasn't going to work, I'd just have to take things into my own hands! I jumped up and grabbed on to the little troublemaker.

"Gyaooooo!"

"Whoa!"

Gaelion smashed into me with the weight of his whole body. The impact had managed to just knock me away and I fell down on my butt.

"Ouch . . ."

Wait a second. He'd caught me off guard, but even so, would Gaelion really be able to knock me away? It went without saying that it would take a ridiculous amount of attack power to overcome my defense rating and break free from my hold. That would mean he was at least as powerful as Ren or Raphtalia.

"Gyaoowwww . . ."

Gaelion glared at me with bloodshot eyes. They were no longer the slightly goofy eyes I'd seen only moments before. They were the eyes of a wild dragon driven by feral instinct. I could feel a pressure emanating from them that sent shivers down my spine.

I held my shield out in front of me and glared at Gaelion

as I readied myself to grab him for real this time. Sadeena and Raphtalia were right there. It could be dangerous for them, if he used that breath attack that blew my roof off again.

"Gyaooooo!"

Gaelion let out a loud screech and then flew off somewhere into the distance.

"Something was clinging to Gaelion. What in the world was that?"

Atla showed up from out of nowhere and began to comment, but I dashed out of the building to see which direction Gaelion had gone.

"Wh . . . what was that?"

The slaves that were still in the village heard the ruckus and came running over.

"What's going on?"

"What in the world happened here?"

"What is it? What happened?"

Rat and Wyndia both looked in the direction that I was looking. So did Fohl and Atla.

"Well, actually . . ."

I told them about Gaelion eating the dragon emperor core and ending up like he did.

"Emperor core, you say? You sure have some strange items, Count."

"You have any idea what might have happened?" I asked.

"The biology of the dragon species is still largely shrouded in mystery. I've heard of dragons wanting cores from other dragons, but I wouldn't have thought it would go on a rampage like that."

"Little Naofumi, where did you get your hands on that dragon emperor core?"

Sadeena grabbed my shoulder and began to interrogate me.

"It was originally from a dragon that lived in the mountains near a village in the east."

"In that case, it's highly likely that Gaelion's body was commandeered by the soul of the dragon emperor that was in that core."

Sadeena sure seemed to know a lot about this kind of thing.

"Inside of that dragon emperor core is something like an organ that contains the soul of the dragon within it. I've heard that other dragons can use such cores to boost their own powers or absorb the memories of the dragon it came from," she went on.

"Does that mean . . . Gaelion absorbed the memories of the dragon zombie and that's why he went on a rampage?"

"No way . . ." mumbled Ren.

He staggered backward, unable to say anything else.

"The dragon that you defeated is the one that turned into the dragon zombie, right?" I asked him.

"I have to stop it, no matter what!" he shouted.

"If you try to do that, it may just come back to life, fueled by its hatred for you," I said.

"In that case . . . We can still stop it! Naofumi! You raised that dragon, didn't you?!"

"He did seem fond of me, but it was the villagers who raised him. This one was in charge of him."

I pointed at Wyndia. Still, he was a cute dragon and I didn't want to give up on him if possible. It would depend on where he had run off to. We needed to go find him and capture him.

"How do you feel about having killed that dragon, Sword Hero?"

Wyndia glared at Ren as she questioned him with a stern tone of voice. She was a dragon fanatic, so she probably just didn't want Ren to be the one to kill the dragon.

"I'm sure he probably just killed it because it was an easy target. He probably knew about it from some quest in a game he'd played or something," I said.

"That . . . That's true. But I know I caused a lot of people problems by killing it. I've heard that region is plagued by disease now. I do feel bad about killing it."

Ren got depressed so easily.

"I can't apologize enough. I don't know how to make up for it," he went on.

Ren cast his eyes downward regretfully. It didn't seem like Wyndia was going to push the issue, but something about Ren's response bothered me.

"You know . . ." I said.

"Huh?"

"I'm only saying this because you seem so naïve, but did you ever stop to think that the monsters you've killed might have had families? That they might have been leading happy lives?"

The blood slowly drained from Ren's face. I guess that thought had never occurred to him.

"Do you plan to go around to all of those families and tell them, 'I'm the one that killed your family member. I take full responsibility,' or something? And if you're going to draw a line and say monsters are monsters, then what about our monsters over there in the monster stable?"

"Umm . . . uhh . . . I . . ."

I sighed. Adolescents were such a hassle to deal with.

"It's the same whether you eat plants or animals. In the end, you have to take other lives in order to go on living. In fact, it would be even better if you just accept that trampling over others is a part of life," I explained.

"Isn't that a contradiction?"

"Huh? What the hell are you talking about? You're a hero. We have to brutally murder monsters to get stronger so that we can save the world, you know? It's the law of the jungle."

I'd heard that even killing humans gave experience in this world. If he wanted to try to insist on some kind of idealistic rubbish, like monsters and humans being different, he would just have to wait until he got summoned to an ideal world.

"So, Ren, whenever you kill a monster, do it with full awareness of the choice you're making. That is, if you're serious about wanting to save the world."

"Fine . . . I understand."

He didn't look very convinced. Ren had been spending a lot of time with Eclair, after all. That was probably making him even more of an idealist.

"But even so . . . I want to apologize and try to protect everyone."

"Uh huh, whatever."

The guy had a problem. If I didn't sort him out eventually, he was probably going to go off the rails again.

"We have to go after him," said Wyndia.

Her icy gaze was fixed on Ren and she had a sense of urgency in her voice. Gaelion was her beloved dragon. I needed that dragon emperor core for my armor too. Worst-case scenario, I might even have to defeat Gaelion to get it back.

"I know. We just have to call Filo back and then we'll head out," I said.

We could have gone after him without waiting on Filo. But having her take us would make things much quicker. Sheesh. I hadn't even gotten to ride my dragon and now I had to put him down.

"Here's a horse to ride to the neighboring town," a soldier announced.

I mounted the horse that one of the soldiers had prepared and was about to head off to get Filo. Just then, Eclair come riding up on her own horse from the direction of the town.

"Mr. Iwatani!"

"What is it? I was just about to head your way."

"It's an emergency! Melty is calling for you! Something is wrong with Filo!"

"What?!"

"What? Why Filo?"

"Fine. Raphtalia and Ren, you two start making preparations to head out," I said.

"Understood!" Raphtalia replied.

"Okay. There's nothing I can do to help treat her, so I'll get started on preparations like you said," said Ren.

I left things at the village to Ren and Raphtalia and headed toward the neighboring town.

I followed Eclair to the clinic that had been built in the town. When I stepped into the clinic, Melty came running over. She looked like she was about to cry.

"Umm . . . Filo just started writhing in pain all of a sudden. Please help her, Naofumi!"

"You know I'm not a doct . . . healer, right? Still, I'll do what I can, of course."

"Promise you'll save her!"

Even if I did promise . . . If it was something really serious, all I could do was use the Elixir of Yggdrasil and hope that helped.

"Let's take a look at her first," I said.

"Okay."

Melty and one of the clinic doctors took me to the examination room. Filo was inside, lying there limply in her filolial form.

"Ugh . . . uuugghh . . ."

Filo's whole body was undergoing the same kind of change that always happened when I used the Shield of Wrath. It looked the worst near her stomach. Actually, it was worse than usual. The sinister aura was flowing out of her body like a dense cloud of smoke. I guess that would have been an apt description. The crest feather on the top of her head was glowing like it was trying to fight back, but the sinister aura seemed to be winning.

"Rafu . . ."

Raph-chan was trying to help by batting at the aura with her hand, but it didn't seem to have much effect.

"What's happening to her? Would using the Elixir of Yggdrasil stop it?"

"That's unclear. However, whatever it is, there seems to be a strong curse component to it. It would probably be best not to expect much, even from the Elixir of Yggdrasil."

The clinic doctor's voice was filled with uncertainty.

"Oh, it's you, Master . . ."

Filo moaned painfully. She looked at me and reached out with her wing. I stroked her cheek gently. Even though she wasn't in her human form, Filo squinted contentedly when I stroked her cheek. She continued to moan painfully.

I checked Filo's condition using my status magic. It would notify me of basic abnormalities, like if she were paralyzed by a poison or something. Filo's status screen was all fuzzy and kept flickering. Something was obviously not right.

And that's when I noticed it. Filo's level was lower than I remembered it being. Had she leveled down? What was going on? Several possibilities came to mind, but from what I had to go on at the moment, it was impossible to determine which one was most likely.

"Go get Rat and Sadeena from the village and bring them here," I told Melty.

"Okay," she replied.

After a few minutes, Rat and Sadeena showed up, along with Fohl, Atla, and Wyndia too.

"Filo! What happened?!"

Wyndia ran over to Filo, clearly worried. Were the two of them even close? Or maybe that's just how a monster fanatic would respond in a situation like this.

"Rat. Sadeena. What do you think?"

"We just got here. All I can say is that it looks like she's experiencing the effects of some kind of curse. Mind if I do a quick examination?"

Rat looked over the doctor's medical report and then started poking at Filo.

"I checked her status and her level is gradually dropping, bit by bit," I said.

"Judging by this aura, I'm guessing it has something to do with little Gaelion going on a rampage."

Sadeena's conclusion seemed to match up with mine.

"But why would little Filo be showing symptoms like that?" she asked.

"Leveling down? That means it's a really powerful curse. Even so, I've never seen symptoms this bad," Rat responded.

"What do you think, Rat?"

"I think Sadeena is right, without a doubt. But . . . Is there some kind of connection between Filo and Gaelion? I know they don't get along, but it has to be more than that," she said.

"If we assume that the cause is not the dragon emperor core, but rather the previous dragon zombie core, then there is a connection."

"What do you mean?"

"When we faced the dragon zombie, Filo ended up eating the dragon's core. What I had was just a single fragment of that core."

In fact, Filo had basically defeated the zombie dragon, and she'd done it by eating its core. It would make sense that it had to do with what was going on now.

"I see. So Gaelion going on a rampage would also affect Filo, since she ate the core that caused his rampage."

"That's my guess."

"In that case, check Gaelion's status. I have a feeling that there's more going on here."

I checked Gaelion's status. Just like with Filo, the screen was all fuzzy and many of the details were unclear. But . . .

"His level is rising."

Gaelion had only been level 36 before, but now he was level 45. He'd soared right past the class-up level limit.

"Umm . . . I can sense a sinister power flowing out of Filo," said Atla.

"Yeah, we can see that."

"That's not what I mean."

Atla pointed at something. But there was nothing there.

"Little Atla can sense things that can't be seen, so she might be able to determine the direction that the power is flowing."

"Hmm . . ."

That was certainly possible. Her abilities were surprisingly useful. The problem was figuring out where the power flowing out of Filo was going. It seemed to be heading in the same direction that Gaelion had gone.

"Can we make Filo throw up the core?"

"Not possible. It seems like there are fragments circulating throughout her whole body."

I checked Filo's status. Judging from the speed that her level was dropping, she had around two days left. She would probably return to level 1 before we could find Gaelion. Actually, that's assuming we were lucky enough for it to stop there. Worst-case scenario, she could end up dying.

"Also, I can sense power leaking from you too, Mr. Naofumi," Atla said.

"What?"

I checked my own stats. From the looks of it, nothing seemed out of the ordinary.

"It's coming from somewhere near your left arm."

That's where my shield was. That meant that power was leaking out of my shield. Now that I thought about it, hadn't I absorbed part of the core into my shield? Could it possibly be leeching off of my shield's abilities? I checked my list of shields just in case, but everything seemed normal.

"It . . . seems to be leaking out and amplifying something."

"Amplifying?"

I had no idea what Atla was talking about, but it was clear that we needed to be on our guard.

"Where is the old lady? She's always useful at times like this."

"The master took Rishia on a trip to go train, along with some of the village children and soldiers!" Eclair replied.

"She needs to open up a training hall here in town, damn it!" I shouted.

Why the hell did she have to go off to train at a time like this?!

"Where is S'yne?!"

"She said she was going to Zeltoble to earn some money!"

"Oh, come on! Why can nothing go my way?!"

S'yne would most likely show up when she noticed something was off though. I'd call for her if I needed her.

"Anyway, someone needs to figure out where the old lady went and tell her to come back. We're going after Gaelion immediately."

We would run out of time otherwise. Atla stepped forward. She had a determined look on her face.

"Mr. Naofumi, I would like to try something on Filo," she said.

"What?"

"What are you doing, Atla?" asked Fohl.

"I'm going to do what I can to try to slow the power leak."

Atla reached out to Filo, who was still lying on the floor, and placed her right hand, and then her left hand on Filo's chest.

"Ughh . . . aaah . . ."

Filo had been moaning painfully, but she stopped. She opened her eyes and slowly stood up.

"That feels a little better," she said.

"Filo!"

"Rafu!"

Melty ran over to Filo. Raph-chan was squeaking happily.

"That should buy us some time," said Atla.

"Alright. Get the carriage and . . ."

Damn it! We didn't have a quick means of transportation. I'd sent our other filolial, Filo Underling #1, out with the peddling division. We would just have to borrow one of the filolials from the town.

"I'm going after Gaelion. Raphtalia, Fohl, Atla, Sadeena, Ren, and Eclair, you're coming with me. Umm, valley . . . I mean . . . you and Rat—"

"Pulling Master's carriage . . . is myyyy job!"

Filo put Atla on her back. She had a strong sense of determination in her voice.

"No, Filo! You need to rest!" Melty shouted.

"She's right. You should take it easy," I said.

But Filo shook her head in refusal.

"Nooo! I'm going! No matter what!"

She didn't have her usual energy, but she stepped forward and made it clear that she intended to come with us at any cost. If that were the case, she'd probably just chase after us, even if I did try to leave her behind. Filo could be really stubborn.

"Fine, but if anything happens, I'm going to leave you at a

clinic and have someone else pull the carriage."

"Mr. Naofumi?!"

"Can you keep the leak under control, Atla?"

"Y . . . yes!"

"Alright then."

"I'm going too!" shouted Melty.

She was clearly fighting back tears. Her best friend was in a predicament. Like Filo, she'd probably do whatever it took to come with us, ignoring the fact that she was the princess, of course.

"You better not do anything reckless. You're the princess, you know."

"I'm Filo's friend, first and foremost!"

"Alright then."

Before, it had been Filo whining about wanting to protect Melty. Filo sure had made a good friend.

"Alright, we're heading out first to go after Gaelion. I want you castle soldiers to hurry up and get word to the old lady."

"Yes, sir!"

We loaded up into the carriage, which Filo stubbornly pulled back to the village. There, we picked up Ren, Raphtalia, and the others and then headed out.

We had been on the road for four hours. Thanks to Atla, we had just barely managed to keep Filo's stats from dropping any further. Even so, her experience points were still seeping out of her body, bit by bit. The leveling down had slowed, but the situation was still bad. Just as I had expected, the direction that Gaelion had gone was leading toward the town in the east where we fought the dragon zombie.

Pant! Pant!

"Filo . . ."

Atla was riding on Filo's back and Melty was steering the carriage. Rat and Wyndia were sorting out the details of the situation, and Sadeena was keeping an eye out at the rear. Ren and Eclair were both ready to engage at a moment's notice.

Filo was clearly exhausted. We needed to hurry, or things were going to get ugly. Motoyasu! Your beloved Filo is in trouble! Where the hell was that creep when we needed him? There couldn't be a better time than this to come rushing to Filo's rescue. Sheesh. The guy wouldn't go away when he was unwanted, but he was nowhere to be found when he might actually be able to help.

"If worse comes to worst, we may have to put Gaelion down. You understand that, right?"

I was talking to Wyndia. She had been the fondest of Gaelion. He might have belonged to me, but I figured she deserved some say in the matter. She had looked after him, so I owed her that much.

"Yeah . . ."

"You consented pretty quickly there. I expected you to argue a bit more."

"It's not like you've given up already, right?"

"You're right. I haven't."

"I understand. I know it's not your fault. But . . . No. If it does come to that, I'll probably argue more then."

"I see. But I won't let you stop me."

"I know that! But that's our last resort, right?!"

She knew she couldn't stop me, but she had to try. Even if she knew that Gaelion was the reason that Filo was in pain, she was still fond of him. Of course putting him down was a last resort. I wanted to avoid doing that, if at all possible.

"I hate the heroes!"

Tears were streaming down Wyndia's face.

"I'm used to being hated."

She made it seem like the other heroes had somehow wronged her too. Ren was acting kind of fidgety. Maybe he knew something I didn't.

"And? What do you want me to do?" asked Sadeena.

She was still keeping an eye out at the rear. It's not like I expected anyone to ambush us from behind, but we were more likely to run into monsters, since we were traveling at night. Several had already come chasing after us, in fact. Sadeena made quick business of them with her harpoon and a few magical spells. Atla and Melty were covering the front. Filo was basically unable to fight. Just pulling the carriage was already a struggle for her right now. I didn't want to push her limits.

"That's it. Very good," Atla said.

"Rafu!"

Atla seemed to be showing Raph-chan how to control the leakage of power from Filo's body. The speed that her level was dropping seemed to slow even further.

"I'm busy thinking about how to get Gaelion to return to his usual self. Just keep an eye on our surroundings, Sadeena."

"Will do!"

Rat broke her silence and jumped in on the conversation.

"If you want to save Gaelion, I think making him throw up the core might work. It would be best to do it as soon as possible too."

"I would imagine so."

"You'll probably just have to hold him down by force and stick your hand down his throat. Normally you would use a special tool to keep him from biting your hand off, but . . ."

"That shouldn't be a problem. Don't underestimate my defense rating."

"Yeah, I guess we don't need to worry about that with you, Count."

"Hey, Rat, can't we use medicine to sedate Gaelion?" I asked.

Rat held up a syringe full of some drug and showed it to me.

"This is a really strong anesthetic. It's strong enough to knock out even a dragon for a bit."

"I see. I'll be counting on you then."

Gaelion's level was slowly rising. His stats got a boost from the adjustments on my shield too. And now, he was even leeching stats from Filo. It would be like fighting a dragon version of Filo. I was just lucky that I had Raphtalia and Ren there with me. If nothing else, we had plenty of firepower.

"We should talk strategy before anything else. Rat, it's probably a good idea to weaken Gaelion a bit, right?"

"Yeah. If possible."

"Alright. Sadeena, when we find Gaelion, your job is to weaken him up a bit. After that, Raphtalia and Ren can use their skills to pin him down."

"What about me?" asked Wyndia.

She was trembling.

"You can't fight, can you?" I asked her.

"I can! If Gaelion might end up getting hurt, then I should be the one to do it! Things could get dangerous, otherwise."

She sure had a strong sense of responsibility.

"Even if that's true, what can you do?"

"Now, now. Little Wyndia is quite the magic user. Right?"

"Yeah!"

Oh? I guess she could be our resident sorceress then.

"Not to mention, she can use the Way of the Dragon Vein," Sadeena added.

"What?!"

Did she just say Way of the Dragon Vein?!

"What kind of magic is that?! I want details!" I shouted.

"Hmm . . . It's magic that you use by borrowing power from things around you. I guess you could say it's magic that borrows power from the Dragon Vein. Learning it makes it easier to use cooperative magic and counter-magic."

Ost had used a similar type of magic, now that I thought about it. I'd just assumed that she was using her own power, but apparently that wasn't the case.

"You'll understand what kind of magic it is later, so let's focus on coming up with a plan right now."

"Fine. I'm going to consider you part of our offense," I told Wyndia.

Alright, that should be enough to put up a good fight. In fact, I was even a bit worried that Raphtalia and Ren might end up killing Gaelion.

Several hours passed, and we arrived at the town in the east. The morning sun was just starting to rise. Filo was a quick runner, but Gaelion sure could fly fast. On another note, dark clouds seemed to be gathering over the mountains near the village.

"Oh! It's the Saint!"

"You mean it's the Shield Hero!"

The villagers noticed us and started making their way over. Wyndia grabbed some sheets and . . . hid under them, for some reason.

Facing the villagers probably wouldn't be comfortable for Ren either, so I told him to stay hidden in the carriage. He seemed okay with coming out, but it wasn't hard to imagine things getting messy if he did. Although, to be completely honest, a lot of it had been the villagers' own fault. They had no right blaming Ren if they couldn't even be bothered to get rid of the dragon corpse before it ended up causing problems.

"We heard a dragon howling this morning. All of the villagers came outside to see what was going on, and the mountains already looked like that."

"I see. I saw a dragon fleeing toward this direction and followed it here," I said.

"Hooray!" shouted the villagers in unison.

I didn't tell them it was my dragon. I had a reputation to keep, after all. The others seemed to realize that and kept their mouths shut.

"Alright, Filo. You've done enough. You, Atla, and Raph-chan, stay here and rest."

"But Master . . ."

"We don't have far to go. Gaelion should be just over there.

Don't push yourself, Filo."

"But . . . I want to go too."

"No. If you push yourself, it's only going to make things worse. You're already near your limit. I'm not going to take you any further."

"B . . . buuuut!"

Filo started whining. What could I do to calm her down? The way things were, she would probably just end up following us without permission. If I used my portal to send her to Zeltoble or something, there's no way she would be able to make it back here in time, but . . . hmm.

"Little Filo, you realize that little Naofumi is just thinking of your well-being, right?"

Sadeena started trying to persuade Filo to back down.

"But I—"

"We're all worried about you, little Filo. You understand that, right?"

"But . . . buuut . . ."

Filo felt helpless. She covered her face with her hands and began to cry. I'd never seen Filo like this before. The way she was crying now was different than the way she cried when she was put on display in Kizuna's world. It showed just how powerless she felt now.

"Filo, wait for us here. I promise we'll put a stop to whatever it is hurting you!"

Melty chimed in to help convince Filo. That must have done the trick, because Filo slumped down compliantly.

"Just stay here and relax. We'll go take care of this and be back in a flash," I told her.

"Rafu!"

"I'll stay here with you," Atla told Filo.

"Sounds good. Atla and Raph-chan, I'm leaving Filo up to you two."

"You can count on us!"

Atla and Raph-chan both responded confidently.

"Alright. Let's go bring that knock-and-run prankster back."

The rest of us walked off toward the mountains covered in dark clouds.

Chapter Seven: Plagued Earth

"I'm pretty sure it was somewhere around here. Ren, do you remember?"

"Umm, yeah . . ."

As we climbed up the mountain, it was clear that the surrounding ecosystem was still in a state of disarray. The land appeared contaminated, and it was obvious that there was some kind of magical disturbance. I never imagined that we would end up back here. Wyndia looked back toward the village and glared with hate in her eyes. What in the world had happened to her?

The last time we'd been here, Filo had just plowed through any monsters that stood in our path. We hardly had to fight at all. But this time was different. Fighting off monsters was taking up a lot of our time, and they just kept coming too.

"I call upon the power of the Earth to come to me and take form. Earth Vein! Lend me your power!"

"Dark Fire Palette!"

When Wyndia finished her incantation, black flames sprang forth and engulfed the monsters in front of us. Her magic seemed slightly different than the magic Ost had used, but something about it did feel similar. I guess this was the Way of the Dragon Vein.

"That sure is strange magic," I said.

"Yeah. I was never taught the more difficult spells, but they all borrow power from our surroundings," Wyndia replied.

"I see."

"Father could use much more difficult spells."

I wondered if her father had been some kind of wizard or something.

"Let's see if we can get you using some spells that are slightly more difficult," said Sadeena.

She began twirling her harpoon around. She turned toward a different monster that had just appeared and pulled out a flask that she had bought at the village down below.

"I, Sadeena, draw forth the power of this holy water that it may manifest itself. Dragon Vein! Vanquish the enemies before me!"

"Saint Aqua Blast!"

Sadeena used an incantation similar to Wyndia's and called forth a glowing mass of water that smashed into the monster and killed it.

"Do you understand? Borrowing power from your surroundings means that sometimes there will be compatibility issues. When that's the case, consider using the items that you have on hand."

Sadeena handed the flask to Wyndia.

"That has holy water in it, so it works really well against the monsters here. But the effects will weaken if you overuse it, so be careful."

"Oh . . . okay."

"That . . . was really impressive," Melty mumbled.

She was staring in awe, not sure what to make of the unfamiliar magic.

"Oh, I might have you help cast some cooperative magic, little Melty."

"Huh?!"

I'm pretty sure Melty had taught Filo how to cast cooperative magic, so she could probably pull it off.

"Don't worry, little Melty. You've got more than enough potential. It even shows in the color of your hair. I'm counting on you!"

"No, no, no, no!"

Melty was refusing like her life depended on it. I guess the magic really was difficult to use. Sadeena and Filo made it look easy, but they were probably just abnormal. Wait a second. What did the color of someone's hair have to do with their potential to use magic?

"You'll make a perfect match! You can do it, little Melty!"

"Ugh . . ."

Melty's level wasn't very high though. Sadeena probably shouldn't expect too much of her.

"Let's prepare for it, just in case. Come, we'll talk it over as we move along," Sadeena said.

They continued talking as we made our way up the mountain. Before long, we came to the spot where we'd found the corpse of the dragon zombie. It had taken us three whole hours to get there. The land was completely and utterly barren. To think that the area would still be contaminated . . .

". . ."

Ren stared silently at the plot of land. This was where he'd left the corpse of the dragon he slayed. I guess you could say he was staring his own mistake in the face.

"Ren, keep your cool."

"I know . . . I decided to take responsibility for my mistakes. I'm prepared to live with what I've done. That's why I'm fighting."

Wyndia was glaring at Ren . . . I think. Her expression seemed to be a complex mix of emotions. I couldn't tell if she was upset, sad, or if she had just given up caring. Whatever it was, it was safe to assume that she had some kind of personal connection to Ren's issues.

"I wonder where Gaelion is," I mumbled.

"Over there, probably."

Wyndia pointed to a recess deep in the mountains. As if in response, a black haze began gathering in that direction.

"Oh my! That sure looks dangerous," said Sadeena.

"I guess we have no choice but to go check it out," I replied.

I looked over at Wyndia.

"You know how to get over there?"

"Yeah. This way."

Was Wyndia from around here or something? Maybe she'd been from a hidden village of dragon-worshipping demi-humans that was wiped out by an epidemic after Ren killed the dragon. Then she got caught and ended up a slave, or something like that. And that magic she was using earlier was unique to the secret village. Raphtalia's story wasn't all that different, so it was possible.

"There!"

We'd been walking for another two hours or so. Wyndia looked back at us and pointed ahead. Of course, that two hours included time spent fighting monsters. Filo didn't have much time left, so having to waste it clearing out monsters pissed me off.

Gaelion was lying on the ground in front of the entrance to a cave. Was he asleep? He was absolutely motionless. We stayed hidden in the shadows as we approached. Our plan was to get close and then trap Gaelion in my Shield Prison. Then we would close in on him, and just as the prison disappeared, we would hit him with our magic to weaken him. After that, Rat would knock him out with her anesthetic. If that didn't work, Raphtalia and Ren would restrain him, and once he was anesthetized, I would take the core back. And that would be the end of it. Assuming things went as planned, anyway.

Shield Prison had a range of five meters. Gaelion was still around twenty meters away. We had to get closer. I used status magic to check his level. He was level 55. That meant he had already stolen 20 levels from Filo. And he was still doing it. He wasn't going to stop.

"Gyaaoooo!"

Gaelion suddenly awoke and disappeared into the cave.

"Damn it!"

I guess we'd failed. Then again, closing in on the cave would be a lot easier now. Once there, I kept my back against the wall of the cave and peeked inside. Gaelion was looking all around the cave, as if he were searching for something.

"I wonder what he's doing."

"He's probably searching for his treasure. Treasure that the villagers stole," Wyndia replied.

"It must be some unfinished business of the spirit in the core that commandeered Gaelion's body," said Rat.

"All because I . . . killed . . ." Ren mumbled.

Wyndia started yelling at him.

"Stop brooding already! It's annoying! Get over it, like the Shield Hero said!"

"Yeah, I know I need to. But . . ."

"Oh my god! Hurry up! Let's go!"

Wyndia dragged him into the cave. She did have a point.

Taking action would be better than standing around brooding indecisively.

"Alright, let's go," I said.

We began to approach Gaelion.

"Gyaaooooo!"

Gaelion roared, and some kind of black sludge began oozing out all over his body.

Throb!

My shield throbbed when Gaelion roared. What the hell?! Nothing like that had happened before when he roared.

"Mr. Naofumi . . ."

"Rafu!"

I heard voices behind us. I turned around to see Filo dragging Atla and Raph-chan toward us. Her eyes were glazed over.

"Atla?! What are you doing all the way up here?!"

Fohl called out to Atla in surprise when he saw her.

"What the hell are you three doing here?" I asked.

"Shortly after you all left, Filo suddenly began writhing in pain. We tried to get things back under control, but it wasn't working. Then she took off running."

"Rafu! Rafu rafu!"

Raph-chan was smacking Filo on the head and trying her best to bring her to her senses, but Filo was in a stupor. She showed no sign of responding.

"Every now and then, Filo would come to her senses and start to turn back. But whenever she did, some kind of power would come flowing toward her and draw her back this way. Then she would end up like this again," Atla explained.

"What about all of the monsters you must have encountered on the way here?"

"They kept their distance, almost as if they were trying to avoid us. We didn't have to fight at all."

Damn it. I guess Filo did have the dragon zombie core circulating throughout her whole body. Maybe that was why I couldn't use my portal in an area with this level of corruption. Shit. I should have sent Filo back to our village before we came up here.

My shield was doing some kind of weird throbbing thing, Gaelion was right in front of us, and now Filo had shown up here in a weakened state. What the hell was I supposed to do?!

"Ugh . . ."

"Filo, do you recognize me?" I asked her.

"M . . . Mas . . . ter . . . Mel-chan . . ."

"Yeah, it's us. We've got this. You need to get out of here. You can't be here right now. Who knows what could happen."

"Filo!" Melty called out.

"Ugh . . . I'm . . . scared. Something inside of me . . . ugh . . . Stop . . . uuuughhh!"

Filo grabbed her chest and started writhing in pain. And

then, just like Gaelion, black sludge began to ooze out of her body.

"Whoa!"

"Ahh!"

"Rafu?!"

Atla and Raph-chan lost their hold on Filo and were sent flying. The black sludge engulfed Filo and began rapidly creeping toward Gaelion.

"Hurry up and stop that sludge!"

Clearly, something really bad was about to happen. Bad for us and bad for Filo too.

"B . . . but Filo is inside of there!"

"She's right!"

Raphtalia and Ren were hesitant to act. Deep down, I felt the same. If we attacked the sludge, we might end up harming Filo. Was there nothing we could do to stop it?

"Sadeena! Can you paralyze it with your lightning magic?"

"I'll give it a try!"

Sadeena quickly began to cast a spell and pointed her harpoon at the sludge engulfing Filo.

"Zweite Thunderbolt!"

Sadeena's magic landed a direct hit on the sludge engulfing Filo. But the sludge simply jiggled a bit and kept on moving. Sadeena took out the flask filled with holy water and began to cast another spell. She must have been using the Way of the Dragon Vein this time.

"I, Sadeena, call forth the power of this holy water to manifest itself. Dragon Vein! Vanquish the enemies before me!"

"Saint Aqua Blast!"

Sadeena spun her magic into the water to form a mass in the palm of her hand. It went flying and smashed right into the sludge.

"—!"

Oh! That one seemed to have an effect!

"Just as I expected. That thing is derived from some kind of curse. Normal attacks aren't going to be effective against it," she said.

"What should we do?" I asked.

"Well, little Filo is the host, and without a host . . ." Sadeena replied.

"No way . . ." whispered Melty.

"That's not an option!" I shouted.

"In that case, our only option is to attack using divine magic," said Sadeena.

Eclair stepped forward. She held her hand to the blade of her short sword and it took the form of a magic sword.

"That I can do! Hiya!"

Ah, that's right. Eclair had an aptitude for using light magic.

"I'll give it a go too!"

Raphtalia had an aptitude for illusion magic, which was a mixture of light and dark magic. I guess that meant she could use light magic too. Although, not as well as Eclair.

"Light Stardust Blade!"

Eclair's sharp thrust, along with a cloud of twinkling stars that shot out of Raphtalia's katana, went smashing into the sludge. Eclair's sword created a small opening in the sludge. Raphtalia's skill made a much larger opening.

"—?!"

But Raphtalia pulled her katana away before the skill completed.

"Any more than that could be deadly for Filo. I could see her through the opening in the sludge, and she was writhing in pain every time the stars hit it."

I checked Filo's fuzzy status screen. Her life force had dropped substantially. Shit! Just when I thought we might be able to stop this thing!

"We still have to stop the sludge somehow," I said.

"Naofumi! The sludge from Gaelion!" Ren shouted.

I looked over just in time to see the masses of sludge engulfing Gaelion and Filo come crashing together at breakneck speed. Damn it! We hadn't been able to stop them! They oozed together to form a single mass, which began to swell up.

"Gaelion! Listen to me! Please!" Wyndia called out.

"Stay back! Do you have a death wish?!" I shouted.

The throbbing of my shield intensified. Something black rushed out of the shield and engulfed Gaelion. He began absorbing even the surrounding air, or perhaps "cloud of corruption" was a more accurate description. Cracking sounds came from all over his body as Gaelion slowly grew more and more massive.

"I have a feeling this is starting to get really dangerous. You have any idea what's happening, Rat?" I asked.

"Why would I know?! It looks like your shield is just making things worse!"

"Yeah, I got that. There's some kind of throbbing coming from the shield."

We retreated from the cave, and the sludge came crawling out after us. Then it took on a clear, physical form. Standing a massive twenty meters tall, a fully-grown dragon was towering over us. The dragon's eyes were filled with darkness. I didn't know what to make of its expression. Nothing about it reminded me of Gaelion anymore. Filo . . . was nowhere in sight.

Damn it! Don't die on me, Filo!

"GURUUUUUUUUU!"

Gaelion took in a big gulp of air. I recognized that motion. That was his breath attack for sure.

"Everyone, get back! Shooting Star Shield!"

I cast Shooting Star Shield and got ready for the breath. The others got behind me and took a defensive stance. Sadeena pulled out a second flask and began casting a spell.

"I, Sadeena, call forth the power of this holy water to

manifest itself. Dragon Vein! Protect us!"

"Saint Aqua Seal!"

Sadeena's magic engulfed me.

"Little Naofumi, that should boost your fire resistance and help protect you against curses, just in case."

"Thanks."

If I could withstand this first attack, then we had a chance of winning. Surely the dragon wasn't as powerful as the Spirit Tortoise. Black flames poured out of Gaelion's mouth and shot toward us. Shooting Star Shield dissolved instantly.

What the hell?! Shooting Star Shield had been able to withstand the full weight of the Spirit Tortoise stepping on it for several moments. His breath had melted it away in an instant! The flames continued barreling toward me. I summoned Air Strike Shield, Second Shield, Dritte Shield, and E Float Shield to protect us.

It felt like my whole body was being incinerated. I almost passed out from the pain. If nothing else, the intensity of the attack was on par with the Spirit Tortoise's electric attack.

"Mr. Naofumi!" shouted Raphtalia.

"Holy hell . . . What's with this intensity . . ."

"Saint Aqua Seal is peeling away. The power of that breath and curse must be incredible," Sadeena said.

I had managed to withstand the attack somehow. I cast healing magic on myself and glared at Gaelion. These burns . . . There was no doubt about it. Those were dark curse burning

S flames. The dragon standing before me looked like Gaelion, but the monster seemed to have the same abilities as my Shield of Wrath. On top of that, Filo was stuck in there somewhere. This enemy might prove more difficult to deal with than the Spirit Tortoise had been. I had to consider that withdrawal might be our best option.

"Hey, Rat. Can we weaken that thing and pull Filo and the dragon core out of its stomach?"

"I'm pretty sure you'll be eaten."

"You're probably right. It might be better if someone just cuts Gaelion's stomach open."

Wyndia was calling out to Gaelion and trying her hardest to get through to him, but it didn't seem to be working. I'm sure he would have responded . . . if this had been an anime or something.

"We can't afford to hold back anymore! Raphtalia, Ren, and everyone else! Attack him all at once! Weaken him!"

"Understood!" Raphtalia shouted.

"Got it! I'll do my best to save Filo and Gaelion!" exclaimed Ren.

"Of course!"

"Wh . . . what kind of monster is that thing?! Can we really beat it?!"

Fohl had waited until now to start wavering.

"What are you saying, Brother? This is Mr. Naofumi's life

we're talking about. As his subordinates, it is our duty to carry out our mission, even if it means risking our own lives."

"I won't let you sacrifice yourself, Atla!"

These two . . . This was no time for silly banter!

"If we injected that anesthetic now, do you think it would stop him?" asked Sadeena.

"I'm pretty sure your lightning has a better chance of stopping him," I said.

"Oh? I'll do my best then!"

She needed to stop messing around and attack already.

Anyway, even the strongest enemy probably wouldn't be able to withstand the ridiculous amount of firepower that Raphtalia and Ren could dish out. That's why I was glad Ren was on our side now.

"Go!"

When I gave the signal, Raphtalia and Ren crouched down low and then rushed at Gaelion. They each used their weapon to unleash their respective skills. It was just as I'd expected. Ren's curse didn't interfere with his combat, and he'd powered up his weapon, so he was faster than Raphtalia.

"Stardust Blade!"

"Shooting Star Sword!"

The two attacks were essentially the same skill. The skills crossed, and their streams of shooting stars went flying toward Gaelion.

Of course, Raphtalia and Ren both followed through and swung at Gaelion's shoulders. Ren's sword failed to penetrate Gaelion's scales. Raphtalia's katana sliced through the scales but stopped just after cutting into Gaelion's flesh. With a loud clang, sparks flew from both of their weapons . . . and they bounced off?! But Raphtalia's attack had managed to penetrate more deeply and sent black sludge splattering into the air.

"What?!"

"He . . . he's tough!"

"Ouch . . . my hand . . ."

Raphtalia and Ren both shook their hands painfully. Gaelion swung his hand at them forcefully in retaliation, but they both dodged and returned to my position.

"Hold on a second . . ."

Ren and Raphtalia were both heroes, technically, and they hadn't been holding back. And yet their weapons had been stopped? What the hell?

"Lightning Strike Harpoon!"

Sadeena leapt high up into the air and threw her harpoon at Gaelion's stomach. When she did, a bolt of lightning went smashing into Gaelion. The flash of light blinded me momentarily.

The harpoon had gone hurling toward his stomach at lightning speed. I was sure the attack landed. But Sadeena's harpoon failed to pierce it. It made a hollow thud, similar to the sound my shield made when I defended against an attack, and the harpoon bounced off and went flying through the air.

"Oh my . . . My finishing move didn't even pierce his scales, did it?"

Sadeena landed on the ground and caught her harpoon out of the air. She back-stepped and returned to our position.

"Ren's and Raphtalia's attacks were ineffective! Of course yours would be too, Fohl and Atla! Get back here!"

It didn't make sense. Ren and Raphtalia were both suffering from the effects of curses, but I still couldn't imagine anything being this tough!

The flash of light had blinded Gaelion. He was groaning and rubbing his eyes with both hands. Seeing if magical attacks would be effective was an option, but I wasn't going to hold my breath. Still, nothing good would come from standing around and twiddling our thumbs.

"Shit! He's fast!"

Gaelion was moving really quickly now, and that only made things worse. It took all Raphtalia, Ren, and I had just to keep up with the speed of his attacks.

I stood at the forefront and took the impact of Gaelion's claws. Ugh . . . One of his claws dug into my shoulder. He had a good amount of attack power too, apparently. I guess I was just lucky that it wasn't enough to deliver a fatal blow. Gaelion took in another big gulp of air. He was going to use his breath attack again.

"Oh, no you don't! Everyone, hide behind me!"

"Understood!"

I called out and had everyone gather behind me. They would be easy targets otherwise. Gaelion's breath was on the same level as the Spirit Tortoise's electric attack. If it'd hit anyone other than the Shield Hero, they would have been vaporized.

Flames worthy of being called hellfire engulfed my body.

"Count! Zweite Heal!"

Rat started healing my wounds. It sure was nice having someone other than myself around that could help heal.

"Should we try using cooperative magic, Sadeena?!"

"But, little Naofumi . . . If you're busy assisting me with magic, who's going to protect us?"

She had a point. If I tried to cast cooperative magic with her, I wouldn't be able to focus on defense. Gaelion was surprisingly strong. If I switched my focus to casting magic, he would break free from my hold. I could tell everyone to avoid his attacks, but I wasn't confident Melty and Rat could pull that off. It would have been nice if Ren could take over defense temporarily, but I had a feeling that wouldn't work either.

"Little Melty and little Wyndia! You two help me cast cooperative magic! We're going to stop little Gaelion!"

"Umm . . . okay! We have to save Filo, no matter what!" Melty replied.

"Naofumi! Watch out!" Ren shouted.

I was holding on to Gaelion's claw and he was clearly upset. He opened his mouth and tried to bite down on me. I took one of my hands off of his claw and used that hand and my foot to keep his jaws from closing on me.

"Crazy . . ."

Ren was staring at me with a look of amazement on his face as I stood there in the mouth of the dragon.

"If you have time to stare, then fight!"

"Sorry!"

Ren leapt toward me and Gaelion and swung his sword.

"Dragon Buster!"

Flames burst out of his sword, took the shape of a dragon, and shot toward Gaelion. It was the first time I'd seen that skill. It was probably especially potent against dragons.

"GURUUUUUUU!"

Gaelion turned his attention to Ren. Or was Ren his target to begin with? Maybe a leftover fragment of consciousness that belonged to the dragon emperor Ren had killed was driving Gaelion to take revenge.

"Ren, if you feel like you can't dodge an attack, use me as a shield."

"I will!"

I could sense hatred. Gaelion seemed to be primarily focused on Ren now. But I still had to focus on defense. Ren's defense rating wasn't high enough to keep him safe. I'd really expected him to put up a better fight. It's not that he wasn't fast. But it still only felt like perhaps two-thirds of my own speed. He was always one step behind. I wasn't sure if it was because of his curse or if there was some other reason.

"Raful!"

Raph-chan used her illusion magic to back Ren up. She was making Gaelion see multiple copies of Ren, which made it hard for him to concentrate on any single one. Thanks to her help, Ren seemed to be able to attack without much danger of being harmed.

"Cursed earth! Cursed Dragon Vein flow! Let us expel this congestion by . . ."

I looked back to see Melty, Sadeena, and Wyndia chanting their magical incantation in unison. Little flickers of light that looked like fireflies began to gather around them.

"GURUUUUUU!"

Gaelion clearly didn't intend to let them finish the incantation. He took in a huge gulp of air and prepared to unleash another one of his breath attacks. I stood in front of Melty and the others and readied my shield. When I did, Gaelion leapt high up into the air, faced me, and opened his mouth. He planned to attack from above!

"Shooting Star Shield! Air Strike Shield!"

I jumped up onto the Air Strike Shield and shielded Melty and the others from the breath. Ugh . . . My whole body was engulfed in the flames. Burns began to form on my skin. I was already weakened by a curse to start with, and these cursed flames only added to the pain. Gaelion followed up by thrusting at me with his claws. I could tell he was going to try to bite down on me again.

"Dragon Vein! Hear our petition and grant it! As the source of your power, we implore you! Let the true way be revealed once more! Give us the power to overcome the obstacles before us!"

The flickering lights began to draw together. It was clear that the three of them had their awareness focused on me.

"This might surprise you at first but stay calm. You'll be fine. Trust me! Now, little Melty!"

"Cooperative magic!"

"The Great Deep!"

"Zee Wille!"

Maybe it was just my imagination, but it seemed like they had cast different spells.

Water suddenly appeared around us, with the three of them at its center. It was like we were in a massive aquarium. Gaelion seemed to be choking. He looked like he was in pain as he swam around trying to escape from the aquarium. Something like this had happened to us before at the coliseum. But maybe something was different this time. For some reason, Ren was writhing around and choking too.

Gurgle, gurgle . . .

That reminded me! Ren sunk like a stone in water! He couldn't swim!

"Little Ren, you're going to be fine."

Sadeena put her arms around Ren, who seemed to be drowning. She brought him over to me.

"The spell doesn't affect anyone that isn't considered an enemy, so you're not going to drown," she told him.

"Huh? Oh . . ."

I guess that meant it could be used to choke enemies.

Pant . . . Pant . . .

"I'm exhausted . . ." Melty whispered.

"Yeah . . ." Wyndia replied.

The two of them were slumped down on the ground, out of breath. I took some magic water out of my shield and tossed it to them.

"I guess you would be. Leave the rest to me," Sadeena said.

Sadeena floated up weightlessly into the water of the magic aquarium and began swimming toward Gaelion, who was still struggling to escape. She was incredibly fast. Gaelion thrashed about and finally managed to leap out of the water. He prepared to spit fire, but before he could, Sadeena burst up out of the water in front of him. She was enveloped in a mass of water that was shaped like a Chinese dragon.

"Dragonfury Dual Blades!"

A loud splash echoed out and Gaelion fell back into the

water and sunk to the bottom of the aquarium. The attack must have damaged him, because blood was dribbling out of his stomach.

"Gaelion . . ."

Wyndia whispered his name quietly, and then stood up and screamed out.

"Gaelion!"

"One more! Orca Strike!" shouted Sadeena.

The water swirling around her formed a tail that smashed into Gaelion's stomach.

"He sure is tough!" she said.

"We'll help! While we're attacking, you and Mr. Naofumi can cast that spell!" Raphtalia exclaimed.

She and Ren headed toward Gaelion.

"Will do!"

"Gaelion!"

Wyndia continued to call out to Gaelion repeatedly.

"Please! Come back to us!" she screamed.

"Hey! Wait!"

I called out for Wyndia to stop, but she ignored me and ran to Gaelion. It wasn't that I couldn't understand how she felt, but she needed to think about the situation we were in.

"GURUUUUUUU!"

"Gaelion! Listen to me! I'm begging you! Return to your normal form!"

Wyndia's voice echoed out, but Gaelion wasn't listening. I rushed toward Wyndia to get in front of her and protect her. But Gaelion was too quick. He opened his mouth wide and was about to swallow her whole.

"Air Strike—"

I tried to summon my Air Strike Shield as quickly as I could. But before I finished . . .

"Father! Stop this already!"

Wyndia screamed out at the top of her lungs.

"GURU?!"

Gaelion stopped dead in his tracks.

Chapter Eight: Demon Dragon

"Father?"

"Huh?"

"I had a feeling that might be the case. I guess I was right," Sadeena said in a whisper.

She and Rat were nodding as if everything suddenly made sense.

"Yes. The dragon that lived here . . . was my father."

Wyndia nodded and faced Gaelion as she responded. Huh? Did that mean Wyndia was raised by a dragon? She looked exactly like a dog-type demi-human, the same as Keel. Nothing about her looked like a dragon. Well, her hairdo did strike me as a bit odd. It was strange. It reminded me of both a dog and a lizard at the same time. But could a dragon zombie even . . . No, wait. I guess her father was probably still a normal, living dragon when he raised her.

"No way . . . That means . . . I . . ."

Ren was stumbling over his words. Wyndia glared at him.

"Your brooding is so annoying! Just shut up for now!" she shouted.

Ahh, so that was why she glared at him every now and then. And that was why his masochistic desires annoyed her so much.

"It's extremely rare, but it's not unheard of. There are stories of wild monsters raising human or demi-human children. Usually it's either a wolf-type monster or a dragon," said Rat.

"Oh jeez, don't tell me you have some kind of wolf-boy here too . . ." I mumbled.

"Stop this, already. Father, there's nothing left here. I know you probably feel hatred for the hero that stole everything from you. But that doesn't mean it's okay to hurt others. Stop this before you do something that you'll regret!"

"GU . . ."

Gaelion let out a tortured groan and backed away. He covered his ears with his claws, as if to say he didn't want to listen.

"I refused to let it go before now. I couldn't bring myself to forgive the heroes. They stole my happiness. They stole Father's happiness. But the Shield Hero is . . . different. He's kind to everyone at the village. He's not like the other people in this country. The people that whipped me. He's not like the villagers that stole your treasures and laughed about it!" Wyndia explained.

She was crying as she told Gaelion about what she'd been through, in an attempt to get through to him. The reason he was covering his ears was because it was working . . . or was it?

But to think a dragon would raise a demi-human child . . . Maybe he'd planned on taking advantage of her after she'd grown up. Did the fact that I was even considering that just prove I'd spent way too much time playing games?

"Please. Return that body to its owner. That baby dragon is named Gaelion, just like you, Father. And he's still alive in there! Return the power that you stole from Filo too. Father . . . You don't belong in this world anymore!"

"GYAOOOOOOO!"

Gaelion started clawing at his forehead. Had she convinced him?!

But just when I thought it had been a success . . .

"Watch out!"

Ren leapt forward and guarded Wyndia from Gaelion's claw.

"Gaelion!" she shouted.

Her attempt to talk some sense into Gaelion had failed. Of course things wouldn't work out so smoothly. He still had Filo trapped inside of his body, after all.

"I guess that didn't work. Wyndia! I—"

"Let me go! Gaelion! Listen to me! Please!"

And then Wyndia suddenly fell motionless, as if she'd just seen something unbelievable.

"Who . . . are you? You're not Gaelion!" she shouted.

"Huh?"

Wyndia glared at Gaelion with hostility burning in her eyes.

"Gaelion and Father were just there! What did you do with them?!"

Wyndia's demeanor changed completely. She was seething with rage now. I looked over at the massive dragon that had been Gaelion. Its black body began to turn purple, and the mass of black sludge that had been surrounding it began to disappear.

"Oh? So you noticed my presence, did you, little girl?"

The dragon spoke, and I joined Wyndia in glaring at him. I thought it might be the voice of the dragon that had been her father before he died, but that wasn't the case, judging by her reaction. I needed to figure out who this new enemy standing before us was.

But wait . . . I'd heard this voice before. It was the same voice that had whispered to me when I cast All Sacrifice Aura.

"Who the hell are you?!"

I shouted at him with menace in my voice. The enormous dragon slowly puffed his chest up proudly. After a brief pause, he replied calmly.

"Hmph. I guess I should introduce myself," he muttered.

The dragon placed a hand on his chest and gave a patronizing bow.

"I come from another world. There, I was the Dragon Emperor. I've been referred to as the Demon Dragon as well. I am the ruler of all monsters. Shield Hero, this should all sound familiar to you."

That brought to mind what had happened in Kizuna's

world and the weapons that Raphtalia and I were always using. They both had "demon dragon" in their name.

The Demon Dragon had asked me a question. If there was any chance of talking things out, maybe this was it.

"Yeah. You're the dragon that tried to take over Kizuna's world, right? I'm pretty sure Kizuna said she defeated you."

The Demon Dragon confirmed my suspicions with a nod.

"I'm glad you seem to understand. That's right. The Hunting Hero and her party crushed my aspirations once."

"And why would that Demon Dragon be here now?"

"Hmph . . . Shield Hero, are you really going to pretend like you have no clue?"

I had a really bad feeling about this. Romina told me that the dragon emperor core she used in my Barbaroi Armor had been created by combining fragments of the dragon emperor and dragon zombie cores. And going by what Rat and Wyndia had said, as well as Gaelion's current state, the corruptive tendencies of dragon emperors extended even to their consciousnesses. As a result, the remnant of the demon dragon in my core fragment, which had commandeered Gaelion's body, went out of control. It made sense.

"So your consciousness remained in the core fragments, which I used in my shield and armor. And now you've taken over Gaelion's body."

"Very good. You catch on quick, Shield Hero," he replied.

"And? I'm guessing you're not here because you decided to help us out by suppressing my rampaging twit of a dragon."

"You guess correctly. I've finally found a body that will allow me to act freely! Surely you don't think I'm going to just relinquish it to you, do you?"

The dragon clearly didn't have friendly intentions. In that case, dealing with this opponent would likely be even more dangerous than fighting a dragon that was merely causing a violent disturbance.

"What have you done with Filo?! Return her at once!"

Melty stepped forward and shouted at the dragon angrily.

"You must be referring to the monster that people call a filolial in this world."

Rip!

I heard a tearing sound and the demon dragon's chest split open. Something crept forward into view. I could see Filo being held in place by tentacles or something. Her arms and legs were tied down. It looked like she had been stitched onto the dragon's beating heart, as if she were now a part of his body. Filo seemed to groan with each beat of the heart. The tentacles were pulsating and glowing, as if to signify that they were stealing her power.

"Ugh . . . ughhh . . ."

"Filo!"

Melty started to take a step forward. But before she could

move, the Demon Dragon cast a spell instantly, without even reciting an incantation. A black beam of light shot out toward Melty's feet.

"Watch out!" I yelled.

I instantly grabbed Melty and pulled her back. It was clear that the dragon didn't intend for the beam to hit her, but the way she had lunged forward made it a close call.

"Naofumi! Let go! That's Filo!"

"Calm down! Charging at him recklessly is not going to convince him to give her back!"

The Demon Dragon placed a hand on his chest, as if to signify his agreement.

"Ugh . . . Mel-chan . . . Master . . . It hurts . . ."

Filo opened her eyes ever so slightly and called out to us. But the Demon Dragon clearly had no intention of returning her. He smirked.

"The Shield Hero is correct. The filolial is a sacrificial offering that gives me power. Do you really think I'll just hand her over to you?"

"Nooo . . . Ugh . . ."

With a cracking sound, the Demon Dragon slowly drew the exposed Filo back, deep into his chest.

"Filo!"

Melty reached out toward Filo and grasped at the air. I held her back and glared at the Demon Dragon.

"Do you really think we're going to just accept that and leave?" I asked.

"I have no plans of letting you leave like this, of course. However, perhaps we can make a deal."

"What do you want?"

Whenever there was mention of negotiating in a situation like this, it always ended up being a ludicrous proposal. It reminded me of that famous line from a certain dragon: "If you want to be my ally, I'll give you half of the world." Even if you accepted the offer, things turned out badly.

But there was always a possibility that the Demon Dragon might be reasonable. It wouldn't hurt to hear him out.

"My aspiration is to rule the world. Humans are weak, stupid, and selfish. Why should the world belong to them?"

"Such a cliché. You're going to complain about humans being unfit to rule the world?"

How predictable. The triteness of it all made me roll my eyes.

"But surely you understand, Shield Hero. You were selfishly summoned to this world, and then framed and persecuted simply because someone didn't like you. Surely *you* understand the arrogance of the people of this world."

". . ."

He wasn't wrong. The countless injustices that I had suffered were all a result of that arrogance.

"Those fools reign over this world like it belongs to them. Deep down, you know that their savage deeds are unforgivable. I could feel it when I was in your shield."

"Well, you're not wrong."

It was a selfish, rotten world where they relied on the heroes to fix things any time something went wrong. If I could, I'd abandon my mission, immediately return to my own world, and forget it all. Like it had all been a bad dream.

"Of course, I will take care of the waves as well. Having the world destroyed is no good for me either. But that's only if the world belongs to me."

His offer sounded good so far. But there were always strings attached when things sounded too good to be true. He'd referred to Filo as a sacrificial offering, and he was sucking away her power. He'd hijacked Gaelion's body. That was plenty of evidence that things wouldn't all be so rosy.

"Mr. Naofumi . . ."

Raphtalia had been trying to calm the frantic Melty down. She placed her hand on my shoulder. I knew what she wanted to say. It was a dirty, rotten world, but there were still people here trying their best to do what was right. I couldn't care less if the worthless fools all died. But there were people that deserved my protection too. Of course I understood that.

"What an arrogant creature! I should defeat that thing, right, Atla?!" Fohl shouted.

He started to step forward, but Atla stopped him with a quick poke in the stomach.

"Ugh . . . Why did you do that, Atla?"

"We're not strong enough to face that creature yet. Our opportunity to act will come, but right now, we need to wait for Mr. Naofumi's instructions. We should focus on mustering up as much power as possible until then."

Atla began focusing her awareness as soon as she finished speaking.

"A . . . Atla?"

Her focus was incredible. She stood there motionless, as if she could no longer even hear Fohl's voice. Her position was somewhere around two meters behind me.

"That's enough of a prelude. Let's hear your conditions already," I announced.

Even if the negotiations were going to end in failure and we had to continue fighting, it still made sense to hear him out. This enemy was too strong to just try and settle things our own way, without considering what he had to say. Ren's and Raphtalia's attacks were ineffective.

Such incredible strength. There had to be something to it. If I could find out what that was by talking to him, I was sure I could figure out a way to deal with him.

"Right down to business. I like that. These are my conditions. Everyone here—other than the Shield Hero—will pledge their allegiance to me and become my minions. And then you will snuff out the Hunting Hero and her companions who shattered my aspirations once before!"

What a joke. Was he really going to present it like that and still expect us to agree? He might have been a powerful dragon, but he had absolutely zero potential as a politician. And what did he mean by everyone other than me pledging their loyalty?

"Do you really think they would agree to that? And why did you specify everyone other than me?"

Everyone around glared at the Demon Dragon and nodded. In situations like this, it was only normal to force the leader, which was me right now, to pledge their loyalty too. The Demon Dragon stared at me. The look in his eyes . . . It wasn't quite contempt. It sent a shiver down my spine. His eyes reminded me of a starving monster staring at its prey.

"Like the filolial offering, you are nothing but another source of power. I need no pledge from you. You, too, will become a part of my body and continue to supply me with power for all eternity. In return, I will exact revenge on the rotten humans for the both of us!"

"Huh?!"

So the bastard intended to make me a part of his body and use me as a power source, just like Filo!

"Surely you didn't think that the filolial was my only source of power. Take a good look at the situation. It is your rage that gives me power!"

"That must be what Atla was talking about when she said there was some kind of power leaking out of you and amplifying something," said Raphtalia.

"No wonder the dragon is so strong . . ." Rat mumbled.

She had a look of annoyance on her face. Wyndia glared at me.

I looked at my shield. My rage . . . I pulled up the Shield of Wrath on my status screen. The screen was all fuzzy. A lot about the dragon reminded me of the abilities of my Shield of Wrath, including the breath attack Gaelion had used before turning into the Demon Dragon. In other words, the Demon Dragon must have been using me as a medium to sustain such massive power. And since I was the source of that power, he wanted to assimilate me into his body to continue leeching that power.

"Go to hell! Do you really think anyone would agree to such terms?!"

"Oh, not at all. I fully understand that you will try to resist. This is not a negotiation. This is the strong exploiting the weak."

The Demon Dragon let out a fierce roar. When he did, a rain of magical attacks poured down upon us.

"Damn you! We won't let you take Naofumi! Shooting Star Sword!"

"That's right! We won't let Mr. Iwatani fall sacrifice to such wretched aspirations!"

Ren intercepted the Demon Dragon's magical attacks with

his Shooting Star Sword skill, and Eclair cast a spell that formed a shield of light. It formed a barrier around me that would help protect me, even if only a bit.

"We will let you do no such thing!" shouted Raphtalia.

She used Light Stardust Blade with her magic sword to help crush the onslaught of magical attacks.

"Give Filo back!" cried Melty.

She must have summoned up some great, latent power in the face of imminent danger. She started rapidly casting spells and firing them off at the dragon's magic.

"Damn it . . . Even if our attacks hit him, they only send sparks flying!" grumbled Ren.

Ren's attack power must have been higher than the Demon Dragon's, because he was successfully quashing the dragon's magical attacks. But Ren's attacks weren't powerful enough to pierce the Demon Dragon's armor.

"Mr. Naofumi, please protect the others. Ren, let's take the fight in close quarters," said Raphtalia.

"Got it!" Ren replied.

Raphtalia gave Ren the signal, crouched down low, and then sprang at the Demon Dragon.

"Hiyaaaa!"

She thrust her katana at him with incredible force. Ren followed her lead and swung his sword.

"Thunder Sword!"

Lightning shot out of Ren's sword and went hurtling at the Demon Dragon. But it failed to even scratch the dragon's scales. Raphtalia's attack, on the other hand, made a sharp slicing sound, as if she had cut through something. There was a cloud of black, noxious gas surrounding the Demon Dragon and it looked like she had cut through that.

"Ugh . . . I suppose I should launch a counterattack too. Try not to die. I'd like to try to gauge my own strength."

The Demon Dragon didn't have a single scratch on him, and yet he had groaned in pain. Just what had Raphtalia cut? I had no idea, but it certainly seemed to have an effect. The Demon Dragon flapped his wings and lifted up off of the ground. He began to shine as brightly as the sun, and a cloud of black flames filled the air.

"Raphtalia! Ren! Get back!"

I summoned my Air Strike Shield and Second Shield in front of Raphtalia and Ren to protect them from the attack. As instructed, they both fell back. Good. That should be enough.

"Experience my power firsthand! Flames of Purgatory! Solar Prominence! Dark Nova!"

The Demon Dragon's mouth snapped open, and near his chest a black sun took form. Black flames showered down toward us. I held my shield up toward the sky and cast E Float Shield, Shooting Star Shield, and Dritte Shield.

"Melty! Sadeena! Anyone! Cast whatever defensive magic you can!"

"O . . . okay!"

Melty nodded and began casting along with the others. Scorching flames poured out of the black sun and exploded.

Ugh . . . The intensity of the attack was even greater than when I'd been hit with the ceremonial magic spell Judgment. On top of that, the flames would curse anything they touched, and now they were engulfing my body. Bit by bit, my skin melted away. The pain followed moments later.

"Little Naofumi! Keep holding on! Saint Aqua Seal!"

Sadeena used the holy water to reduce the amount of damage I took. I could tell that the flames would delay any healing. There was no doubt about that since my Shield of Wrath was the source of their power. The holy water was clearly very effective against curse elements. Healing wouldn't be a problem as long as the curse effects weren't delaying it. Thankfully Rat was helping a bit by casting her own healing magic.

After several moments, the flames died away. The area in front of me had been transformed into a field of smoldering ash.

"Hmph. Killing you would mean losing a source of power. That attack is not quite powerful enough to deliver a decisive blow. That's its downside."

"Ugh . . ."

I cast healing magic on myself and got ready to continue

the fight. I had no doubt that he was trying to weaken me so that he could assimilate me into his body.

"Naofumi, you're his target! You need to stay back, no matter what!" Ren shouted.

"Mr. Naofumi! The Sword Hero is right! Be careful! The dragon is clearly trying to weaken you!" Raphtalia added.

The Demon Dragon was taking a moment to recover after unleashing such a massive attack. Raphtalia and Ren took advantage of the opportunity and leapt at him to resume their attacks. Earlier in the fight, the two of them had attacked at the same time and the compounded effect had left a faint mark on the Demon Dragon's scales.

Was there nothing I could do? If I paired up with Sadeena, we could cast our cooperative magic spell, Descent of the Thunder God, on Raphtalia and Ren. That should increase their attack power. Sadeena must have realized what I was thinking, because she nodded and took my hand into hers. But was that really all I could do? I couldn't help but wonder.

The job of a shielder was to block the opponent's attacks and to create openings for allies to attack. If they had some leeway, they could assist the other party members while helping to keep them alive. Naturally, that's exactly what I had always done. There was nothing else I could do.

"Hmph . . . It looks like I'll need more power. Let's try this then," whispered the Demon Dragon.

He started to concentrate. Naturally, his movements also slowed, but Raphtalia and the others still couldn't land a decisive blow.

If he was leeching my abilities, then . . . Wait. Leeching my abilities? It was safe to assume that he was using the abilities of the Shield of Wrath. Ren had implemented the power-up methods, and yet his attacks were still ineffective. I was the only one with a high enough defense rating to pull that off. The Demon Dragon even said that he was using the Shield of Wrath as a medium. So what would happen if I intentionally failed a power-up attempt on the Shield of Wrath?

"He's using my shield as the source of his power. I'm going to try intentionally failing a power-up attempt on the shield."

Ren turned to me and nodded.

"That makes sense! I hadn't thought of that! Give it a try, Naofumi!"

"Huh? What do you mean?" asked Rat.

"Failure is always a possibility when powering up our weapons. If I intentionally cause it to fail, then the Shield of Wrath will be weakened. In other words, the shield that is supplying his power will become weak. And that means . . ."

"The dragon will be weakened too!" she exclaimed.

"Exactly. If he's getting his defense from my shield, then that should make it possible to harm him with our attacks. I'm sure of it!"

I made up my mind and got ready to power up my shield.
And that's when it happened!

"Did you really think I hadn't thought of that?"

Chapter Nine: Forced Power-Up

"What?!"

The Demon Dragon cast a spell and magical symbols appeared on my shield. The power-up screen suddenly appeared in front of my eyes.

Would you like to attempt to power up Shield of Wrath from +7 to +8?

Huh? Wait! I hadn't done anything! The cursor moved to "yes" on its own and the power-up attempt initiated.

"What did you do?!"

"Heh . . . I'm sure you're smart enough to have figured out what's happening. I'm not against trying my luck either, you know."

Warning: Power-up level will be reset to 0 upon fail—

The Demon Dragon selected "yes" before the warning even finished displaying. There was a clunking sound and the power-up symbol appeared.

+8 power-up successful!

Shit! Why the hell did it have to be successful at a time like this?! Ugh . . . I nervously looked over at the Demon Dragon.

"Bwahahaha! I enjoy a good gamble from time to time! Heroes! Feel my power!"

The Demon Dragon swung his tail. He was even faster than before! He flapped his wings and a powerful wind rushed through the air!

"Ugh . . ."

Damn it! Just when I thought things couldn't get any worse! At the very least, I needed to cast support magic on Raphtalia and the others.

"Zweite Aura!"

I wasn't prepared to lose to this powered-up Demon Dragon. I cast my support magic on Raphtalia and Ren.

"Air Strike Shield! Second Shield! Raphtalia! Ren! Use those as footing and to protect yourself!"

"Understood!"

"Thanks!"

The Demon Dragon's scales were glistening. In MMOs, it was common for a shiny effect to be added to a weapon's appearance whenever a high-level refinement was successful.

"Umm, hey, Count. Is it just me or . . . Did he not just get stronger?"

"Yeah. He's interfering with my shield. But I'm not just going to stand by and watch!"

Two could play this game.

"Careful now! I can't have you going and causing trouble, my little medium."

Locked.

When I tried to power up the Shield of Wrath, that was the message that appeared on the screen. Shit! I couldn't power up my own shield! What the hell?! In MMOs, every now and then someone's account would get hacked and they would lose control of their character. That's what this felt like!

The Demon Dragon immediately attempted another power-up. Once again, he chose "yes" for both prompts immediately.

+9 power-up successful!

. . .

"Whoa!"

Ren was unable to dodge the next attack. He went flying and smashed into the wall.

"Ren!"

"I . . . I'm okay!"

He and Raphtalia could no longer keep up with the Demon Dragon's attacks. They were lagging one step behind now.

"Count?!"

This piece-of-shit shield! Did it want to kill me?! This was its chance to fight back by failing and weakening that bastard! If he succeeded again, we were screwed. And of course, the Demon Dragon attempted another power-up.

+10 power-up—

I immediately jumped out in front to protect Raphtalia and Ren. The swipe of the Demon Dragon's tail threw me flying through the air.

"Ugh!"

My surroundings spun around before my eyes at high speed. As if to finish me off, a second swipe sent me smashing toward the ground.

"Mr. Naofumi!"

"Naofumi?!"

I had been tossed around like a ragdoll. Tossing me through the air was a feat that not even Kyo or the Spirit Tortoise had been able to manage. The Demon Dragon's scales were glittering brightly now. Or was I just seeing stars after being tossed through the air?

Shit. The Demon Dragon was steadily powering up to a

level far beyond anything we could handle. But powering up was a double-edged blade. *Go ahead, keep making attempts!* The power-up level was sure to reset before long. And I was running out of power-up materials, so when it did fail, that would be the end of it.

"Hmph. I guess that's enough powering up," he announced.

"You're running away from a little power-up? I expected more of a demon dragon with aspirations to rule the world," I taunted.

I'd just have to taunt him and force him to power-up until he failed. But the Demon Dragon looked at me scornfully and puffed up his chest.

"I will not fall for your weak attempts to taunt me. I'll have plenty of time to make more attempts after I make you mine!"

He saw through my plan!

"Count, is everything okay?"

"Does it look okay to you?"

What the hell? He'd hacked my account and now he was powering up my equipped weapon a ridiculous amount. It was like he stole my weapon and managed to turn it into an ultra-rare item, after it was no longer mine. This really sucked. It made me want to curse the whole world.

"Zweite Heal!"

"Healing again? Don't think I'll let you do that so easily. Anti-Zweite Heal!"

The Demon Dragon sighed and nullified the healing magic that Rat had cast.

"Naofumi!"

"*As the source of your power, I command you! Let the true way be revealed once more! Unleash an attack like a blade of water and slice him through!*"

"Drifa Aqua Slash!"

Melty focused her attention . . . Wait, since when could Melty use drifa-level magic?

"Anti-Drifa Aqua Slash!"

Once again, the Demon Dragon sighed and nullified her magic effortlessly.

Damn it! He was obviously adept at using magic. I wouldn't have been surprised if "Magic" were his middle name. Now that I thought about it, I hadn't really seen Kizuna or any of them use much magic. They probably could, but they might have gone without, when fighting the Demon Dragon. It wouldn't do much good if he just nullified the spells as soon as they were cast.

"Now then, I guess fighting you without holding back is the least I can do."

The Demon Dragon began to cast a spell. The speed of his incantation was even quicker than before.

"Superb! With the power of the holy weapon, nothing is impossible!"

Would you like to attempt to increase rarity from SR to SR+?

Once again, he ignored the warning and continued. Something told me things were not going to get any better.

"Umm, he seems to keep growing scarier and scarier . . ."

"Goddammit!"

"Ugh! Shooting Star Sword!"

Ren's Shooting Star Sword went flying at the Demon Dragon, but it didn't even make him blink. The attack wasn't even making sparks anymore.

"What was that? Are you trying to tickle me?"

"I have no choice. I'll over-power-up my weapon too!" Ren shouted.

He opened up his settings and started attempting to power up his weapon, but he was forgetting one very important thing. He was still suffering from a curse with effects that reduced his luck.

"Ugh . . . It keeps failing!"

"Stop trying! You're being reckless! If anyone should try, it should be you, Raphtalia!"

"U . . . understood!"

Maybe Raphtalia could catch up to the abilities of the Demon Dragon, even if only a bit. I would have her attempt a power-up with a possibility of failure. Wait, did she even have something like that? I had no idea.

But damn, when my luck was bad, it was really bad. What the hell was with this string of successes?! I'd lost track of how many times the Demon Dragon had been successful now. If it had been the Soul Eater Shield, things sure would have been a lot easier on me!

Around the time I saw the letters "LR" appear, I jumped out to protect Raphtalia and Ren and was tossed through the air, once again. Success again?! What the hell?! The likelihood of that being successful was probably even lower than powering up to +11! But dodging wasn't a choice with the others there behind me. I had no choice but to guard against the attack.

"Ugh!"

I took the full brunt the attack, which had been bolstered by the newly increased weapon rarity. Damn, that hurt. I just wanted to go home now. It was bad enough when he was just feeding off of Filo's ridiculously high attack power, but now he had powered himself up and even increased his rarity. Could it get any worse? Was there no end to my bad luck?

This wasn't funny anymore. The next attempt to increase the rarity had to fail! He would be weakened this time for sure!

Increase to AF successful!

Was it impossible for this bastard to fail?!

"Hahahaha! No one can stand up to me now!"

The fiendish Demon Dragon was covered in a bright, blinding gloss from head to toe. He towered before us, calm and confident.

"Surely you have no chance of stopping me now. Shield Hero, accept your fate as an offering and give me your power!"

Damn it . . . I'd always relied on the Shield of Wrath to save the day when the going got tough, and now I was paying for it, with interest. I was facing a beast that had all of the same abilities as I did. If I didn't overcome this obstacle, everything I had worked so hard for would have been for naught. But what could I do against such a savage enemy?

"Feel my wrath!"

The Demon Dragon swiped at me with his claws. I cast Shooting Star Shield and summoned all of my skill-based shields to guard against the attack.

"Impudent fool! Hmph!"

His claws smashed right through all of the summoned shields and even shattered my Shooting Star Shield. I went flying through the air.

"Ugh!"

"Mr. Naofumi!"

"Now then . . ."

The Demon Dragon squinted and puffed his chest up, as

if to say he was merely toying with us. He began to cast a spell.

"Great power in this core stone of mine! Hear my plea and . . ."

An unfamiliar incantation echoed throughout the air surrounding the Demon Dragon. Actually, the incantation seemed to follow a pattern similar to what Therese had used for her magic.

"I won't let you!" shouted Raphtalia.

She leapt forward and swung her katana in an attempt to interrupt the incantation. Ren followed her lead. But the Demon Dragon continued to focus on the incantation, as if to imply that their attacks would have no effect on him.

Their attacks couldn't harm him because he had my defense rating. There was no doubt about that. But there had to be something we could do. There just had to be! I imagined what it would be like to fight myself. I tried to think of what attack would annoy me the most right now.

"Sadeena! Help me cast Descent of the Thunder God! As quickly as possible!"

"Sure thing!"

I started reciting the incantation with Sadeena.

"What are you doing, Naofumi? Things are completely one-sided now. We can't win like this," said Melty.

"Don't worry! Ren, Raphtalia, imagine you're fighting me. Use any defense ignoring and defense rating skills you have!" I shouted.

"G . . . got it! I'm pretty sure I have a few!" Ren replied.

"Understood!" shouted Raphtalia.

". . . *show yourself! I am the Dragon Emperor, ruler of the world. Form a barrier to obstruct them!*"

"Demon Dragon! Encompassing Mirrors!"

When the Demon Dragon heard my plan, he twitched and stopped reciting for a brief moment. Immediately after, he initiated the spell.

"Life Force Blade! Guard Breaker!"

"Eagle Blade!"

Raphtalia and Ren each focused their attention on their own blades and then fired off their skills. Both of their attacks smashed into a transparent wall before reaching the Demon Dragon.

"Damn . . . A barrier!" Ren shouted.

"It's like your Shooting Star Shield, Mr. Naofumi!" Raphtalia added.

With a loud crack, the barrier shattered and dispersed.

"Hahaha! Did you think I wouldn't be prepared for this? Fools!"

That Demon Dragon bastard! I assumed he had been casting a magical attack, but it had been defense magic! Raphtalia and Ren tried again using different skills, but those attacks were also blocked by the barrier the dragon had created. It was safe to assume that there were multiple layers.

"Raphtalia."

"Yes? What is it?"

I used my eyes to communicate my intentions to Raphtalia. I looked at Raphtalia's and Raph-chan's tails several times and acted like I was focusing my attention. Raphtalia seemed to understand what I wanted her to do. She nodded. Next, I looked over at Wyndia and Melty. Wyndia just stood there looking confused, but Melty sighed and nodded. She must have understood what I was asking her to do.

"Power of two, lend your strength to support them! Re-spin the threads of fate and turn their defeat into a victory!"

"Now then, I suppose it's time to add the finishing touch. One that will kill all but the Shield Hero, of course."

Having secured himself from attack, the Demon Dragon began reciting another incantation. But his oversight was the chance we needed to win. Only worrying about attacks from Raphtalia and Ren was a big mistake. He paid no attention to the fact that Sadeena and I were reciting an incantation. At best, it would just be a buff for Raphtalia, and he would have no problem dealing with that. I'm sure that's what he was thinking.

But he was forgetting something important. Sure, Eclair hadn't reached her full potential and probably couldn't even keep up with his speed. Rishia and the old lady weren't here, so it probably seemed like there was no one else to worry about. But . . .

"Dragon Vein! Hear our petition and grant it! As the source of your power, we implore you! Let the true way be revealed once more! Give us the power to overcome the obstacles before us!"

"Descent of the Thunder God!"

The Demon Dragon kept his attention focused on Raphtalia and slowly continued to recite his incantation. It was obvious that he considered her to be the primary threat. But had he not noticed while he was in my shield that there was someone else who could unleash a barrage of the attacks I feared most? And this whole time, she'd been focusing her mind to prepare herself!

"ATLA!"

I turned to Atla and cast Descent of the Thunder God on her. With the slave maturation adjustment, Atla was level 45. But she had an inherent grasp of the essence of the Hengen Muso style. She was a fearsome opponent that had impressed even the old lady!

"My time has come!"

Lightning poured down onto Atla. Bolts of electricity jumped from her skin and turbocharged her speed.

"I've only observed Eclair, Rishia, and the master, but I'll do my best to mimic their movements!"

"I'm counting on you!"

"Bwahahaha! To think such a low-level weakling would dare face me! Insolence!"

"We'll see about that! First Mirage!" Raphtalia shouted.

"Raful!"

Raphtalia and Raph-chan used their illusion magic, and *poof!* Multiple copies of Atla appeared.

"What?!"

"*. . . show yourself! I am the Dragon Emperor, ruler of the world. Strike down these foolish mortals that would defy the Dragon Emper—*"

The Demon Dragon swiped at Atla and her copies violently with his tail and wings, but Atla parried the attacks as easily as if she were waving off flies. In fact, the attacks might not have even been making contact at all. Forgetting that any one of those might be the real Atla would be a dire mistake.

"Annoying little insect! So be it. I'll stop this incantation and buy some time."

The Demon Dragon stopped reciting his incantation. I could feel the partially-formed magic hanging in the air.

"*Great power in this core stone of mine! Hear my plea and show yourself! I am the Dragon Emperor, ruler of the world . . .*"

He began to cast a different spell. Incredible! To think he could pause one spell midway and cast another at the same time!

"Take this!"

Atla thrust at the Demon Dragon. There was a loud cracking sound and his barrier shattered in an instant.

"I'm not finished!" she shouted.

I have no idea how or where she had been storing up

energy, but she continued to launch a string of fierce attacks without pause.

"Demon Dragon! Explosive Assault!"

Explosions filled a wide area surrounding the Demon Dragon. He planned on just blowing Atla away!

"Not on my watch!" I shouted.

I leapt in front of Atla—I didn't know if it was the real Atla or just a copy—to protect her.

"You underestimate me! It will take more than that to stop me!" she shouted.

Atla ignored the explosions and held her hands out in front of her. That was all she had to do to shift the direction of the Demon Dragon's explosions. It was as if she had altered the direction of the wind or something. Incredible.

"There you are!" shouted the Demon Dragon.

He swung his arm at me. I leapt backward without even looking. If it were the real Atla behind me, I knew that she would respond accordingly. Atla seemed to ignore me. She jumped sideways, right into the Demon Dragon's claws and then disappeared.

"Too bad. I guess that wasn't the real one," I taunted.

"Indeed. Don't think that you can see through my illusions so easily. And if an attack like that is all it took to defeat Atla, my life would be a lot easier," Raphtalia added.

I had the urge to make a wisecrack about that last comment,

but in a way, I guess it was proof that she was confident in Atla's abilities.

"Grr . . . Do not interfere!" shouted the Demon Dragon.

"You're gravely mistaken if you think such haphazard swipes can stop me!" Atla taunted.

The Demon Dragon was holding his claws and tail out and spinning around in an attempt to hit the real Atla. She deftly hopped up onto the tip of his tail and stood there confidently with her hands on her hips. Incredible. It was like in a manga or anime, when a warrior would jump up on top of the enemy's blade mid-swing.

"This is the last one!"

Atla didn't attack the Demon Dragon's tail, but instead charged at the dragon himself and thrust the heel of her palm into the final remaining barrier. When she did, a loud crash echoed through the air. Using the same movement as the old lady had when she destroyed Kyo's barrier, Atla shattered the Demon Dragon's barrier completely.

"But I'm still not done!"

Atla landed on the ground for a brief moment, but then shot back up like a bullet. She delivered a sharp jab to the Demon Dragon's shoulder, and instantly the Demon Dragon's shoulder burst open!

"Wha . . . Gaaahhhhhh!"

The Demon Dragon seemed confused for a moment, but

then immediately began writhing in pain from his split-open shoulder.

"I'm far from finished!"

The Hengen Muso attacks, and Atla's imitations of them, could be fired off continually. That was something that neither Raphtalia nor Ren could do with their skills.

"Wyndia! Let's do this!" shouted Melty.

"Okay! Give us back Father and Gaelion!" Wyndia replied.

Their cooperative magic began to take form around Wyndia. She took aim at the Demon Dragon, who was still thrashing around in pain.

"Cooperative magic! Saint Rain!"

Small droplets of rain began to fall throughout the area. Their spell used the rainclouds that had been formed by the cooperative magic Sadeena and I had cast, so the incantation and evocation had both been quick. Black smoke billowed up out of the Demon Dragon's wound each time one of the droplets made contact.

"You insolent fools!"

Moments earlier, the Demon Dragon had been confident of his victory, but now his eyes were burning with hatred. Flames erupted from all over his body. That sure looked like quite the feat!

"You won't hit me with an attack like that!" Atla exclaimed.

Atla was unscathed, and the rain that Melty and Wyndia had called forth showered the flames.

"Now then, Demon Dragon. Want to guess what I was doing while Atla, Melty, and Wyndia were making a fool of you?" I asked.

Sadeena and I had been reciting an incantation continuously this whole time. This kind of magic was a hassle since it required you to solve a little puzzle, but there was no way around it if you wanted to cast the spell. Still, I was able to keep my eye on what was happening while doing it, so I guess I had gotten used to it.

"Wha—?!"

"Time for the second wave! Go, Eclair!" I shouted.

"My turn, is it? Leave it to me! Mr. Iwatani and Ms. Atla, feast your eyes on the true essence of the Hengen Muso style!"

Sadeena and I finished casting Descent of the Thunder God on Eclair and she charged forward. But I noticed that she had been focusing herself before springing to action.

"Oh! That's the Muso Activation technique that the master was lecturing about the other day! I didn't know Eclair could do that!"

Ren was playing the narrator character.

But that explanation didn't tell me anything! Why the hell was he acting like Rishia now?! I was still stuck sparring with Raphtalia and Atla. Nothing he was saying made any sense to me!

"Haaaa!"

Oh! Eclair started moving ridiculously fast! Well, about as fast as Ren anyway. She was still a bit slower than Raphtalia or me when we got serious. But Eclair must have mastered the Hengen Muso defense rating attacks, because the Demon Dragon's scales went flying with each of her thrusts.

"Grr! Do you not realize who I am?! Weak, pathetic humans!"

The Demon Dragon seemed to be struggling now. He let out an infuriated howl. His regenerative capacity must have been incredible though, because I could see his wounds closing up almost immediately after they had been inflicted. That was a bit worrying.

"It doesn't matter how impressive your support magic is if I remove it!"

The Demon Dragon began reciting an incantation. I guess he was going to try to nullify the support magic that we had cast on Atla and Eclair. The effectiveness of their attacks began to decrease. Had the support magic expired? I checked Atla's status screen and the effect was still in place. That meant that he must have used magic to . . . Ah, he must have lowered his own defense rating.

"Alright, Demon Dragon. Now you get to experience the struggle of being the Shield Hero. Raphtalia, Ren, you're up!"

"Understood!" shouted Raphtalia.

"Will that work?" Ren asked.

I gave him a silent nod.

"Instant Blade! Mist!"

"Shooting Star Sword!"

Raphtalia's powerful quick-draw attack and Ren's specialty, Shooting Star Sword, split the Demon Dragon's stomach right open.

"Gah! You make light of me . . ."

"If you raise your defenses, we use defense rating attacks. If you lower them, we use brute force by switching to pure attack power. I'm sure you realize that producing more barriers is useless too."

The same tactics had been used on me before. I'd managed to survive somehow by using cheap tricks. But if L'Arc and the others had been able to fire off those attacks repeatedly, I would have been in the same situation as the Demon Dragon. He was experiencing firsthand the very scenario that I always worried about.

The black sludge around the Demon Dragon had been regenerating immediately before, but now, for some reason, Raphtalia was slicing through it like it was soft tofu and it was disappearing each time she did.

"Grr . . . Stop struggling! You belong to me! Resistance is futile!"

The Demon Dragon suddenly began making awkward movements. What was going on?

"Grr . . . I won't let you escape! Stop trying to fight! Grrraaaaahh!"

He started thrashing around as if something was fighting back from within his body.

"Grr . . . urgh . . ."

Something near his chest seemed to be . . . trying to escape? The Demon Dragon pressed down on his chest, but a beam of magic began to leak out from under his claw.

"Ugh . . ."

"Everyone, attack! It looks like this is our chance!" I shouted.

"Weak, pathetic humans! Don't get . . . cocky!"

"Hmm? Are you sure it's okay to be paying attention to us? I don't know what's going on with your chest, but attacking you there can't be a bad idea!"

"Here I go!" shouted Atla.

"Indeed. That seems to be his weak point. Let's go, Ren!" said Eclair.

"Okay!" Ren replied.

"I'm not in the mood to lose!" Raphtalia exclaimed.

On my signal, Atla, Eclair, Ren, and Raphtalia all attacked and sliced right through the arm that the Demon Dragon was using to press against his chest.

"Urghhhh . . . gahhh!"

The Demon Dragon nearly fell over backward from the

pain of having his arm severed. The arm began to regenerate immediately, but the pressure on his chest was gone. With the restriction removed, the thing that had been struggling inside burst through the dragon's chest wall and showed itself. A tiny baby dragon—Gaelion—came flying out, holding Filo by the nape of her neck.

"Gaelion!"

"Gy . . . gya!"

The Gaelion that appeared looked like he had just hatched. The experience points that had fueled his growth had been sucked right out of him. Even so, he had fought back to protect Wyndia. To protect all of us. The fact that he brought Filo out with him was proof of that.

"Filo!" shouted Melty.

"Ugh . . ."

Nice! Filo was still alive. I held her up in my arms and cast my healing magic on her. The Demon Dragon was busy fighting Raphtalia and the others and couldn't afford to pay attention to what we were doing.

The thing about magic was that casting spells required a certain amount of concentration. The pain the Demon Dragon was experiencing most likely made that impossible for him. And now, two sources of his power—Gaelion and Filo—had escaped, which would undoubtedly weaken him even further.

And then the Demon Dragon's already black appearance

grew several shades darker and he glared over in our direction. He was staring at Wyndia. Wyndia returned to where Melty and Sadeena were standing and took in a deep breath.

"Sadeena. I . . . I'm going to defeat that Demon Dragon!" she shouted.

"Okay!" Melty replied.

"It looks like that's our only choice," said Sadeena.

The three of them began casting cooperative magic. They were reciting the incantation incredibly fast this time, as if driven by Wyndia's determination. And then, before I knew it, a tiny Gaelion was flapping his tiny wings and hovering over them, assisting with the incantation.

"Grr . . . I'm not going to play nice anymore! Gaaaaaaa!"

The Demon Dragon started to lose form. He began to look more like a mass of black sludge than a huge dragon. On my status screen, I noticed that his name changed from Demon Dragon to Wrath Dragon. The abilities of my powered-up Shield of Wrath had combined with a fiendish dragon to create the Wrath Dragon. Was Wyndia's father in there too? What a miserable dragon.

I stepped forward to protect Wyndia and the others. Gaelion flew over to me and hovered right behind me.

"It's dangerous here. Stay back."

"*I can't do that.*"

"Wha?!"

Gaelion spoke! But it must have been telepathic communication, because the voice seemed to come from within my head.

"*Don't act so surprised. You'll give me away to Wyndia and the Sword Hero.*"

"You must be . . ."

It must have been the father Gaelion. He was still occupying the body of baby Gaelion.

"*It makes me happy to see how much my daughter has grown, Shield Hero.*"

Umm, daddy getting emotional is not what I was interested in. I'd have to ask why he was still inside of Gaelion later. That issue obviously hadn't been resolved at all.

"*You've noticed, haven't you? Your rage has coalesced with the Dragon Emperor from another world.*"

"Yeah, I got that . . ."

"*That thing is the embodiment of your anger. Now that it has lost this host body, it is sure to come chasing for you. You must defeat it before the true rampage begins. If you do not, it will pursue you to the ends of the earth and beyond.*"

"Got it. Ren, Raphtalia, let's finish this!"

"Understood!"

"Okay!"

My companions were the whole reason I'd been able to push the enemy into such a tight spot. The gold star went to Atla this time.

"You need not worry. I'm going to help you attack now. Once we force that thing to spit up the demon dragon core, your sidekick can finish it off!"

"So the usual game plan."

"You've got this!"

Sheesh. I couldn't help but feel like we still had other unresolved issues, but maybe it was just my imagination. Gaelion joined the party, which increased the speed of our incantations. The Wrath Dragon unleashed a breath attack. It was weaker than before, but still too powerful to take head-on.

"Haaa!"

Atla simply held her hands up and the Wrath Dragon's flames were parried away. How did she do that? That girl had some formidable defense capabilities. The Wrath Dragon persisted in attacking me. It needed a new host.

"There's no rule that says I can't dodge just because I have a shield, right?"

The Wrath Dragon came at me with an onslaught of entirely straightforward attacks. I maneuvered back and forth, dodging them. The attacks were focused solely on me, so there was no need to guard against them in an attempt to protect the others. Since his attack pattern was so straightforward, dodging the attacks wasn't too difficult, as long as I kept an eye on his speed.

"Here I go! Stardust Blade!"

"Shooting Star Sword!"

Gaelion had produced vanished.

"D . . . did that do it?" Sadeena asked.

She landed on the ground and looked back at the Wrath Dragon. She was breathing hard. Of course, I checked the Wrath Dragon for signs of life too.

"Not yet! Also . . ."

Atla immediately dashed toward the Wrath Dragon and leapt at him like a lion pouncing on its prey. She dug her fingers into his windpipe.

"The core is here! Without this, he'll be nothing!"

The core was floating there in midair and shining brightly.

"Leave it to me!" Raphtalia shouted.

"It's in your hands, Raphtalia! It would seem you're the only one here that can defeat this dragon-shaped black mass of emotion!" Atla replied.

Raphtalia must have already been preparing to attack, because her katana was glowing brightly. With the demon dragon core exposed, the Wrath Dragon opened his mouth fearfully when he saw Raphtalia. He turned his back to her and prepared to flee toward the sky.

"You're not getting away!" she shouted.

"Air Strike Shield! Second Shield! Dritte Shield!"

I summoned my shields to form steps. Raphtalia dashed up the steps and sliced at the Wrath Dragon.

"Instant Blade! Mist!"

"Gyaaaaaa!"

Still in midflight, the Wrath Dragon was split clean in two. He let out a nightmarish shriek and his body fell back down to the ground. It was as if Raphtalia's blade had created a blast of air that sliced the dragon's body right in half.

"Father . . . Forgive me. I will dwell on the past no more," Wyndia whispered.

". . ."

Wyndia pressed her hands together and cried. Gaelion looked on silently from behind. Seeing his daughter grow up was probably making him feel emotional.

Chapter Ten: Purification

Raphtalia landed back on the ground, shook the sludge from her blade, and sheathed her katana.

"You're the MVP today, Atla," I said.

Her training had been limited to sparring with me and Raphtalia, and yet she had managed to pull off a performance like this. She got a passing mark, for sure. On the other hand . . . I looked over at Fohl. To think that I had expected so much more from him when I purchased the two of them.

"Wh . . . what are you looking at me like that for?! Damn it! Atla! I swear I'm going to get stronger! You just watch!" Fohl shouted.

"Please do try," Atla replied.

She gave her brother a word of encouragement, but it was clear she had little interest in whether or not he was actually motivated.

"Umm, thank you, Atla," said Raphtalia.

"Everything I did was for Mr. Naofumi."

It was exactly the kind of response I'd come to expect from Atla.

Thank goodness. I guess that took care of this mess. Well, I still needed to have a talk with Gaelion later.

"Kwa?"

Gaelion flew over to Wyndia and started licking her face. Had he returned to normal? Or was daddy putting on an act?

"Gaelion, are you okay?" Wyndia asked.

"Kwa!"

"Give me back what you stole!"

Filo stood up and started shouting at Gaelion.

"Settle down, Filo. You still haven't fully recovered," said Melty.

She tried to calm Filo down.

"Kwa!"

Gaelion glared back at Filo for a brief moment, but then looked over at the Wrath Dragon.

"I think he says what you're looking for is over there," said Wyndia.

"Is this tiny baby dragon really Gaelion?" asked Raphtalia.

"Yes. He pushed himself too hard and ended up like this, I think."

"Give me back my experience points!"

Now Filo was shouting at the liquified corpse of the Wrath Dragon. She'd had a real streak of bad luck lately. It felt like her luck had been on the decline ever since around the time we went to Kizuna's world. They made a freak show out of her there. Motoyasu latched on to her after that. Then he stole her carriage. And now she had leveled down after being forced to become a sacrificial offering to the Demon Dragon. Maybe I should treat her to a really good meal.

"Now then, all that's left . . ."

I looked at the demon dragon core stone that Atla had pointed out. Without a doubt, that core is what had been the driving force of the Wrath Dragon. That thing had been in my shield and in Raphtalia's katana too. Absorbing it back into my shield would be dangerous, but just leaving it lying around would be even more dangerous. I would just have to store it away somewhere very carefully. I could use it as an armor core stone or something.

Filo was still shouting at the Wrath Dragon's corpse when it suddenly turned into a black light, which then made its way back into my shield. Some of the light also enveloped Filo and then disappeared. Once most of it seemed to have finished returning to my shield, I suddenly heard an extremely unpleasant voice.

"There will always be rage in your heart. I will retreat . . . this time."

I guess we might not have completely defeated it. I'd just have to hope that there was no next time. I'd do my absolute best to avoid relying on the Shield of Wrath from now on. It was a beast of a shield, powered up beyond belief. If I used it again, it was likely that I would finally lose myself to it.

"Kwa!"

Gaelion jumped up onto my shoulder playfully and began frisking about.

"Heeeey! Master is supposed to play with me!" Filo shouted.

"I don't have time to play with pets right now! Let's go home already."

"Buuut . . ."

"How do you feel, anyway, Filo?"

"My body feels better. But Gaelion didn't return very much of what he stooooole."

I checked her status. She was level 41 now. That was quite the drop. Gaelion, on the other hand, was level 60 now, despite having fled from the curse of the Demon Dragon, without looking back. Their levels had basically been swapped.

"Give it back!" Filo shouted.

"Kwa!"

Gaelion jumped off of my shoulder. He and Filo began fiercely glaring at each other.

"Kwa! Kwa kwa!"

"I think Gaelion says he has no idea what you're talking about. He says he's the Shield Hero's favorite," said Wyndia.

"Boo!"

Gaelion made the opening attack. He slapped Filo on the cheek with his tiny tail and laughed.

"Give it back! Give it back! Give it back!"

"Kwa! Kwa! Kwa!"

"Rafu?"

Gaelion and Filo started exchanging blows. Raph-chan stood between them with a look of disgust on her face. This had all been Gaelion's fault to begin with, and he didn't seem to feel bad about it at all. In that case . . .

"Now, now, then. We'll just give Gaelion back to Filo, body and all. Maybe she can get some of her experience back if she eats him," I said.

I grabbed Gaelion, forced Filo to turn into her filolial queen form, and then pried her mouth open and stuffed Gaelion in.

"Kwaaa?!"

"Stop that!"

"What are you thinking, Naofumi?!"

Wyndia and Melty interfered.

"Boo! Stop trying to make me eat weird things, Master!"

"But you love eating. Eating a dragon might make you feel better."

"Noo! Dragons are yuuucky!"

So the little glutton was complaining, was she? She needed a more balanced diet.

"Filo, stop being a picky eater."

"Nooo!"

"That's not the problem here! Think about what you're saying, Naofumi!" Melty shouted.

"Mr. Naofumi, let's not encourage Filo to pick up any strange eating habits," said Raphtalia.

"Yuuucky!"

"Stop trying to make Filo do weird things!" Melty exclaimed. She hugged Filo and then started glaring at Wyndia.

"This mess is all that thing's fault! We should get rid of him!" she said.

"He's back to normal now!" Wyndia replied.

Oh, jeez. What a hassle. I needed an escape from reality. I hugged Raph-chan and started petting her showily in front of Filo and Gaelion.

"Boo!"

"Kwaaaa!"

Filo and Gaelion glared at Raph-chan with envy in their eyes, but that wasn't my problem.

"What are you trying to do?!" Raphtalia snapped.

"They're both causing trouble! Raph-chan is well-mannered, cute, and unselfish. She's the best!"

"Rafu!"

Raph-chan waved her hand at Raphtalia. For some reason, Raphtalia looked at Raph-chan with the same look in her eyes that Filo had.

"You know, I feel sorry for you, Naofumi," said Ren.

Frankly, this was all his fault, when it came down to it.

"You bastard. You better not try to say this was all some quest triggered by leaving that dragon's corpse to rot. That would just piss off everyone that got tangled up in this mess."

"I . . . I wouldn't!"

Ren shook his head back and forth violently. But I really could imagine him saying that. That it was a quest with a rare boss encounter and defeating that boss would get you an epic weapon . . . Something like that.

"Anyway, we're going home!" I shouted.

"Things sure are always exciting with you around, little Naofumi!"

Sadeena cackled. This kind of thing was nothing to joke about. Sheesh.

"Filo, let's go home."

"Okay!"

"Kwa!"

Gaelion crawled between my legs.

"I can't walk with you there! Get out of the way!"

"Kwaaaa!"

Gaelion started glowing brightly and then suddenly grew to the size he had been before swallowing the demon dragon core. No, he was a bit bigger. Around four meters long. With me already on his back, he used his tail and arms to grab on to Wyndia, Sadeena, Rat, and Atla, and then took flight. Just before lifting off, Raph-chan jumped on to his head and was hanging on to his horns.

"Wha?! Boooo!"

Filo cried out with disappointment in her voice.

"Mr. Naofumi!"

Raphtalia looked awestruck. I didn't know what to say either! I had no idea he could transform.

"Kwa!"

"Boo!"

Gaelion flapped his wings loudly and flew up into the air.

"Big sis! Sword lady! We have to hurry and go after them! Carrying Master is my job!"

Filo wasn't going to let Gaelion win. She took off running in an attempt to get the remaining party members to hurry up.

"You look comfortable up there. It reminds me of riding Ethnobalt's boat in the other world," said Raphtalia.

"A . . . Atla!"

Fohl had a look of urgency on his face. But without a carriage, I'm sure there was no way he would be able to catch up with us.

"You never get a break, do you, Mr. Iwatani?" asked Eclair while looking up at us.

"Jeez . . . This little guy sure is pushy," said Rat.

"Rat, did you know that dragons could transform like this?" I asked her.

"I've read about it happening on very rare occasions, but I've never heard of a case surpassing what filolial variants can do."

From up in the air above, I looked down at the area

below us. I noticed that the dark color of corruption had faded away from the land.

"Did you notice it too, Count? Gaelion was sucking up the corruption from the surrounding area while he was running amok. This seems to be the result," Rat said.

So that was what happened. I wondered if this area would finally become truly peaceful. It occurred to me that I could probably use Portal Shield now. I gave it a try.

"Portal Shield!"

Nice. It seemed usable, as far as I could tell. A little warning message popped up to let me know that if I registered this location, it would teleport me to the ground. I chose to continue with the teleport and focused my awareness on the surrounding area. Raphtalia and the others were out of range. It probably wouldn't be a good idea to leave them behind.

"Leave Master here!"

Oh? Filo was running after us in a mad dash below. She seemed faster than she should have been after having lost so many levels. I checked her status again just to make sure. Huh? Her stats that had been reduced by the curse were back to their normal values. Ah, no wonder! That's why she didn't seem to be weakened that much.

But why was Filo the only one that had the effects of the curse removed? Maybe the Demon Dragon had leeched away the remnants of the powerful All Sacrifice Aura. That had been the source of the curse, so the consequences would have gotten sucked away with it. I was super jealous. That meant that Filo was no longer cursed. If she leveled back up, she would be faster and more powerful than before. All's well that ends well, I guess.

"Kwa!"

"Gaelion, you're on your way to becoming a fine dragon. Keep it up, and someday you'll be as great as my father was."

"Your father is hiding in plain sight, you know."

"What are you talking about? My father . . . is dead."

Wyndia brushed me off. She didn't believe me.

I had Gaelion put us down near the eastern village. I teleported everyone back to the village from there. I guess there's no need to mention that the eastern village residents were thrilled that the mountain had returned to its initial state of beauty.

"*You sure are something, Shield Hero!*"

That's what they said. I sure had fooled them. But to be honest, from what Wyndia and Gaelion had said, the villagers only got what they deserved. I thought a lot less of the eastern village residents now.

"Master rides on my back!" Filo shouted.

"Kwaaa!"

The heated battle between Filo and Gaelion resumed as

soon as we got back to the village. Gaelion had transformed back into his baby form again.

"Oh, whatever. It makes no difference who I ride."

"It does too!"

Filo sure was stubborn. I sighed.

"Whatever. Play time goes to you for the next few days, so settle down."

"Yaaaay! But Master is supposed to—"

"You're going to lose your play time if you keep pushing the issue."

"Kwa . . ."

"You're the one that caused that mess, so you're grounded. But I might let you join me and Filo for some extra play time if I'm not busy, so behave yourself."

Gaelion tottered off to Wyndia and started crying.

"Kwaaa!"

"Why are you nice to that bird, but you bully Gaelion?" Wyndia snapped.

"Is it that hard to understand? He has to be punished."

"Well, Mr. Naofumi does have a point. That was no small incident," said Raphtalia.

"Rafu!"

Raphtalia and Raph-chan both nodded in unison.

Sob . . .

Gaelion was hanging on to Wyndia and crying, but I saw

him steal a glance at me. It reminded me of a bully feigning tears whenever a parent showed up. That just pissed me off.

"That attitude just got you in more trouble."

"Kwaaaa . . ."

Now he was crying for real.

"Ha! That's what you geeeet!"

"Filo!"

Melty and I both shouted at Filo together. She looked away and started singing. Sheesh . . . This one acted just like a little brat too.

"Anyway, Filo, your curse is gone now, so I want you to get out there and level."

"Okaaay! I'll go with Mel-chan and we'll level together! Then you can play with me, Master!"

I had no idea why she was dragging Melty into this, but she sure seemed excited. Oh? Melty didn't look too enthusiastic.

Melty spoke up. "Listen, Filo. I don't have time for that. I have a ton of work I have to take care of back at the town that Eclair is running."

"Buuut, Mel-chan! You were just saying you were too weak and wanted to level uuuup!"

"I didn't mean right this instant!"

"But, Mel-chan! When the townspeople were being lazy and said they'd do something the next day, you got mad at theeeem! You said, 'If you can do it tomorrow, then you can do it now!'"

"I have other things to do!"

"Buuuut, Mel-chan! Before, you said, 'You'll never get anywhere in life if you don't do the things you want to do just because you're busy!'"

Oh, boy. Filo was in her but-but-but mode. When she got like this, the back-and-forth would just go on and on until she either got her way or the other person just refused to respond anymore. Still, who knew when Filo would get another chance to level if she didn't go now.

I looked at the assistant that had come to fetch Melty and motioned him over with my eyes. We talked quietly so that Melty couldn't hear us. The assistant was worried about Melty's level being so low too. She was a hard worker, so her magic proficiency was far ahead of her level. But regardless of that, many of the higher-ups wanted her to raise her level before she was put in charge of running the country. Really, the fact that a child was spending so much time on public affairs probably wasn't a good thing either.

"Rafu!"

Raph-chan called out from on top of Filo's head. She stood up on her hind legs and slapped her hand against her chest, as if to say, "Leave it to me!"

"Alright then. Knowing you'll be there is reassuring, Raph-chan," I said.

"What's so reassuring about that?" Raphtalia snapped.

I was sad to see Raph-chan go, but Melty and Filo should be fine if she went with them. I was sure she would make it more enjoyable anyway. It was time for Melty and Filo to realize just how cute Raph-chan was.

"Eclair."

"What is it, Mr. Iwatani?"

"You've been relying on Melty too much. Melty is going out to level now. You're the town governor, so I'm ordering you to take care of your own busywork while she's gone."

"M . . . Mr. Iwatani?!"

"I don't want to hear any complaints from you either, Ren. Melty has been taking care of all of the tasks that Eclair has been putting off."

"F . . . fine. But I can help her out a little bit, right?"

I guess if he really wanted to help, that was fine.

"Mr. Naofumi, what are you trying to do?" asked Raphtalia.

"This is a good chance to address the issue of Melty doing all of Eclair's work for her," I replied.

Raphtalia sighed.

"Well, it's true that Melty is working much too hard for her age," she said.

Melty needed to go out and play every now and then too. Filo would watch out for her, I'm sure.

"It's decided. Allow me to make the proclamation. Melty, Her Royal Highness the Second Princess, has set out on a journey of personal growth with her cherished bird!"

"What's going on, bubba?" asked Keel.

I made the announcement in front of Keel and the other villagers. Keel looked tired. She was yawning the whole time.

"N . . . Naofumi? What did you just call me?" Melty grumbled.

"It's just your official title. Eclair, you tell the residents of your town the same thing."

"U . . . understood."

"So that settles it. Filo, take Melty and go level."

"Yaaaay!"

"Wait a second, Naofumi! You can't just decide something like that on your own!" Melty complained.

"It's okay, Melty," I replied.

"What's okay?!"

"I didn't decide on my own. Your assistant agreed to it too. And Eclair is going to take care of your work for you. Go play with Filo and have a little bit of fun."

"Stop messing around!" Melty shouted.

"All that's left is to decide whether or not to set you up with the slave maturation bonus. I'm pretty sure the queen would give us the go-ahead."

The queen apparently wanted me to marry Melty, so she would probably let me do anything I wanted to her. I just needed Melty to agree to it.

"No thanks!"

"Oh? That's too bad. Oh well. Off you go!"

"We'll be back, Master!"

"Wait, Filo! I never agreed to—"

Before Melty could finish, Filo grabbed her by the collar with her beak and threw her on her back. With Melty on her back, Filo flapped her wings and took off running while yelling, "Here we gooooo!"

"Naofumi! I won't forget this!"

Melty's voice trailed off as she got further away.

"Melty, Her Royal Highness the Second Princess, we eagerly look forward to your development!"

I made an exaggerated saluting motion. In a final display of spite, Melty nonsensically tore an accessory off of her outfit and threw it at me. Of course, since she was riding on Filo's back and Filo was sprinting away, it didn't actually hit me. It just fell on the ground. That girl was always screaming so hysterically. Did I really upset her that much? All in all, she wasn't that bad though.

"Raful!"

Raph-chan was sitting on top of Filo's head and waving to me. I was counting on her to watch those two helpless dolts.

"Now then, it's morning already. I'm tired . . ."

"I'm sure Melty is tired too. We were still fighting just a few hours ago," Raphtalia said.

"Filo is in good spirits, so they'll be fine. I'm sorry, but I don't have the time or energy to be worrying about those two right now. Raph-chan is a different story, of course."

I decided to cancel my training for the day. I would just make breakfast for the slaves and then take a nap. I was completely exhausted.

"Alright, everyone. Once you finish eating breakfast, I want you all to get to work."

And then, out of nowhere, S'yne suddenly appeared at the village.

"Did something————?"

Oh, yeah . . . I had totally forgotten about her.

And just like that, things had finally returned to normal for us.

Chapter Eleven: Perfect Hidden Justice

It was the day after Filo and Melty set off on their journey to train. I gathered up the slaves from the village who had been making an earnest effort to level up, and I used my portal skill to teleport us all to Zeltoble. When the old lady had gotten back to the village, she told me that it would be good practice for them if they fought against some unfamiliar opponents, like mercenaries. She said they were at least strong enough to fight in the coliseums now.

"Bubba! Bubba! Do we get to fight here?!"

Keel was excited. We were watching a duel at a coliseum in Zeltoble.

"Yeah. This is the open coliseum, so it's relatively safe. I want you all to fight hard, but do your best not to get injured too."

"Sure thing, bubba!"

"Keel, do you really understand?" asked Raphtalia.

"Of course! I don't want to get injured and get left behind!"

I was glad that Keel seemed to be in her usual good spirits.

"Besides, with Sadeena here, we'll be fine no matter what happens!"

"Oh my!"

"Yeah, I've heard she used to rake in the money here in Zeltoble. Speaking of which, where's S'yne?" I asked.

Apparently, S'yne hadn't noticed that something was happening when we were dealing with the dragon incident recently. She had been asleep or something. Sheesh . . . She was never around when we needed her the most. Maybe she would have come if I'd called her though. I guess it was partially my fault for forgetting about her. She may not have even been able to teleport to that corrupted mountain in the first place.

"I hear little S'yne is busy in the underground coliseum," Sadeena replied.

"Does she ever take a break?"

"And of course, she's donating half of her profits to you, little Naofumi."

"Nice! Keep it up, S'yne!"

"You prioritize profits too much, Mr. Naofumi," Raphtalia said.

"An impressive attitude, Mr. Naofumi!" Atla exclaimed.

"What part of that is impressive?!" Raphtalia retorted.

The two of them went back and forth in their usual manner.

By the way, Fohl had realized just how weak he was and went out to train with the old lady. On top of that, he'd apparently asked for the no-holds-barred course and the old lady got really excited or something. The group of slaves with me now had nothing to do while the old lady was out, which is why I'd brought them to Zeltoble to fight in the coliseum.

We were at the coliseum that the slave trader managed. The bets here were on the small side, but we still had to pull some strings to participate, just like when we had fought Sadeena. My slaves had stat adjustments. They were far stronger than their levels would imply, and their histories had to be touched up a bit too. The Lurolona slave price bubble had burst, but they were still being traded on the high side.

"Fehhh . . ."

"Rishia, are you still making that pathetic sound after all of your training?"

"I . . . I can't help it!"

Her talents had finally blossomed, but she was still the same useless Rishia. Sheesh . . . I'm sure we would have been able to defeat the Demon Dragon a lot easier if she had been there. Whenever faced with an opponent bent on world domination, Rishia's true powers would awaken and she'd defeat the enemy like some kind of heroine saving the day.

"Alright, everyone. Be careful while you're out there fighting," I told the slaves.

"Okay!" they shouted back in unison.

I left the slaves with Sadeena and the rest of us made our way to the gallery seating.

The tournament that we'd entered was a short one that would only last one or two days. In general, the open coliseum was meant to entertain guests with straightforward fights. That's why there was a greater emphasis on rules than in the underground coliseum. There were all kinds of restrictions, like level classes and only being able to use dulled weapons. Of course, you never knew what might happen since betting was still part of it. The current tournament had level classes, and killing opponents was strictly forbidden. It felt more like a sports tournament than underground fighting.

I considered having Raphtalia or Sadeena enter, but it was likely that someone would recognize them, so I decided to hold off on that. As for myself, this tournament was one-on-one matches only. I might have been able to win without breaking the rules, but you couldn't win by forcing the opponent out of bounds, so I decided not to enter. Even though I couldn't attack, I might be able to win by restraining the opponent, but that would be a real hassle. It made more sense to just have the slaves get some real-world fighting experience.

"Alright, we'll be watching from the gallery. You all do your best!"

"This way, Shield Hero," said the slave trader.

He had been silently standing nearby. He led us to our seats in the gallery. On the way to our seats, I caught sight of the other contestants getting ready for their matches. The majority of them looked like degenerates. Many of them had brutish or muscle-bound appearances too.

And then I saw it. I couldn't believe my eyes.

"I . . . Itsuki?!"

"Huh?!"

"Feh?!"

There was Itsuki, mingling with the other contestants like he was just another ordinary mercenary. When Raphtalia and Rishia heard my outburst, they looked over and saw him too. They both cried out in surprise.

"Is something wrong? Yes sir."

"No, it's just . . ."

I explained to the slave trader that Itsuki, the Bow Hero, was here in the coliseum. We needed to talk to Itsuki before we did anything else. S'yne's adversaries were trying to kill the holy heroes. I wasn't going to let Itsuki slip through my fingers here.

"Let's see . . ."

A brawny man whose face was concealed by a piece of cloth brought the slave trader a list.

"Contestant #982. He's registered as Perfect Hidden Justice."

I almost fell over backward. Perfect Hidden Justice? That had to be a joke. That was so blatantly obvious that it would have sent even the most delusional escapist running back to reality. Even I couldn't help but feel embarrassed.

"Can we talk to him?" I asked.

"Yes, I can grant you permission under my authority."

The slave trader instructed his assistant to take us to the contestant waiting room. I didn't want to alarm Itsuki, so I approached casually and greeted him.

"Hey. Long time no see," I said.

"Mr. Itsuki!" exclaimed Rishia.

Itsuki just stood there vacantly and showed no sign of responding.

"I . . . Yes . . . Everyone . . ." he mumbled.

"Hey," I repeated.

"Everyone is counting on me. Yes. Everyone . . . is counting on me. This prize money will help save people."

"Are you listening?!" I shouted.

Itsuki just kept mumbling to himself quietly. It was hard to make out what he was saying. He had a vacant look in his eyes. I couldn't even tell where he was looking.

"I . . . I'm not inferior. I'm . . . Actually . . ."

"Hey! Listen to me!" I shouted at him.

"Mr. Itsuki! Umm . . . I—" Rishia began.

I grabbed Itsuki by the shoulders and shook him back and forth, but he showed no response. I heard the sound of a gong echo throughout the coliseum.

"I . . . fight for justice!"

"Mr. Itsuki! Ahh!"

Itsuki shoved Rishia out of the way and sprinted off, as if he hadn't heard a word we said.

"What's up with that jerk?" I grumbled.

"Are you okay, Rishia?" asked Raphtalia.

She had caught Rishia before she fell.

"Fehhh . . ."

It was like we didn't even exist to Itsuki.

"So . . . I looked into that contestant a bit more, and it seems he's been making the rounds at all of the Zeltoble coliseums for a while now. Yes sir."

"Really? This is the first I've heard of that."

"Yes. I've been told that he started showing up a day or two after you left Zeltoble."

We'd just missed each other! That put me in a mood to complain.

Still, I don't know what had happened to him, but something was clearly wrong with Itsuki. It probably had something to do with losing to the Spirit Tortoise coming back to haunt him though. That was easy enough to guess. That reminded me, the queen had mentioned receiving several eyewitness reports from when he fought the Spirit Tortoise. Going by those and what Kyo had mentioned, Itsuki's party had a falling out.

When the coliseum matches began, I focused on Itsuki's match. I'd assumed that attacking from a distance would be much more advantageous for Itsuki than close combat. But the rules restricted combat to a small area. An opponent would be able to close the gap in a flash. That would make using a bow disadvantageous. Regardless, Itsuki was advancing through the tournament with ease. He actually seemed pretty skilled at one-on-one combat.

But there was something strange about his expression. And every time the audience cheered, he threw his hands into the air and howled ecstatically. Was that really Itsuki? The Itsuki I knew was a bit more reserved. He was a hypocrite who was always trying to act like a real man of character.

"Fehhh . . ."

My slaves were fighting in a separate tournament, so I wouldn't have to worry about them getting hurt. But I still needed to figure out how to take him into custody. Also, something about the way his bow looked really bothered me.

"How can we take him in without letting him get away?" I wondered out loud.

We'd already figured out how to interfere with the portal skills. Magically generating a magnetic field in the area would cause the portal skills to malfunction. It would be possible to keep him from running if we used ceremonial magic, like Sanctuary or Judgment.

Luckily for us, this was Zeltoble, the country of merchants and mercenaries. If I gave the order, I could have the slave trader arrange to obstruct portal usage in the coliseum Itsuki was fighting in. But if we did something that went against the rules, it was likely that Itsuki would feel threatened and run away. And things could turn really bad if he took hostages from the audience and started getting violent.

Just as I expected, the slave trader wasn't prepared to agree to a plan that might result in people getting injured in a coliseum full of visitors. He said we'd have to be extremely careful and make advance preparations if we were going to try anything.

"We can just knock him out, no questions asked, and then take him into custody," Atla said.

"Why are you always so violent?! Jeez . . . We should at least try talking to him, right?" Raphtalia replied.

"Yeah. I'd like to take him in on amicable terms, if possible," I said.

More of S'yne's old enemies might have still been hiding out in this world. We couldn't know when or where to expect them. I wanted to convince Itsuki to stick with us, if possible.

"Mr. Naofumi, perhaps we should try to find out what he's after by talking with our fists. I'm sure we would be able to get through to him that way."

"What are you, Atla? Some kind of martial arts master?"

It was hard to believe she was a sickly little girl not too long ago. Everything she said made it sound like she only knew how to think with her fists. At least her brother had a little common sense.

"Mr. Itsuki . . ."

Rishia was watching Itsuki fight with a really worried look on her face. Hmm . . .

"What do you think we should do, Rishia?" I asked.

"I . . . I . . ."

Rishia put her hands together like she was praying and spoke hesitatingly.

"Mr. Itsuki seems very troubled. I would like to help him resolve whatever is bothering him."

"Even though he discarded you like a piece of trash?"

Incredible. Rishia must have been some kind of saint. Her devotion was unwavering. Itsuki sure was a lucky guy.

"Either way, it seems like Itsuki is fighting in the coliseums to earn money."

I had the slave trader do a bit more digging. He confirmed that Itsuki had been fighting day after day to earn money in coliseums around Zeltoble, both open and underground. It was clear that he wanted money. But we still hadn't been able to figure out where he was staying. It was probably a good idea to look into why he was trying to make all that money too. Knowing Itsuki, I'm sure he was fighting to fund some kind of hypocritical scheme or something.

Maybe I would tail him and see where he went after the tournament ended. Or maybe we could lure him out somehow later.

"Hey, Perfect . . . I'm going to beat you this time!"

Itsuki's opponent spoke to Itsuki.

"No, the victory will be mine again."

"Like hell it will! I've seen all of your attacks now!"

Oh? It seemed like Itsuki would respond to his opponents.

So the reason he had ignored us earlier is because he had been focused on the tournament . . . perhaps. But I could tell that something was off by the look in his eyes, even from a distance. His bow looked strange too. It was an unnaturally pure white, and yet it had a really sinister design. I could sense a strange aura coming from it.

"So we can assume that he'll respond during combat . . . I guess," I wondered out loud.

"Naofumi!" Rishia called out to me.

"Umm . . . I . . . I want to talk to Mr. Itsuki. So please, let me fight in the coliseum!"

"I think that's a good idea. I have a bad feeling about that weapon of his," said Raphtalia.

She nodded in agreement with Rishia's proposition.

"Isn't that pretty much the same as Atla's idea? Then again, it did work for Ren. I guess we should try it sooner than later this time."

"In that case, I have a suggestion, Shield Hero."

The slave trader seemed to have a plan.

"What's that?"

"There's an underground fight arena that isn't being used tonight. You could lure the Bow Hero there and then capture him. Yes sir. I could give him a written invitation when I present him with the tournament prize money."

Something seemed off. I couldn't help but feel like there was some kind of ulterior motive at play here.

"Let me guess. The queen is offering a reward to anyone who assists with the capture of a hero or something, right?"

"Impressive! You understand our true intentions well. My hat's off to you! Yes sir!"

"There's nothing impressive about it . . ."

His intentions were painfully straightforward.

"You better not try to turn this into a hero-deathmatch spectacle or something. I can't guarantee anyone in the audience will make it out alive."

"Of course. I will ensure that no guests are invited."

The real problem would be if he had unlocked a curse series. Eclair had been able to get through to Ren, but there was no guarantee the same thing would work for Itsuki.

"Is it possible Itsuki might think the invitation seems too good to be true and not come?"

"I suppose it is possible. Yes sir."

Still, it would be a good way to get him to talk. If he did show up, we could just make it look like a real match and then ask him what was going on . . . Right?

"What about the rules?"

"The Bow Hero seems to prefer one-on-one matches. Yes sir. There have been exceptions though. I've been told that he has fought alone in team-battle tournaments when the prize was large enough."

Hmm . . . In that case, inviting him to a one-on-one fight in the underground coliseum would be our best bet. If we made it a team-battle tournament with a huge prize, it was possible that he would get suspicious. That would be risky. It would be completely pointless if he didn't show up.

"Alright. Since you say you want to talk to him, Rishia, you'll fight him in the first match. Then it's our turn. I'll take care of filling out the audience with fake onlookers."

I'd just use the village slaves. We could put Sadeena or S'yne in the lineup of fighters, and that would make it all the more appealing.

"Understood! Thank you!"

Rishia thanked me. I gave her a small wave to say it was nothing.

"I hope you're able to talk some sense into him and convince him to come with us," I said.

"Me too!" she replied.

"What would you like us to do?" Raphtalia and Atla asked, looking at me questioningly.

"If Rishia happens to lose, you can go fight next and just pretend like it's a coincidence."

"Understood!" Atla exclaimed.

"Not you, Atla . . . You stay in the gallery," I replied.

I was afraid she might end up killing Itsuki.

We went about setting up a fake tournament to lure Itsuki out into the underground coliseum. Itsuki was given a flyer along with his prize money, and we had someone follow him back to his place. That was a partial failure though, because his tail lost him in a crowd on the way. But we did have a general idea of where he was staying now.

The underground coliseum that the slave trader prepared for us was a cozy little arena in the basement of a small tavern. It felt like the kind of place where you might expect to see underground wrestling or something. There was nothing there but a barely adequate waiting room and a slightly cramped arena.

The slave trader had arranged for several magic users to cast a ceremonial magic spell called Sanctuary on the arena. That would make it impossible for Itsuki to flee using his portal skill. The invitation that Itsuki was given clearly specified that would be the case. If he noticed anything strange going on, he was likely to run. We needed to be extra careful about not making him suspicious.

Itsuki had showed up earlier that day, completely unsuspecting, and registered himself as a fighter. He was standing by in the waiting room now. Luring him there really had been so simple that it was almost disappointing.

"Luring him out was a success, but we still need to find out what he's doing here and why he's trying to make money," I said.

"You really did find Itsuki?" Ren asked.

I'd returned to the village earlier and brought Ren back to Zeltoble with me. I figured there was a chance Itsuki would listen to Ren, even if he refused to listen to me. The two of them had been fairly close and talked with each other frequently before, apparently. Ren agreed to come without hesitation too.

"Yeah. Rishia is going to fight him in the first match. After that, I want you to go out there and try to talk to him, Ren."

"Got it! I'm sure that Itsuki . . . is suffering just like I was."

Ren was eager to do as I told him. I guess Itsuki was in the same type of situation he'd been in, after all. He probably wanted to do whatever he could to help out.

"You've got this, Rishia."

Raphtalia was trying to encourage Rishia, who nodded enthusiastically in response.

"R . . . right! This time I really will do my *besht!*"

There she went with that annoying, cutesy pronunciation. I would've thought she'd be taking things seriously now, of all times. But maybe that's just what made Rishia who she was.

"Rishia, go show Itsuki how strong you've become. Show him that you're more than strong enough now."

"I will!"

Rishia responded enthusiastically to my encouragement.

It was true. She was more than strong enough now. She'd really blossomed, both stats-wise and skill-wise. From joining our party at the Cal Mira islands, to training with the old

Hengen Muso lady, and even taking on Kyo in her awakened state during the Spirit Tortoise incident, she had never given up on fighting. She'd gained self-confidence from everything that happened in Kizuna's world, and she'd experienced a real life-and-death battle.

Rishia had changed. She wasn't the same person that Itsuki had used as an errand girl. Now was her chance to show him that. The gong sounded and Rishia started walking to the arena. After seeing her off, Raphtalia, Atla, and I headed to some ringside seats with a good view.

"And now, a faceoff between Perfect Hidden Justice and Rishia Ivyred! Let the battle . . . BEEEEGGIIIINNNNN!"

The same announcer from when we fought Sadeena shouted out and gave the signal to start. I was surprised he'd agreed to take part in a fake tournament. My slaves all started clapping loudly. I'd ordered them to get out of there immediately if anything went wrong. Sadeena and S'yne were there to help guard them though. They would be able to buy them some time, even if things turned ugly.

"Mr. Itsuki!"

Rishia called out to Itsuki. He was mumbling to himself under his breath, but he stopped and looked up, his gaze fixed on Rishia.

"Oh? So my opponent is Rishia? This will be an easy win."

Rishia was clearly a nobody to Itsuki.

"Mr. Itsuki! Please listen to me! The situation is extremely serious! Your life is in danger! Please listen to what Naofumi and Ren have to say!"

Rishia pointed over to me and Ren at our ringside seats. I waved at him, just to let him know I was there. All of a sudden, Itsuki's expression grew incredibly grim.

Chapter Twelve: Justice vs. Justice

"Naofumi . . ."

The malice in his eyes was unbelievable. Never before in all of my fights against other people had someone's icy, murderous intent felt so tangible. But why was he glaring at me so menacingly?

"Your actions! They are absolutely unforgivable!"

"What are you going on about all of a sudden?"

Had I done something wrong?

"Then again, if you asked me to come up with something I'd done wrong . . . I could go on for hours."

"I wish I could argue with that. I really do," Raphtalia whispered with a sigh.

It was nothing to be ashamed of. I'd just done what was necessary to survive.

"Mr. Naofumi is the embodiment of justice. He can do no evil," Atla replied.

"I'm not so sure about that . . ." I said.

I thought about what Atla said. Saying that I made the rules would put me on the same level as Itsuki. It was hard to tell whether he was under the effects of a curse or just showing his true colors now.

"Then let me spell it out for you. You've gathered up slaves, forced them into hard labor, and you're keeping all of the profits for yourself! Am I wrong?"

"Isn't that the whole point?"

That's what slaves were for, right? Of course, it was only natural to compensate someone for their labor. But once you owned a slave, that was manpower that belonged to you. You didn't have to pay them for every little job they did. Did I have any qualms about purchasing another human being? Sure I did, but I was just doing what needed to be done.

This was taking the argument to the extreme, but to put it in terms of modern society, slaves were kind of like vacuum cleaners. No one was going to look at a vacuum cleaner and feel sorry for it because it was sucking up dust every day. Slaves were a convenient tool, just like a vacuum cleaner or a washing machine.

"What is that guy with the bow talking about?"

"Hard labor? Has Bubba Shield ever made us work that hard?"

"He never orders us to do more than we can handle. On the contrary, it's always just the right amount."

The slaves started whispering among themselves. They sounded like a bunch of shills.

"More importantly, this popcorn stuff that you made for us is super good, bubba!" Keel shouted.

She was sitting in the gallery and chomping on some imitation popcorn that I'd cooked up to help set the mood for the match. It really wasn't all that good.

"Let's go do something fun after this is over!"

"Yeah, let's do something fun!"

Oh, damn it! They were distracting me. I wished they would just shut up!

"Oh my, look at that unquestioning obedience, little Naofumi!"

That killer whale wench, Sadeena, needed to keep her mouth shut!

"The village children enjo————"

"She says that despite being slaves, the villagers enjoy the work that they do."

S'yne weighed in and her stuffed-doll familiar translated for her.

Letting them get to me would be a waste of energy!

"You're making them act like they enjoy laboring for you! That's even worse! And I heard about how you gave a sickly young girl expensive medicine to force her older brother into hard labor! The same slave siblings that Princess Malty was trying to rescue!"

"There's no way Witch would be trying to rescue anyone!"

I reflexively shouted back in anger. But it was the truth. Doing a good deed was impossible for that woman. That, I was sure of.

"Who is this 'Witch' you speak of? We must not be the only pair of siblings that you have rescued," Atla said.

"No, you're the only ones," I replied.

Atla was sitting next to me looking confused, but I was pretty sure Itsuki was referring to her and her brother. I don't know where he'd gotten his information, but he sure was spouting off nonsense. Witch rescuing a demi-human? Even if hell did freeze over, that still wasn't going to happen.

But wait . . . Why the hell was he mentioning Witch?!

"Itsuki! You just said Witch's name, didn't you?! Why are you bringing her up?!"

I couldn't even imagine how it all fit together. Surely Witch wasn't pulling Itsuki's strings now, was she? But Itsuki clearly wasn't listening to me. He just continued on with the accusations.

"I also heard that you sold your medicines to rich nobles but did nothing for the poor!"

Was he talking about my peddling operations? Or did he mean before . . . when I was traveling around Melromarc as the supposed saint of the bird god?

"I'm no saint. No one expects a merchant to sell goods to someone with no money, do they?"

Every now and then, some entitled jerk would show up and demand that I grace them with some medicine, like it was their God-given right. Maybe he was referring to those people.

"I heard about the evil noble who had fallen ill and was destined to finally meet his end. Thanks to you sticking your nose where it didn't belong, he escaped death and the people's suffering was prolonged!"

"Now you're really barking up the wrong tree. I only sell the stuff. It's not up to me to decide how people use it. And anyway, refusing to sell someone medicine because they're a bad person, or trying to say that someone is better off dead, would be even worse."

What the hell? Since when was selling medicine to rich people wrong? Besides, even if I had refused to sell to those rich people, it would have just been them doing the badmouthing. In the end, I was the bad guy no matter what I did!

"As a hero, you have the power to save others, and yet I spoke with a lamenting mother who told me about how you refused to save her son!"

"I have no idea who you're talking about . . ."

That wasn't ringing any bells. I didn't save someone? I always did my best to save anyone that was seriously ill. Just like I had done with the old Hengen Muso lady. That's not to say I didn't demand those people pay for it afterward with anything they owned, but still . . .

"The woman clung to me, crying and saying she could never forgive you!"

Who would still be holding a grudge against me after all

that I did? Oh wait, I think I understood.

"That son that you mentioned . . . He was already dead, wasn't he?"

"That's right! She told me that your shield had the power to perform a miracle, and yet you still refused to help!"

"Are you even listening to yourself? There's no way I could bring the dead back to life, even if I do have the legendary shield. The people that can do that kind of thing are from another world."

I knew of people that could come back to life. Although, we had still managed to kill them. That was getting off topic though.

I had pretty much figured out who Itsuki was talking about. It was really rare, but people like that did show up every now and then in villages and towns. They would bring me a corpse and ask me to bring the person back to life. Based on the rumors that I was a saint, and my actual feats as the Shield Hero, they would insist that I should be able to do such a thing. They would come begging to me, expecting miracles.

"Please, bring this poor soul back to life!" they would plead.

Those kinds of people never listened to reason. It would be one thing if they just burst into tears and gave up after being told I could do no such thing. But so, so many of them would just get pissed off and start trying to attack me. That's why I started putting up signs at the entrances of the towns and villages that said I couldn't bring people back to life.

"It seems like you're just going out in search of unjustified resentment based on misunderstandings, and then using that to condemn me as evil. Instead of wasting your time doing that, why don't you just fix all of those problems yourself? You're a hero too, right?"

"No, Princess Malty told me that these were special powers that only your shield possesses!"

I guess that Witch bitch really was telling Itsuki what he wanted to hear now. She was exactly what he needed to convince himself that I was evil. Itsuki was more close-minded than ever. He clearly wasn't going to listen to me, no matter what I said.

But seriously, was it really necessary for Witch to go and deceive every single one of the heroes? It had been the same with Ren. She must have swooped down on Itsuki when he was in a bad place. Now I really wanted to capture Itsuki. We needed to make him tell us where Witch was. Actually, there was a good possibility she was lying low at the same place Itsuki had been hiding out. I'd just have to hope that the slave trader's protégés could figure out where that was.

"Itsuki, that makes no sense. Naofumi and I spent some time comparing the abilities of our weapons. Some of the effects are different, but the type of skills they possess are basically the same. If Naofumi's shield had such an ability, I'm sure that my sword would have an equivalent ability. Or are you claiming that your bow has some kind of unique ability that our weapons don't?"

Ren interjected with a sound argument. Indeed, my shield was meant for defense and Ren's sword was meant to attack, so there were fundamental differences. But in general, the weapon skills all worked the same. It was just as Ren had said.

Well, I couldn't deny that some kind of resurrection skill might exist, but we still hadn't confirmed the details. If one of the legendary weapons did possess such a skill, it probably would be the shield. But if I did have that kind of ability, you can bet I'd be using it. Hell, I'd be making a killing by charging people ridiculous prices to bring other people back from the dead. Actually, if I could resurrect people, I'd bring Ost back to fight on our side in a heartbeat. Waves or otherwise, I'm sure we could overcome pretty much any problem with the almighty Spirit Tortoise fighting for us.

"He has committed countless other crimes! I cannot forgive you, Naofumi!" Itsuki shouted.

"Nonsense. On the contrary, what about all the people you couldn't save because you were too weak to defeat the Spirit Tortoise?" I asked.

He completely ignored his own failures and preached to me about justice. What a joke!

"That's beside the point. If you're not willing to repent, then I won't go easy on you!"

Itsuki readied his bow.

"This is my new bow. It's a truly superb piece of equipment. It's called the Justice Bow. And now I'm going to use it to defeat you!"

Itsuki fired a barrage of arrows into the gallery. Was attacking innocent bystanders his idea of justice?!

"Like hell you will! Air Strike Shield! Second Shield! Dritte Shield! Shooting Star Shield!"

I summoned my Float Shield, as well, and made sure none of the slaves in the gallery were harmed.

"We won't let you," said S'yne.

"Let's do this!" Sadeena shouted.

The two of them used their skills and magic to knock the magic arrows out of the air.

"Itsuki! Stop this!" shouted Ren.

He was batting the arrows away with his sword to protect the slaves. Raphtalia and Atla sprang into action too. Fortunately, none of the slaves were injured. But that announcer, who always shouted so passionately, had been hit by one of the arrows.

"Urgh . . ."

"Are . . . are you okay?!"

The announcer fell to the ground with a thud, but then stood back up immediately.

"Mr. Naofumi, I felt some kind of sinister force swell up and shoot through that man. What was that?" Atla asked.

"I have no idea."

He looked like he was okay.

"Mr. Itsuki, as announcer for the underground coliseum, I've aided the Shield Hero in his plot to deceive you. Please forgive me!"

Huh? What was the announcer up to? Did he have a change of heart and decide to turn on me? Something wasn't right.

"You are forgiven. Reflect on your sins and wash your hands of this shady business."

"Yes sir, Mr. Itsuki!"

The announcer had a crazy look in his eyes. It was as if he had been brainwashed.

"Itsuki . . . That bow of yours . . ." Ren muttered.

He pointed at the bow and Itsuki grinned happily.

"It's amazing, isn't it? By unlocking the power of this bow and shooting an opponent, I can liberate them from brainwashing so that they can finally understand me!"

Did he really think he was liberating people from brainwashing so that they could understand him? There's no way people would sympathize with others so easily. Case in point, Itsuki was making zero effort to understand my side of the story. On the contrary, he was the one brainwashing people. Justice Bow, my ass.

"This bow that Princess Malty entrusted me with possesses divine power! With this weapon, I can rescue even irredeemable trash!"

I decided to try thinking about things from Itsuki's point of view.

He was defeated by the Spirit Tortoise and lost everything. That's when Witch showed up and instigated him, which awakened new powers in the form of a curse series. If it were a mecha anime, it would be like the excitement of switching to a new robot suit. And then, before Itsuki came down from that high, Witch had sent him out to earn money by fighting in the coliseums. But he was being careful about how he used the power since it was his trump card. Something like that.

Either way, it was clear that Itsuki had unlocked a curse series weapon.

"Itsuki, let me tell you how it really is. That bow may seem like a tool of justice to you, but things aren't that simple. The truth is, that's a sinister bow with the power to brainwash others."

"You're wrong! This bow . . . is the embodiment of justice!"

I'd seen anime and manga where the hero went around spouting off nonsense. The hero would defeat an enemy and that enemy would be forced to sympathize with the hero. It seemed reasonable at first, but thinking about it from another perspective, the whole idea of trying to make someone understand something by fighting them was pretty warped. If a little violence is all it took to make someone abandon their beliefs, then those weren't worthy of being called beliefs in the first place.

"Everyone, fight me! Open your eyes to that which is just!"

He was on a completely different level than Ren had been. Ren had still been aware that he was in the wrong. But that wasn't the case for Itsuki. Itsuki was charging forward, blindly following his own sense of justice to the very end.

In terms of the seven deadly sins, this would probably fall under pride. But that wasn't a perfect fit either. Another possibility would be vainglory, which was one of the eight cardinal sins. Or maybe it was one of the eight deadly sins that popped up in anime or manga every now and then as an alternative take on the concept. This was getting into real escapist, nerd territory.

I'd seen two instances of an eighth deadly sin. The first was justice. It was a justice that had been taken too far, becoming cold and merciless. Even the slightest of sins was deemed unforgivable and had to be paid for with one's life. The second was fanaticism—sticking to one's beliefs no matter what. Even if it meant one's own ruin.

Then there was also the possibility that it was all four of those. Ren had unlocked multiple curse series too. It had been gluttony and greed in his case. We'd only seen two at once so far, but three or four at once might be possible too. I felt like I was starting to understand what this "justice" was that Itsuki was chasing.

"You're wrong!"

Rishia lashed out at Itsuki in a surprisingly loud voice.

"You misunderstand Naofumi, Mr. Itsuki!"

"Is that you, Rishia? You, too, have been brainwashed by Naofumi."

"Mr. Itsuki, you said that Naofumi was forcing slaves into hard labor and keeping the profits for himself, right?"

Itsuki nodded with a look of disgust on his face.

"Then tell me. Why is everyone living in Naofumi's village in good health? Have you heard from any slaves that were overworked? Have you talked with anyone who was nearly worked to death?"

"I don't know about any of that. But there's no way that Princess Malty or Mald would lie to me!"

"I'm asking if you verified any of this yourself!"

Uh oh. Rishia had switched into her justice mode. That hadn't happened for a while now. Not since we fought Kyo. If they started fighting while she was like this, we'd get to see the awakened Rishia.

"I've been watching Naofumi rebuild the village from the very start, when he brought the slaves in. Do you have any idea how many people Naofumi has saved after they fell into a life of slavery? And you call that forcing them into hard labor and hoarding the profits? Hogwash!"

"She's right! Not a single child in that village is being forced to do work they don't want to do!" Ren shouted.

He jumped on the bandwagon and tried to help talk some sense into Itsuki.

"That's right! We're all living life to the fullest, thanks to bubba saving us!"

"We're working hard to rebuild our village!"

The slaves all started to speak up in opposition to Itsuki.

"Despite what you all might say, Naofumi has openly confessed to his crimes. There is no denying it!"

"Confessed? Are you talking about when I said I work my slaves like horses? Sure, I confess to doing that."

"Mr. Naofumi, that's not helping your case at all. Besides, you went through all of that trouble to buy up the Lurolona slaves when the prices were skyrocketing, so there are no profits to speak of. You're still in the red," said Raphtalia.

She let out a deep sigh. But I did work the slaves like horses! There was nothing wrong with that.

"The children in Naofumi's village aren't normal slaves. They're always having so much fun while they work. It doesn't even make sense to call them slaves," added Ren.

Umm, I was pretty sure they would be categorized as slaves, from a social status perspective, and considering that they all had slave curses.

"On the contrary, you would think that Naofumi was the villagers' slave if you saw how hard he works for them!" Rishia shouted.

"Wha . . . ?!"

"Yeah! He stays up late every night and spends every last minute doing all that he can for the village and the neighboring town! And he still trains to better himself on top of that! He doesn't even have time to level! Which of those sounds like a slave to you?!" Ren added.

"What the hell?! What are you trying to say, you bastards?!" I shouted.

I was on the verge of activating Rishia's slave curse to punish her.

"Naofumi is the village foster parent," Ren went on.

"Oh my . . . I guess he is. Little Naofumi is the village mommy," Sadeena interjected.

"Not even close! I am *not* a mommy!"

These bastards had it all wrong! Especially Sadeena! Neither Ren nor Rishia were making any sense anymore!

"You're absolutely wrong!" I shouted.

"Mr. Naofumi, I believe in you," Atla said.

What the hell did that mean?! Bastards, all of them! I was going to chew the whole village out later.

"Despite what you may say, the truth speaks for itself! Naofumi is evil, and that's that!"

Itsuki wasn't budging. But Rishia continued on.

"Mr. Itsuki, what about yourself? Are you free of sin? I find that very hard to believe."

"Enough of the theatrics. It's repulsive. You make me want to puke!"

Itsuki glared at Rishia with a scowl on his face. Talk about verbal abuse. Did he really think it was okay to talk to her like that? He'd already forced her to try to kill herself by jumping into the ocean, and yet here he was still pretending like he was the good guy.

"There is only one thing for me to do, and that is to destroy all traces of evil in this world!"

"Yeah, that's not happening," I said.

All traces of evil in this world? As long as there were people, there would be conflict. According to Itsuki's standards, Ren and I counted as evil. Actually, I was sure anyone that didn't bow to him would be considered evil in his book.

"I may possess very little power. But even so, I . . . I will not condone such injustice!" Itsuki shouted.

He was trying to sound like some kind of hero. He pointed his bow at me and drew the string. When he did, an arrow appeared.

"Naofumi! I will shoot clean through that injustice!"

I could hear the whistling sound of Itsuki's arrow slicing through the air as it came hurtling toward me. I moved my Float Shield and blocked the arrow.

"Injustice, you say?"

That was my line. I got summoned here as the hero they didn't like, so they created an elaborate conspiracy to persecute me. It didn't get any more unjust than that. What the hell gave him the right to go on about injustice? Itsuki's words themselves were a big, stinking pile of injustice.

"Mr. Itsuki, it seems you are not willing to listen."

Rishia held her sword out and took a fighting stance.

"Mr. Itsuki, I cannot accept this justice of yours. My justice deems your actions to be unacceptable!"

"Itsuki! This isn't who you are! If you give yourself up to that cursed power, it will only lead to your destruction!" Ren shouted.

"Do not interfere!"

Itsuki aimed his bow up into the air and drew the string. Another arrow went flying. It was headed toward me, of course.

"Mr. Naofumi!"

Raphtalia called out to me, but I held my hand up to signal her not to worry. I snatched the arrow out of the air this time.

"Shining Arrow!"

Itsuki pulled the bowstring back even harder and a bright, shining arrow appeared. It would probably take some time to shoot that one.

"Mr. Itsuki, your intentions have become clear. I am your opponent now. I will fight you with everything I have!"

Rishia readied herself to face Itsuki. She held a hand to her blade.

"Muso Activation!"

The air around Rishia began swirling and created a vortex. Is that what Muso Activation was? This was on a completely different level than what Eclair had done. I knew it was the same skill thanks to Ren's commentary, but this time I could clearly see something visibly jetting outward.

"She's absorbing life force from her surroundings. I've seen the master do it too. Rishia's doing it the same way," Atla explained.

She was sensing the life force and trying to figure out how the technique worked. Atla could get stronger just by watching others fight. I was jealous. It made me feel bad for Fohl though. His little sister was a prodigy and yet he still had to prove himself stronger than her.

"Haaah!"

Rishia charged at Itsuki. Her speed was incredible.

"Hengen Muso Small Sword Technique! Spiral Slash!"

A flow of life force began spiraling out of Rishia's sword.

"Argh!"

Itsuki must have realized that getting hit by that would have caused some damage, because he dodged by a hair's breadth and then fired off his arrow. Why the hell did it curve around and come flying at me?!

"Shooting Star Shield!"

I cast Shooting Star Shield to generate a defensive barrier that would guard against Itsuki's arrows. The shining arrow split into multiple arrows that rained down over me. Just to be safe, I held my shield up toward the arrows. I didn't take any damage.

I'd disabled any counterattack effects too.

Rishia was right in front of him! He was supposed to be fighting her! Why the hell was he still aiming at me?

"I won't let you get away!" Rishia shouted.

Itsuki had managed to launch his skill while dodging Rishia's first attack, but she immediately followed up with more. They all seemed to be that same Spiral Slash attack. It was pretty incredible that she could use it so many times in a row. But the base stats of Itsuki's curse series weapon must have been pretty high. He didn't seem to take much damage even when Rishia's attacks hit him. Even worse, his wounds were slowly regenerating.

"If that's all you've got you better not expect to be able to stop me!"

Cursed, toxic fumes erupted from Itsuki, sending Rishia flying into the air.

"Mr. Itsuki, you must not let that power consume you! I guarantee you will regret it!" Rishia yelled.

"You are the one who will regret it! Now open your eyes to justice! Arrow Squall!"

Itsuki's arrow came flying in my direction. What a hassle. Judging by the name of the skill, it would probably turn into a rain of arrows.

"Air Strike Shield!"

I stopped the arrow before it multiplied.

"I may be outnumbered, but as long as I defeat you, Naofumi, the victory is mine!" he shouted.

Umm . . . He did know he was fighting Rishia one-on-one, right? On the contrary, he was the one choosing to attack the audience without provocation. Did he even feel like he was being driven back, in the first place? It wasn't uncommon for the hero of a story to face countless enemies at once. Itsuki was probably imagining himself in a similar situation.

Maybe he thought of Rishia as a soldier that I had sent after him or something. I would have guessed he thought of her as some frightened, little animal that screamed a lot. Either way, she was the obstacle directly in front of him. It only made sense to defeat her before coming after me. Even so, I would be fine just grabbing his arrows out of the air or using Float Shield, along with Ren and Raphtalia intercepting his attacks.

"I've spent a lot of time thinking about what justice means since meeting you, Mr. Itsuki."

"Evil has no place talking about justice!"

"Evil? What is evil? What is justice?"

Rishia continued trying to get through to Itsuki. I thought she was wasting her time, but it seemed important to her to try. I guess I'd just have to accept that and endure Itsuki's vicious onslaught.

"The only thing you consider justice is that which satisfies you personally! Am I wrong, Mr. Itsuki?! Do you really think that using force to suppress others is true justice?!"

Rishia spoke from the heart. Her words moved Ren to join the conversation.

"I'm sure you've heard the saying, 'Justice without power is empty, but power without justice is merely violence.' Itsuki, you've always aspired to fight for justice, right? You never really talked about yourself much, and I never really cared to ask before. But I want to get to know you better now. I want to know what it is that you're after and what it is that makes you suffer. So please tell me!"

Itsuki continued to focus his attacks on me. It would be nice if Ren thought about my situation a little bit before giving a speech. Still, he did have a point. I had no idea what kind of person Itsuki was either. I understood his personality, but I had no idea what kind of life he had led before. What was it that made him go on and on about justice like this?

"Justice is power. It's proof of what is right. Rescue the weak! Crush the strong!" Itsuki shouted.

Huh? Something suddenly hit me. I tried thinking about Itsuki's behavior from the other way around. What if Itsuki had been filled with gloom and feelings of depression in his own world?

It was clear that Itsuki wanted to be a hero. A lot of fictional superheroes had ordinary alter egos, or maybe they were someone that got bullied a lot. But then they would transform or put on a disguise and go out to defeat bad guys. Anyway, that's how it was for most of the famous superheroes, like Superman or that spider guy.

The more tyrannical types of players in online games were basically doing the same thing too. Itsuki was always trying dish out his justice in secret. So that was it. Fighting for justice did indeed mean using one's power to save others. Put all of that together and you get the idea of rewarding the good and punishing the evil. Justice wins, and evil gets stomped out.

"I don't care if you or anyone else tries to call me evil! I fight for justice!" Itsuki went on.

His thirst for recognition and his lofty ideals all added up to one conclusion.

"Itsuki, the way you treated Rishia is no different than the way you were treated. That's why you can't bring yourself to face her, right?" I told him.

"What?!"

"This is a coliseum tournament. You're a fighter in this tournament. If you want to fight me, then you have to defeat Rishia first. Otherwise, you have no right to challenge me."

I had to make the conditions clear now or Itsuki would just keep this up forever. If I was the evil that Itsuki wanted to defeat, then he could do that in our match. I'd seen this kind of thing happen in those battle-type anime and manga. Motoyasu had done something similar to me countless times since coming to this world too. He would challenge me to a fight after specifying conditions that made it completely one-sided. I didn't have any reason to set conditions like that here, but I had promised to let Rishia handle this.

"Damn it!" he grumbled.

I knew it. This was just a guess, but Itsuki had most likely been bullied back in his own world. Rishia had the lowest status of his party members, and they had basically bullied her before running her off. In other words, Rishia's very existence brought back unpleasant memories from the past for Itsuki. He thought he'd cut himself off from his past, but now the embodiment of who he was before was standing right there in his way. It created incontrovertible dissonance with his justice.

"I see. Rishia is clearly brainwashed by your evil, but if I must defeat her, then I will."

Rishia turned to me and bowed her head deeply.

"Thank you, Naofumi. Leave the rest to me. I will get through to Mr. Itsuki. You'll see."

"No problem. That's hard to believe, but I hope you do. You've come a long way, just like Eclair, so maybe you can pull it off like she did too."

I couldn't bring myself to say anything more positive than that, but I actually thought pretty highly of Rishia. Everyone ridiculed her for being weak, but she never gave up. And she had the inner strength to stand up to an enemy even when they were far more powerful than her.

Either way, it looked like Itsuki was finally prepared to accept Rishia as his opponent. Now the problem was what to do if she lost. I wasn't sure what our best course of action would be if Rishia was defeated. But for the time being . . .

"Let's get the slaves out of here. They'll just be in the way if we have to fight. Sadeena, S'yne, and Atla, I'm leaving the evacuation to you three."

"Sure thing, little Naofumi."

"Ok——"

"Leave it to us!"

I gave the order and had all of my shills removed. Itsuki, Rishia, Raphtalia, Ren, and I were the only ones left in the coliseum. But jeez, Rishia was hopeless. Did she really love Itsuki that much?

"Here I come! Haaaaah!"

Rishia closed in on Itsuki rapidly.

"Ugh! Saint Arrow Rain! Spread Strafing!"

Itsuki backstepped away from Rishia and shot several arrows at her. He carefully timed it so that the arrows he'd already shot up into the air came raining down toward her just as he shot another straight at her. It would be difficult to dodge them all.

"Hengen Muso Small Sword Technique! Circle!"

Rishia spun her small sword around in a circle. A shrill noise rang out and all of the arrows were deflected. Both of them seemed to be holding back, but Rishia was holding her own, despite the fact that Itsuki was a hero. Was this the true power of the Hengen Muso style? Eclair mentioned that Rishia had mastered even more difficult techniques than she had. Rishia was definitely a force to be reckoned with now.

Seeing all of his arrows knocked out of the air, Itsuki glared at Rishia with an annoyed look on his face.

"Mr. Itsuki, I am your opponent right now. You're getting distracted."

Itsuki kept glancing over at me every now and then. He considered Rishia to be nothing more than a checkpoint he had to pass to fight me. But he wouldn't be able to defeat her with that mindset. Rishia was one of my top fighters, whether we were talking about stats, technique, or resolve.

"Hmph . . . You've become quite brash, haven't you, Rishia? But do you really think I've been fighting seriously?"

A sinister aura radiated from Itsuki as he raised his bow.

"Law Fanatic!"

I felt some kind of barrier develop around Itsuki abruptly. He let out a wild howl and his eyes began to glow an eerie red. The sinister aura condensed around him and transformed into a full suit of armor. At first glance, it looked like a holy set of armor meant to resemble a winged angel. But I could also see decorative elements of the design that looked like horns and demons in several places.

The skill boosted his own stats. There was no doubt about that. On top of that, it formed some kind of pseudo-armor. It was a full suit of battle armor like you'd see in Power Rangers or Kamen Rider.

Rishia just stood there silently, waiting for Itsuki to attack. Her expression couldn't have been more serious. If anyone tried to interfere, I was sure Rishia would never forgive them. Ren was fidgeting and edging forward like he wanted to give her a hand, so I held my hand out to stop him.

"Here I come, Rishia. Once I'm finished, you will realize that I am right, and then we can defeat Naofumi together!"

"I will not. I will never accept you the way that you are now, Mr. Itsuki. Even if it costs me my life!"

Rishia thrust her small sword into the ground and crouched down low. What was she doing? She was gathering up so much life force from the earth that I could visibly see it. Her small sword was completely enshrouded in life force now.

"Hengen Muso . . . Secret Technique, First Form . . ."

Rishia plucked the small sword from the ground and dashed toward Itsuki.

"Sun!"

Rishia began radiating light as she thrust her small sword at Itsuki. Something about the technique . . . It seemed like some kind of divine ultra-power-up.

"Shooting Star Bow!"

Itsuki fired off his version of the Shooting Star skill that us heroes all loved so much. His was particularly annoying. When he used it, his arrows left a trail of stars flying around in the air behind them. It was safe to assume that the arrows themselves were pretty dangerous too.

"Second Form! Moon!"

The light that was surrounding Rishia intensified. It formed a crescent-moon shape that shot out and cut down Itsuki's arrows. Itsuki had a look of disbelief on his face, having just seen his finishing move quashed.

"I'm not done! I still haven't shown you everything I have!" he shouted.

Then what the hell are you waiting for?!

Ren had said something like that too. I reflexively glanced over at Ren and he averted his eyes in embarrassment.

"Third Form! Star!"

Rishia closed in on Itsuki rapidly. When she was mere inches away, she released a barrage of thrusts. Eclair's Multistrike Demolition skill seemed to last forever, but Rishia's string of attacks would give it a run for its money. With each single thrust, another piece of the armor protecting Itsuki broke away and disappeared.

"Argh . . ."

Rishia kept thrusting at Itsuki. It seemed like the attacks would never end. And I'm sure each one of them was fortified with life force. I couldn't really tell just by watching, but the attacks made a distinct, sharp thwacking sound. Those attacks were no joke. I had no doubt about that, because I was the Shield Hero and just seeing them made me cringe.

"Enough!" Itsuki thundered.

His sinister aura exploded outward and sent Rishia flying through the air.

"Feh—I'm not finished!"

Rishia took a defensive stance while still in the air to soften her fall. After landing, she steadied her breathing and prepared to resume her attacks.

"There's no way that someone like you could possibly thwart justice, Rishia! Don't interfere with my finishing moves!"

What the hell? Was he seriously telling her not to fight back? This wasn't a turn-based RPG, for crying out loud. On the contrary, overcoming the enemy's finishing moves was the key to progressing in something like an action game.

Ah, that must have been it. In a superhero-type setting, the bad guys would always basically just wait for the superhero's finishing move. Laser beams, a super kick, or five people combining their weapons to fire off a special attack, for example.

"Mr. Itsuki, stop this already. Your justice is flawed! Please, relinquish that power before it's too late!"

Rishia's sounded emotional as she forcefully admonished

Itsuki. The battle did seem to be pretty one-sided in Rishia's favor. It wasn't like when Eclair fought Ren. Itsuki was actually taking damage.

"You're wrong! I . . . will use this new power . . . to save . . . the world!"

Itsuki's bow began to change shape. I could see the sinister aura around him change color in response. He'd most likely unlocked another curse series, just like Ren and Motoyasu had done. Even Rishia might be at a disadvantage against Itsuki if he'd powered up his weapon and unlocked multiple curse series. From the looks of it, it didn't seem like he'd implemented all of the power-up methods like Motoyasu had, but I couldn't say for sure.

"Are you going to be okay, Rishia?" I asked.

"Yes. I don't need assistance."

"Alright. Whatever works for you."

Depending on the situation, I might have to step in. But if Rishia said she was fine, then I'd just keep watching for now. We were all on the edge of our seats as we watched the situation unfold.

The thing was, it seemed unlikely that Itsuki would pass out like Ren had. No matter how pathetic he had become, he was still a hero, I guess. But Rishia still lacked a decisive blow that could end the battle, just like Eclair had.

"Take this! Shadow Bind!"

Itsuki aimed at Rishia's feet and shot his arrow. The name of the skill gave me a really bad feeling.

"Rishia—"

The arrow didn't hit her. It landed behind her.

"My . . . my body!"

Before I could warn Rishia, she had been paralyzed. Just as I expected. If the arrow landed on an opponent's shadow, the skill would restrict their movement.

"Bind Arrow!"

Rishia already couldn't move, but Itsuki shot another binding skill at her. When the arrow reached her, it stitched her body to the ground.

"I . . . I still haven't lost!"

"Wrong! You're finished!"

"Let this foolish sinner pay for her transgressions with her being roasted to death in a brazen bull! Let her writhe in pain as her dying screams are converted into the cries of a raging bull!"

"Bull of Phalaris!"

It reminded me of my Iron Maiden. A bull-shaped statue appeared, and its belly opened up and closed around Rishia, trapping her inside. Then the belly was engulfed in raging flames.

"Rishia!" I screamed.

Itsuki was confident he had won. A grin crept across his face. There was no doubt about it. That skill was the equivalent of my Iron Maiden.

"Victory is mine. Now, Naofumi, prepare to meet your doom."

Damn it. I'd thought Rishia might be able to win, but I guess I was being overly optimistic. I needed to figure out how to rescue Rishia before anything else. Ren took off running in her direction without hesitation. But then, all of a sudden, cracks began to form on the surface of the bull that Itsuki had summoned.

"Huh?"

Itsuki had a look of disbelief on his face. A sharp cracking sound rang out and the bull shattered. Rishia leapt out.

"Fourth Form! Demon!"

Rishia closed in on Itsuki again and swiped her small sword at him. What was that? The tip of her sword was glowing, but it left a trail of darkness in its path.

"Ugh . . . My . . . my eyes!"

Itsuki covered his face with both hands and started groaning. The attack must have had a blinding effect.

"Don't think you've won just yet!" Rishia shouted.

She was breathing hard. Rishi had managed to surmount a skill named after an instrument of execution. Her growth was truly amazing. Incredible. I had no idea that someone who wasn't a hero could become so strong. That pathetic, little Rishia who was ditched by Itsuki finally got to show him how much she had grown.

"How long . . . How long do you plan to stand in my way?!"
Itsuki screamed at Rishia while rubbing his eyes.

"This is absolutely unforgivable! I am justice! To think
you would cause me this much trouble! You're nothing but the
opening act! You've overstepped your boundaries!"

Itsuki's bow took on an even more bizarre form. What had
been white wings turned into demonic-looking bat wings.

"Die . . . All who defy me . . . must die!"

"Mr. Itsuki, I'll say it again. Relinquish that power before
it's too late. Return to your normal self. You must not rely on
that power!"

Rishia was crying now. She was crying because the person
she loved was being consumed by corruption and she was
watching it happen. She believed she had enough power now to
stop it, and that's why she was fighting. But to Itsuki, she had
become nothing more than another target of his hatred.

"For justice! Die! This world . . . is defiled by . . . your evil!"

Itsuki jerked the bowstring backward ridiculously hard
and let go. A barrage of arrows went flying toward Rishia. She
knocked them all out of the air, but then I suddenly heard a
sound that I knew was bad.

"Mr. Naofumi!" Raphtalia shouted.

"I know!"

It was the sound of Rishia's small sword—the Pekkul
Rapier—snapping in two. She was still swinging the broken

sword around . . . and using her life force to replace the missing piece of the blade. But the prolonged use of life force to replace a physical object like that was extremely difficult. I pulled a sword drop out of my shield and threw it to Rishia.

"Rishia! You're at a disadvantage like that! Use this sword!"

But Rishia ignored the sword I had thrown and continued her exchange with Itsuki.

"I'm sorry, Naofumi. That . . . would go against my sense of justice!"

Itsuki had a crazy look in his eyes. He smiled.

"What are you smiling about? Mr. Itsuki, I haven't been defeated yet."

"How can you say that? You've already lost."

"No. You told me once, Mr. Itsuki, that justice never gives up."

"Heh heh heh . . . Fool. You . . . are evil."

"Mr. Itsuki, I will never give up, no matter how painful or hopeless things may become. You taught me that when you rescued me from despair, Mr. Itsuki. And Naofumi showed me the same thing too!"

Rishia calmed herself and steadied her breathing. I could tell from her stance that she was about to cast a spell. I guess she decided that she would use magic, since her sword was broken. She wasn't going to cheat, and she wasn't going to give up. That was the mindset she had. Her growth . . . I don't know why, but it made me feel really proud that such a completely hopeless girl could change so much. It surprised even me. It reminded me of the saying, "Where there's a will, there's a way."

"I'll say it again. Mr. Itsuki, I beg of you, relinquish that power. Then you can start over and regain the trust of the people of this world by fighting for them!"

"Why should I relinquish this power?! I . . . I will use this power to save the world!"

"Mr. Itsuki! I can say with certainty that your justice is flawed! After being at Naofumi's side and watching him fight, I am confident of that! Naofumi fights even to save the inhabitants of other worlds! He stands at the forefront to protect everyone, no matter what!"

"Silence, evil! Be gone!" Itsuki shouted.

And then it happened. None of us could believe our eyes. This was on a totally different level than anything like Rishia's growth, strength, or Hengen Muso techniques.

Itsuki's bow began to glow intensely. The brightness forced even Itsuki to close his eyes. I could see all of this because I was watching from a distance. And then the light sprang forward from the bow and flew at Rishia. It had happened too quickly for her to dodge. The light hit her. But she was completely uninjured. The light from Itsuki's bow had leapt into the palm of Rishia's hand.

And then, for whatever reason, Rishia's slave curse icon shattered and disappeared from my status screen.

"What . . . was that?" I muttered.

"Mr. Naofumi."

"Oh, hey, Atla. Is the evacuation complete?"

"Yes. But more importantly, Mr. Naofumi . . ."

Atla was gazing in Itsuki's direction.

"Inside of that sinister aura was a bright, pure flow of power that leapt toward Rishia."

"Pure? Do the legendary weapons have some kind of power that we still don't know about?"

It was clear that some kind of power had jumped from the bow to Rishia. I guess that meant we could assume that Itsuki's bow had lent Rishia its power.

"Rishia?"

Ren called out to Rishia.

"This is . . ."

I couldn't believe my eyes. Rishia was holding a knife in her hand. It was shaped like an ordinary knife, but it had a flashy jewel set in the handle. It was semi-transparent, and its form seemed to waver. Was it some kind of magically formed, unstable weapon? What was it?

Rishia held her other hand to the blade of the knife and it transformed into one of those kunai weapons that ninjas used. Then it turned into a boomerang. So it could change shape like the legendary weapons. What in the world was it?

"Wh . . . what in the world is happening?!" Itsuki shouted.

Even he had no idea what was going on. At the very least,

Itsuki didn't seem to be behind whatever had happened.

"I see now. I understand."

A look of realization came across Rishia's face. She pointed the boomerang at Itsuki and spoke confidently.

"Mr. Itsuki. Even the legendary bow can no longer accept your justice. It has lent me its power so that I may stop you!"

"Lies! That can't be! My bow would never betray me!"

"I will use this power to stop you!"

"Stop screwing around!"

The sinister aura overflowing from Itsuki's bow intensified. He drew the bowstring backward powerfully and an inordinate number of arrows launched toward Rishia. The fletchings of the arrows were shaped like angel and demon wings. The mass of arrows transformed into the shape of a bear as they shot through the air toward Rishia.

"Hengen Muso Throwing Technique! Rolling Spin!"

Rishia channeled her life force into the weapon and then threw it at Itsuki.

"Wha—Why?! I am absolute justice! Why do you still persist in defying me?! Gah!"

The boomerang spun around Itsuki and sliced at him.

"You're wrong, Mr. Itsuki. You're wrong, and your bow is trying to correct that."

Rishia held her right hand up into the air and the boomerang returned to her. Then she transformed it into a chakram. She blinked slowly, and it looked like her eyes changed color ever so slightly. She was drawing life force into her eyes.

"I can see everything clearly now. I see the flow of power that is tightening around you, Mr. Itsuki. I see the parasitic power leeching off of your bow. And now that I can see it . . ."

Rishia threw the weapon at Itsuki.

"Air Strike Throw! Second Throw! Dritte Throw!"

Air Strike? I was pretty sure only the legendary weapons had skills that used that name. Did that mean she was using a legendary weapon? Or maybe it was a seven star hero weapon. Rishia had thrown a different weapon for each of her three skills. There was a knife, a hatchet, and a short spear.

Just what kind of weapon was it? Even assuming it was a seven star hero weapon, the spear belonged to Motoyasu. None of the three weapons she threw even belonged to the same category. Or maybe . . . She'd thrown them all, so maybe it was a throwing weapon.

"Tornado . . . Throw!"

The three weapons started spinning around Itsuki. They created a vortex that was blowing the sinister aura away from him.

"Gaaaahhhhh!"

The chakram appeared back in Rishia's hand and she launched it at Itsuki's bow.

"Mr. Itsuki, this proves that you are not justice. Now please, let's start over and do things the right way."

The chakram smashed into Itsuki's bow and a loud cracking

sound rang out. The chakram returned to Rishia's hand. And then, with the sound of breaking glass, the armor-like outer layer of Itsuki's bow shattered and fell away. When it did, the announcer that had been brainwashed by Itsuki crumpled to the ground, like a marionette whose strings had been cut.

"Gahhh! My . . . my new power . . . the power of salvation . . ."

"I'll say it again. You're mistaken. Mr. Itsuki, please try to understand. There is no one justice. There are as many 'justices' as there are people. The opposite of justice is not evil. It's justice. The losing side is simply branded as evil. That is all."

"No! I . . . I'm not evil! There's no way I could be evil! It's everyone else . . . It's them!"

"Blaming others and rejecting others is easy, even without justice. But the important thing is to accept others. Anyone can change for the better, no matter what kind of person they might be. I believe that."

Itsuki sounded like he was about to cry. The bizarre shape of his bow had dissolved away, and the bow returned to its usual . . . No, I could still see several of the odd designs on it.

"What do you think, Atla?"

"Well, Rishia used that power in her hand to eliminate the sinister aura. However, the roots of the sinister force remain."

"I . . . I have to . . . for the people that believed in me . . ."

Itsuki hadn't given up. He stood back up. He sure was

stubborn. Just then, one of the slave trader's assistants came and whispered something into my ear.

"I see . . . Itsuki, we figured out where you've been hiding. I'm going to leave you here and go check that out. There's no reason I should have to waste my time fighting some noob that can't even stand up to Rishia."

I'd had the slave trader's assistants and some people from Zeltoble's underground guild work together to figure out where Itsuki was staying. They'd dug up enough evidence to be confident they'd found the place. Now all that was left was for me to barge in and capture Itsuki's accomplices.

"I won't let you!"

Hmm . . . This could be a good chance to show him how things really were.

"Itsuki, I guess I can show you a shred of mercy."

"What?!"

"You say your companions are just. Then take me to them. I already know the location, but I want you to lead the way."

"I'm not falling for that! That's how you plan to capture Princess Malty, isn't it?!"

"Itsuki! You'll never know the truth if you only listen to one side of the story! Is that what you call justice?!" Ren interjected.

"I . . . That . . ."

Itsuki tried to reply but stumbled over his words. I'm sure he was in a state of emotional shock after losing to Rishia.

"Think about the games you played back in your world.

I'm sure there was some kind of event where you had to decide which side was right and which was wrong, right?"

". . ."

I was showing him that I was sincere. Itsuki seemed to be trying to decide whether he should compromise. Actually, deep down, he probably knew that I was right. Regardless, I guess it would still be hard to bring himself to just casually lead the enemy straight to his own base.

But why had Witch betrayed Motoyasu, deceived Ren, and then run away anyway? I still didn't know what her motives were.

"Itsuki, Witch is a criminal. Shouldn't she have to pay for her crimes? Or prove her innocence? Or are you going to say that winning a fight to the death is the only valid proof of justice?"

"No . . . That's not it!"

"She can even have a trial or something. If Witch is really doing good on behalf of the country, I'm sure the queen will show tolerance."

If Itsuki felt like he had been deceived and fell into despair, he'd most likely unlock another curse series and go on a rampage, like Ren did. I was pretty sure he hadn't fired off a bunch of curse series skills yet. We needed to intervene before he really hurt himself.

I looked over at Rishia. Right now, there was still a chance that Itsuki would listen. She needed to save him before he completely lost all hope, like Ren had. That's what I told Rishia with my eyes, and she nodded back at me.

"Fine then. I'll prove Princess Malty and the rest of my companions' innocence!"

Itsuki agreed to stop the fight and take us to his hideout.

Chapter Thirteen: Atonement

"No . . . no way . . ."

Itsuki led the way, and before long we arrived at his hideout, which was exactly where we thought it was. It was a residence in a relatively quiet area of Zeltoble. We took a look around inside, and apparently the building even had a secret passageway that led down into an underground tunnel.

Witch must have already made her escape by the time we got to the hideout. The place was deserted. All that was left was a bunch of garbage lying around. It looked like they had been getting drunk and partying every night or something. What a mess. And it stunk of alcohol too.

"I . . . I'm sure they're just out at the moment. They probably sensed you were coming and made a run for it."

"Are you really going to keep trying to ignore the truth? What's this? There's something on the desk here."

Oh boy. This was the same penmanship I'd seen in Ren's letter. I had a really bad feeling about this. Beneath the letter was a rather thick bundle of papers. I really, really did not want to read this.

"Itsuki, can you read the writing of this world?"

The letter was written in the official language of Melromarc.

Every time I saw Witch's writing, I couldn't help but think how messy it was. She had a characteristic way of shaping her letters that was just plain ugly. The queen and Melty both had really nice writing, so why was that bitch's writing so damned crude?

"No. I can't, because you refuse to tell me where to get the skill to understand the languages of other worlds!"

"Not that again! Here, Ren. You read it. Or Rishia. I don't care. And get Rishia to teach you to read already, Itsuki. That girl is a beast when it comes to learning stuff. It would put any hero to shame."

"Fehhh?!"

Rishia let out a pathetic squeal when I called her a beast. It was hard to believe she had been fighting a fierce and heroic battle only moments earlier.

"Mr. Naofumi, I feel like you could have phrased that a bit more nicely . . ." said Raphtalia.

When she put it that way, I did feel like maybe I had been a bit harsh. But taking it back would be bad for my image.

"Umm . . ." Ren began to read.

"It was nice leeching off of you, but it seems we've just about sucked you dry, so we're going to take our leave. Since we're the poor victims here, we'll be taking all of the tournament winnings you brought back every day. Yes, that's right. Thanks to the Shield, we have become poor victims, forced to live hard lives, so your donation is appreciated."

As Ren continued reading the letter out loud, the look of

disgust on his face grew more and more apparent. It was pretty much the same letter she had left him, after all. But really, would it kill that bitch to not leave letters like this?

Ren started reading the second page of the letter.

"Mald and the others have had enough too. Do you really not realize that no one can stand the way you act all high-and-mighty and constantly order people around? You're always going on about justice this and justice that, and yet you fell for my lies so easily. It was hard not to laugh every time I saw your face."

"Hey, Naofumi, I'm not misinterpreting this, am I?"

Ren looked incredibly annoyed, like it was all he could do to not rip the letter up into little pieces. He handed it to me.

"Just skimming over it, it seems your interpretation is fine. Some of the expressions are slightly off, but the meaning is the same."

I took the third page from Ren to read it for him. He was all tense with anger. I wasn't sure how long I would last without losing my cool, but it looked like there wasn't much left of the letter.

"P.S. You're weak, and neither your face, height, nor your personality are my type. If you have feelings for me, then defeat the Shield. We can meet again if you do that. Ha ha ha! Also, I'm leaving you a little gift. Thanks in advance for taking care of that!"

"Damn, she's annoying!"

I crumpled the letter up and threw it at the wall. I took the bundle of papers from the table and passed it to Itsuki. I was sure even he would be able to figure out what those were. He didn't need to study the language to understand a bunch of numbers, after all.

"Itsuki, do you know what those are?"

"Wh . . . what are these?!"

"I'm sure you can tell just by looking. They're promissory notes. And it looks like they're all stamped with your seal."

I'd ask the slave trader later how many merchants had lent money out based on these credentials. There were a bunch of the notes, and the totals were substantial too. Itsuki was red as could be. Financially speaking, that is. Honestly, paying all of those back would probably be impossible for him. Even with all of his earnings from the coliseum tournaments.

"No way . . . I . . . Mald, Princess Malty, and the others all said they wanted to help rescue people. That's why I was working so hard to save up all that money."

"Umm . . . According to information gathered at a nearby tavern, his companions were spending quite lavishly and thoroughly enjoying themselves. Yes sir. I've also been told that they spent quite a bit betting in various underground guild coliseum tournaments."

The slave trader had come to deliver an update. He had the worst possible timing. There were several other merchants standing behind him too. Itsuki fell to his knees and huddled over in despair.

"You sure put your faith in the wrong place. I tried to tell you. Nothing good can come of trusting Witch," I told Itsuki.

I figured I might as well pour some salt on his wounds. I looked over at the slave trader.

"Where are the people that actually created these debts? We should probably go after them if they've fled," I said.

"It's likely that they escaped into the underground tunnels of Zeltoble. Yes sir. The merchant guild is currently on high alert and an order for their capture has been issued to the mercenaries and adventurers. However . . ."

He wanted to say that it was unlikely that they would be found. They had probably prepared to make their escape beforehand. They would most likely get away. I let out a deep sigh and began to approach Itsuki, who was still doubled over in despair. It would just make things harder if he ended up unlocking another curse series now.

"Mr. Itsuki . . . Please, stand up. I . . . I believe in you, Mr. Itsuki. Fighting for justice means always standing up again, no matter how many times you fall, right?"

"Rishia . . . I . . ."

Rishia reached her hand out to the despondent Itsuki.

"This is a chance to start over again. As for the money . . . I'll help you with that. We can work to pay it back together."

"But . . . It's not just that . . . I made an irreparable mistake . . ."

"Everyone makes mistakes. But you can always do something. If you give up now, it will only lead to the suffering of countless more people."

"Countless more . . . people?"

"Yes. We went to another world. And we formed an alliance with the people of that world. They were our enemies. We thought they were evil, but we made peace with them. I'm sure you remember. One of them was the incredibly powerful woman with the folding fan who came out of the rifts during a wave."

Rishia had gone to the other world with us. She'd spent time with Kizuna, who had been trapped in a never-ending labyrinth. She knew about our agreement with Glass and the others, who we had fought multiple times before that.

"I had no idea . . ."

"But we also fought against an unforgivable enemy."

"There was an enemy that even you couldn't forgive?"

"Yes. And right now, Naofumi is preparing to fight another unforgivable enemy. To do that, he needs you and all of the heroes, who give our world hope, to help him. So please, stand up."

I couldn't deny the fact that Itsuki was the Bow Hero. Just like with Ren and Motoyasu, if he powered up his weapon properly, having him on my side would make me feel a lot better.

Keep it up, Rishia! You're getting through to him, just like Eclair did with Ren!

Itsuki started to make sobbing sounds. Rishia's words must have been the final nail in the coffin for the curse, because the last of the sinister designs on his bow broke apart and disappeared. When they did, Itsuki collapsed and fell flat on his face.

"Mr. Itsuki!"

I took his pulse. He was still alive. Hopefully he wouldn't have any consequences to pay for using the curse series.

The slave trader was holding the other merchants back. They were all discussing how Itsuki should be dealt with. Damn it. Witch sure knew how to leave a mess behind! I would kill her for sure the next time I saw her. Or no, maybe I would make her pay back this debt that she had forced on to Itsuki using her own two hands. Itsuki's own party members had been in on it too, apparently. L'Arc had mentioned that they looked like nothing but trouble, and boy, was he right.

"I . . . I'll—"

Rishia stepped forward to stand up for Itsuki, who was still collapsed on the floor. She was going to tell the merchants that she was prepared to take on Itsuki's debts.

"Slave trader, have Itsuki's debts transferred to my name," I said.

I had some money from peddling our goods. If I rounded up all of my Elixir of Yggdrasil and whatnot, and sold that too, I was sure it would work out one way or another. If that still wasn't enough, I'd just have to pay the rest back later. Surely it wouldn't be any more than what I'd paid for the slaves at the peak of the price bubble.

"Mr. Naofumi . . ." Raphtalia whispered.

She had a look of relief on her face. I looked at her and gave the orders to begin the search for Witch. Rishia looked like she was on the verge of tears. She bowed her head to me deeply.

"Rishia, it's your job to give Itsuki a thorough re-education, just like Eclair has done for Ren. Make sure that he never loses control like this again."

"I . . . I will!"

"Aww . . . You really are a good guy, aren't you, little Naofumi?" Sadeena said.

"That's our Mr. Naofumi! Seeing him shoulder the responsibilities of the foolish Bow Hero . . . That's how a real man behaves!" Atla exclaimed.

Foolish? She needed to be a bit more careful about her word choice. Itsuki *was* still a hero.

In the end, we weren't able to figure out where Witch and Itsuki's companions had run off to. But we had managed to successfully capture Itsuki. It had cost me a lot of money, but Itsuki probably wouldn't try to cause any more problems now.

I'd gone ahead and invited Itsuki to my party before heading to their hideout, so I was able to use my portal skill to take him back to the village with us despite him being unconscious. I just hoped things would work out as well as they had with Ren.

It was around noon the following day. Our search for Witch had ended in failure, so I wasn't in a very good mood. Itsuki finally came to. He had been sleeping in one of the camping plant houses. I figured it was about time for him to wake up, so I went to check on him and that's when I heard Rishia call out to him.

"Mr. Itsuki!"

Itsuki stood up and got out of the bed. He looked around. I stood there with my arms crossed and watched as Rishia ran over to him worriedly. I had Filo, Atla, and Ren on standby outside just in case Itsuki decided to cause any trouble.

"Itsuki, you remember what happened yesterday, right? I shouldered all of your debt, but I still expect you to work to pay it all back," I told him.

". . ."

Expressionless and sleepy-eyed, Itsuki slowly turned his head to me and just stood there in silence.

". . ."

The room was completely silent. Rishia was waiting for Itsuki to say something too, but it didn't look like that was going to happen.

"Hey! Say something!" I said.

"Something . . ."

What the hell?! That bastard! He had the nerve to try to pick a fight with me at a time like this!

"Sorry, Rishia. It looks like I'm going to have to break my promise to you," I said.

He obviously didn't regret what he'd done at all. A guy like that didn't deserve to live. I'd just sell him off to the Zeltoble merchants.

"Fehhh! Please, just wait a minute! Go on, Mr. Itsuki. Give him a sincere apology."

"I'm sorry."

Still expressionless, Itsuki obediently bowed his head and apologized. What the hell? Is this what kind of person he was?

"Itsuki, what happened to you?" I asked.

"I don't know. Do you mean yesterday? Why was I so unhappy?"

"Umm . . . Itsuki, don't tell me you don't know who you are."

Surely the consequence for using that ridiculous Justice Bow wasn't amnesia, right? But considering what had happened to the other heroes, that wouldn't have been all that strange. It was going to be a real headache if that were the case though.

"No, I'm Itsuki Kawasumi. I'm the Bow Hero. I aspired to fight for justice, but I was defeated. And I was deceived, on top of that."

"So you don't have amnesia, right?"

"I don't know."

How could he not know?

"You better not be hiding something. What are you up to?"

"Am I up to something?"

"How the hell should I know?! That's why I'm asking you! Don't answer a question with a question!"

What was wrong with him? It was like he'd lost all ambition. He was acting like a spaced-out junkie . . . No, this was different. Just a second ago, when I said, "say something," he replied by saying, "something," didn't he?

"Itsuki, do a handstand and take your clothes off while upside down."

"Okay."

Just as I'd ordered, Itsuki did a handstand and started unbuttoning his shirt with one hand.

"Mr. Itsuki! Stop that!"

When Rishia told him to stop, he got back up on his feet and stood there motionless. Hold on. Did that mean he would do anything he was told to do?

"Itsuki, kill yourself."

"Okay."

Itsuki pulled a rope out of his bow . . . Not the bowstring, but a rope stored inside of the bow, like the one I had in my shield. He started looking for a place to tie the rope so that he could hang himself.

"Fehhhh! Don't do that, Mr. Itsuki!"

"Okay."

"Itsuki, what do you want to do?" I asked.

"What do I want to do? I don't know."

Oh, come on, Itsuki!

Also, Itsuki had always been so secretive and reserved that it was kind of creepy seeing him talk so readily.

"Itsuki, do you not have any idea what's going on? There are all kinds of consequences for using cursed weapon skills. Is that what this is?"

I felt like I could sense some kind of inauspicious presence completely enshrouding Itsuki's body.

"When I was fighting in the underground coliseums in Zeltoble I used some special skills several times when things got tough."

Ugh. So now that Itsuki had been freed from the cursed weapon, the consequences had come crashing down on top of him, I guess. He was in bad shape.

"Well, Rishia is going to take care of you, so just take it easy for now."

"Understood," he replied.

Itsuki gazed at Rishia for several moments and then looked back at me.

"Should I be doing something?"

"Is there something you want to do?"

"Umm . . . I guess I should do something. Or maybe I

should just stay still. If I move . . ."

Yeah, he had obviously become indecisive. The consequence of his curse was probably a loss of volition or something like that. Sheesh. Why did all of the heroes that showed up at my doorstep have to be under the effects of a curse? Motoyasu wasn't here, but he had been pretty messed up too.

"Itsuki, spend some time thinking about what it is you want to do. And pay off your debts."

"Understood. I'll work to pay off my debts."

"Mr. Itsuki, I'll help you fight to atone for your mistakes," Rishia said.

Itsuki nodded at her docilely. Good. She could work and help Itsuki pay off his debts too.

"Thank you, Rishia. I'll do my best."

Itsuki shook Rishia's hand and a single tear rolled down his cheek.

"Mr. Itsuki?"

"Huh? Why am I crying? Rishia . . . I'm sorry . . . for everything," Itsuki whispered.

And then he returned to being completely expressionless, as if he had finished letting out all of the feelings he had pent up inside.

"It's . . . It's okay . . . It's okay, Mr. Itsuki . . ."

Rishia was crying. Of course she was. The guy sitting in front of us was a completely different person who only looked

like Itsuki. He did exactly what anyone told him to do without complaint.

I sighed. It would be easy to get Itsuki to talk, but we had a whole pile of other problems now. I wasn't sure what to do. It seemed like I was constantly worrying about something or other lately. For now, I'd hammer the power-up methods into his head. Then I'd have him go recuperate at the Cal Mira hot springs, since they helped speed up recovery from curses. That seemed like a good plan.

It wouldn't be long before all four of the holy heroes had finally implemented all of the power-up methods.

Chapter Fourteen: Secret Base

"Alright, little Naofumi! You and I are going to have some fun tonight!"

"Like hell we are!"

One night, several days after Itsuki arrived at the village, I decided to have Sadeena teach me the Way of the Dragon Vein. The slaves had gotten over their trauma for the most part, so she didn't have to spend so much time looking after them at night.

"He's right, Sadeena! You need to stop fooling around so much!" Raphtalia snapped.

Raphtalia must have finally gotten her nights back to herself too, because she was sleeping at my house again. I'd asked her to fight Atla off if she showed up during the night.

"Oh, by the way, I figured it might be difficult for me to teach you all of the details by myself, so I asked little Gaelion to help out," Sadeena said.

She stuck her hand out the window and made a beckoning motion. Gaelion came flying over in his baby dragon form and entered the room.

"Hmm . . . So you want to learn the Way of the Dragon Vein, do you? I sense that a divine blessing has already been bestowed upon you."

"Did he just sp—"

Raphtalia was standing there dumbstruck after hearing Gaelion speak.

"I am Gaelion, the weakest of the emperor dragons. I was slain by the Sword Hero. Nice to meet you."

Introducing oneself as "the weakest" was kind of strange, but whatever.

"He's the dragon that raised Wyndia. The Demon Dragon took control of his core, and now he shares a body with baby Gaelion. I didn't have time to explain before now," I added.

"Normally I would have introduced myself right away, but I've had my hands full keeping my presence hidden from Wyndia, since she's always around."

"Little Gaelion can use the Way of the Dragon Vein too. With him helping out, you should be able to get the hang of it in no time."

"That would be nice."

I'd been studying a bit on my own, but it wasn't going very well. Ren and Itsuki . . . Those two still couldn't even use normal magic without relying on crystal balls or something. I was rushing them to master normal magic, while also trying to work on the Way of the Dragon Vein in my own time.

Then again, now that I had Sadeena and Gaelion with me, couldn't they just fire off powerful support magic nonstop? I guess it would still be good for me to learn too.

"Mr. Naofumi! Huh?! Brother!"

"Atla! I'm not letting you get away tonight! I'll show you the fruits of my training!"

"Ha! Do you really think someone like you could stop me, Brother?"

"I'll stop you tonight for sure!"

I heard a loud commotion coming from outside of the house. I peeked outside and saw an imbecilic pair of siblings brawling while the rest of the slaves looked on excitedly. What were all of them still doing up?!

"I have a feeling it's going to be hard to concentrate," I mumbled.

"I think you're right. Atla will probably be here shortly, so I doubt you'll get to learn much magic tonight," Raphtalia replied.

"It would be nice if there was a good place we could go. Should we use my portal and go find a place near the castle?"

"That could work. But if it were only as far as the castle, Atla might still show up riding Chick, for example."

Who was that? Ah, that must have been Filo Underling #1's name. I seemed to recall hearing the slaves call it that while petting it.

Zeltoble could work. But on second thought, Zeltoble wasn't any quieter, and then I'd have to worry about accommodations and dealing with the slave trader. After staring out the window and enjoying the commotion for a few moments, Sadeena suddenly spoke up.

"How about I take us to my secret base then?"

"Secret base?" I asked.

"Yep. There's a little island not far from the village, and my secret base is on that island. I doubt even little Atla could come after you there."

"Hmm . . . If that hakuko girl is going to interfere with our training, then it does make sense to move to a quieter spot," said Gaelion.

"Fine. Raphtalia, don't leave my side, no matter what. You're the only one I can trust," I said.

I could only imagine what might happen to me if I ended up alone with Sadeena and Gaelion. Well, mainly Sadeena. But that would have been pretty much the same as being alone with her, so who knew what she might try to do.

"Mr. Naofumi, I think you're a bit too scared," Raphtalia replied.

"Oh? I wonder who he's more afraid of? Me or you, little Raphtalia?" Sadeena poked.

Seriously? Raphtalia, of course! That went without saying! Raphtalia got really scary whenever Sadeena started hanging all over me.

"Should I swim, and you can all ride me? Or should we have Gaelion fly us out there?"

"Gaelion sounds good."

If something happened, I could sick Gaelion on Sadeena. That should at least buy me enough time to get away.

We all climbed onto Gaelion and departed for the island where Sadeena's secret base was located.

"Wow. So this is where your secret base is, huh?"

It had been around thirty minutes since we climbed on to Gaelion's back. The island finally came into view. It was dark, so I couldn't see well, but it wasn't a very big island. It reminded me of one of those crescent-shaped atolls I'd seen in travel brochures. There didn't seem to be any monsters on the island either. I didn't want to sound like Motoyasu, but it seemed like a romantic little island floating there under the moon.

Once we landed, Sadeena took us to a cave near the edge of the island and lit a torch inside. The cave even had a little hole in the roof, like a skylight. The interior was crude—what I imagined a pirate cave would look like. There was a table made of haphazardly piled-up rocks and a chair that was really just a tree trunk that had been split down the middle. There seemed to be other rooms in the back, but it was dark, so I couldn't really tell.

"Make yourselves at home."

"You used to come here with mom and dad, right? When I was little, they told me they'd bring me when I grew up. I remember lying in bed unable to sleep because I was so excited," Raphtalia said.

I could relate with that. I could remember being little and getting excited when relatives told me they would take me camping. But I had no recollection of ever actually going camping, by the way.

"Oh? So you already knew about this place then?" Sadeena asked.

"Yes," replied Raphtalia.

"Yeah, I'm pretty sure even Atla won't show up all the way out here," I said.

"Right?"

Then again, I couldn't help but feel like she might actually try to swim or take a boat.

"Alright then, little Naofumi. How about we go ahead and get started with the Way of the Dragon Vein lessons?"

"Sounds good."

"This isn't the kind of thing you can learn without having a certain amount of aptitude, right? I'd like to be able to use it too, if possible," said Raphtalia.

"It should be possible if I bestow my blessing upon you," Gaelion replied.

"In that case, you should join us, Raphtalia. If we can learn it together, then that's even better."

Surely that would be a good thing if Raphtalia could use

it too. But Sadeena stared at Raphtalia for a moment and then groaned.

"Hmm . . . Teaching little Raphtalia could be problematic."

"She can't learn?" I asked.

"Hmm?"

Gaelion placed his hand above Raphtalia's head.

"Ah, I see. She already has some kind of blessing bestowed on her. It seems to be far too powerful for me to remove in my current state," he said.

"R . . . really?" Raphtalia asked.

"Does it have to do with the vassal weapon or something?" I asked.

I guess this was a downside to having a vassal weapon from Kizuna's world. How annoying. That reminded me, I'd forgotten to ask Kizuna and the others about what kind of magic they used in their world. I seemed to remember there being something about that in the manuscripts they gave us, but deciphering that stuff was such a hassle. I guess I'd just have Rishia figure it out. Then again, Rishia had been working on deciphering a different manuscript already and was having a hard time. I guess I shouldn't expect much. Not to mention, she had to take care of Itsuki now too.

"If I absorbed the knowledge of that other world's emperor dragon from the core you have, then I should be able to teach her, but . . ." Gaelion suggested.

"It's all too easy to imagine you getting swallowed up instead," I replied.

"I'm just lucky that he was a different class of emperor dragon, which is why he didn't completely assimilate me. If that hadn't been the case, that would have been the end of me."

"I see . . ."

So there could be class differences, even if they were both emperor dragons. I guess that meant he could read some kind of basic information from the core stone, but there were fundamental incompatibilities at a deeper level. The Demon Dragon was the whole reason Kizuna got summoned to the other world in the first place. I'm sure the Demon Dragon that Kizuna fought was stronger than the one we had faced recently.

Gaelion pointed at some water in a jug.

"We'll start by drawing power from that water over there. I'll show you how it's done."

Gaelion placed his hand over the jug.

"*I call upon the power of this water to come to me and take form. Earth Vein! Lend me your power!*"

"Aqua Seal!"

Some kind of power shot up out of the water toward Gaelion and materialized in the form of magic. I'm pretty sure that spell was supposed to create a magic barrier. It would be effective against fire-based magic. That would come in handy at the scene of a fire.

"So there are no magical tomes or anything, I guess."

"With the magic you normally use, you materialize your own power using a fixed process. This magic doesn't work like that. You're borrowing power from other sources," Gaelion replied.

It seemed to employ the same basic system as the magic Therese used. She had told me once that she was borrowing the power of her jewels when she cast her spells.

"Dragons can call upon their own power to conjure the magic, but humans should stick to borrowing power from other sources," he continued.

"Why is that?" I asked.

"We're talking about your own life force, otherwise. If you overdo it, you'll end up drawing out every last bit of your own power. You would die," he replied.

Whoa! That was a risk I didn't want to take.

"On the contrary, when it comes to materializing magic using your own inner resources, the magic you normally use is more than enough," he said.

That was true. So normal magic drew from your own power, and the Way of the Dragon Vein borrowed power from other sources. I'd just remember it that way.

"I'm sure you realize this, little Naofumi, but once you are able to use the Way of the Dragon Vein, it'll be easy to use counter-magic too. You're reading the opponent's power in order to interfere with their casting," Sadeena said.

Oh? So that's why the Way of the Dragon Vein made things like interference possible. Ceremonial magic and cooperative magic were difficult because you had to attune your power to that of others. This would simplify that process. I think that's what she was saying.

Gaelion and Sadeena continued to give me pointers, and I spent the next two hours or so practicing using the Way of the Dragon Vein.

"I told you to stop injecting magic power! I can tell there's some kind of strange magic power going into the water just by watching!" Gaelion lectured.

"You can see that?" I asked.

"The water is vibrating! Not to mention, it's glowing!"

Ugh . . . Therese had scolded me about the same thing when I was practicing magic with her. They really did seem to be similar systems.

"It . . . It seems incredibly difficult," Raphtalia commented.

She was watching me as I struggled to figure it out. She looked concerned.

"Hey, Raphtalia, maybe you remember. The magic back in Kizuna's world was similar. Maybe you can use the same kind of magic that Therese used."

"I'll give it my best shot."

"Little Naofumi, you have to avoid releasing magic power

like you would when using normal magic. Instead, think of yourself as empty and let the power come to you from the water."

"Yeah, that's what's so hard."

It was a sensory type of thing, and those were always the most difficult.

Alright . . . Don't use magic power to draw it out. Let the power come to me from the water.

Nothing was happening. The water didn't respond.

Concentrate! Hey, water! Give me your power!

"Stop releasing magic power!" Gaelion thundered.

Goddammit! This was so annoying! I felt like I was starting to understand why Wyndia could only use the Way of the Dragon Vein. The fact that Sadeena could use both types of magic just meant that she was a bona fide freak. She was a prodigy. I wasn't. I was just a hard worker.

I continued to struggle, and another two hours or so passed. I was starting to get the idea of how it worked. Since I'd developed the ability to see the flow of magic power, watching Gaelion and Sadeena cast spells and then mimicking their flow had done the trick. In other words, I just kept begging them to do it over and over.

While watching, I created an empty space in my own magic power. Then I carefully extended the magic power out until it just brushed the water's surface, like reaching with my hand. A pristine flow of power was sucked up into my body by way of the magic.

"That's it. That's good enough. You're progressing faster than I expected. I'm surprised," said Gaelion.

"Yeah, not bad," Sadeena added.

After that, a little puzzle popped up, like when I'd cast magic along with Ost or Sadeena. I was already familiar with how to do the rest.

"*I call upon the power of this water to come to me and take form. Earth Vein! Lend me your power!*"

"Aqua Seal!"

A target icon popped up on my screen. I chose myself and verified that the magic had successfully been cast.

"Hmph. You sure learned that quickly. I guess heroes really are different," Gaelion said.

"Yeah, you must be a genius, little Naofumi," Sadeena poked.

"Oh, shut up. You have no idea how much time I've spent studying on my own."

Now that I had figured it out, it seemed like it had taken hardly any time at all. But they had no idea how hard I'd worked to get here. Ost had granted me the ability to use it, and I'd been practicing ever since getting Therese to teach me the basics! I'd been racking my brains and trying to figure it out forever now.

"All that's left is to practice, practice, practice. Diligence is key," said Gaelion.

"Yeah. Now that I can manage this much, I guess that's really the only option," I replied.

It was like learning to ride a bike. Being able to just barely pull it off would be pointless. I needed to shoot for becoming a pro cyclist. Well, they didn't have those in this world, but still . . .

"Alright, I guess we should wrap things up and get some sleep," I said.

"Good idea. I completely lost track of time," Gaelion replied.

"You know what that means, little Naofumi. It's time for you and me to have a drink!"

Sadeena brought a barrel of alcohol out from the back and plunked it down in front of us.

"Where the hell did you get that from?"

"I salvaged it from a shipwreck. It's perfectly aged!"

As if I cared. Wherever she'd gotten it, I'm sure the circumstances had been shady. That's probably why she was keeping it here.

"Salvaged it from a shipwreck, you say?"

"Yep."

"Is keeping something like that for yourself allowed? In Melromarc?"

"It's perfectly fine. This barrel falls outside of salvaging law jurisdiction."

"Salvaging law?"

"Salvaging law says that someone who salvages something maintains seventy percent ownership, and the remaining thirty percent goes to Melromarc. It's a pretty useless law actually. It only applies to the territorial waters of Melromarc. I salvaged this in international waters."

Well, I guess it would be impossible to prove who had salvaged what. People could probably get away with it as long as they kept their mouths shut.

"The waves have been high lately, and the currents around Melromarc are strong. Now is the right time to be on the lookout."

I guess the waves of destruction made the ocean waves more dangerous too. Now that she mentioned it, I did seem to recall the captain saying something similar when we were on the boat headed to the Cal Mira islands.

"Do you want me to do a bit of treasure hunting if I get some free time? That might be dangerous if I don't level up some more first though."

"You've already leveled up quite a bit. I could use some treasure right about now if you're up to it."

What I really wanted to know is how she leveled up so quickly. Maybe monsters gave more experience in the water. But underwater treasure sure sounded lucrative. I guess salvaging was kind of like a side job for Sadeena. That must have been how she'd made money before meeting me, apart from her fight purses and other funding from Zeltoble.

"Okay, let's all get our drink on!" Sadeena exclaimed.

"Hmm . . . I could go for a stiff drink," said Gaelion.

He leaned toward the barrel.

"Here! This is for you, little Gaelion!"

Sadeena pulled out a 1.8-liter glass bottle and handed it to Gaelion. Umm, was that Japanese sake? The bottle was shaped the same. I guess one of the previous heroes must have told someone how to make it like that.

"Cheers," he said.

Gaelion starting drinking straight out of the bottle.

"Oh! This is the good stuff, isn't it?"

"It sure is. It's from the region where I grew up. It's strong enough to satisfy even a dragon."

"I see . . ."

Gaelion continued drinking. He seemed to be in high spirits.

"What about you, little Raphtalia? Your parents could really hold their alcohol, so I bet you can too."

"Umm, sure."

She could definitely drink a lot. L'Arc had been totally smashed by the time Raphtalia had only started getting tipsy.

"Drink up, you two. I have some rucolu fruit for you too, little Naofumi."

Sadeena handed me and Raphtalia a drink. It wasn't like I

actually liked rucolu fruit that much. But whatever. Going on about that at a time like this would be tactless.

With a map of the sea in one hand, I discussed our plans, while we all went on drinking. Every time the conversation died down for a moment, Sadeena started prodding Raphtalia.

"Hey, little Raphtalia. What do you think about little Naofumi?"

"I have a lot of respect for Mr. Naofumi."

Oh? She was always getting upset with my crude behavior, so her answer was a bit of a surprise to me. This probably wasn't the kind of thing a person should admit, but I really did do a lot of terrible stuff.

"Is that really how you feel?"

"Yes."

"So you don't want to marry him or anything like that?"

"I . . . uhh . . ."

Huh? Marry me? Was she asking if Raphtalia thought of me in a romantic sense? It wouldn't really bother me if she did say she liked me, but I'm pretty sure Raphtalia had other things much higher on her list of priorities. That was clear from how hard she was working to ensure that more children didn't end up in the same unfortunate circumstances she had, as a result of the waves.

"I . . . That's . . . Umm . . ."

Raphtalia's face turned red. She was looking this way and

that, avoiding eye contact. Chronologically speaking, Raphtalia was still pretty young. She probably shouldn't have been drinking alcohol actually, and she wasn't old enough to be thinking about things like love and romance. She only thought of me as a surrogate parent. Asking her to think about me in that way was probably just getting her worked up.

"I . . . Mishter Nawofoomee . . ."

Raphtalia was starting to slur her speech. I didn't think she would be that drunk already.

"Oh? Little Raphtalia?"

"Whuud I'm shaying ish . . ."

Raphtalia's face fell smack-dab into the table with a loud thud.

"Err . . . I, too . . . am feeling a bit . . ."

Gaelion shook his head back and forth and then lay down on his back.

Hmm . . . Raphtalia was no lightweight, and she was passed out drunk. Meanwhile, Sadeena and I were completely unfazed. Something about that was kind of depressing. I always felt out of place when I went out drinking with a group of people. That's why I didn't really like drinking very much. I just felt more and more alone as everyone else happily drunk themselves further into oblivion.

I had no idea what it felt like to be drunk. I'd never even gotten motion sickness, which was supposed to have symptoms similar to being hungover at least. I guess the closest I had ever come to being drunk was experiencing a state of euphoria. Well, that was an exaggeration, but I'd felt carefree while just having fun before. I guess I'd been drunk with success before, but that was obviously not the same thing.

I don't remember who it was, but someone once told me I drank like a mutant fish. Mutant . . . Really?

"Well, look at that. Dragon Killer and Tanuki are both famous drinks where I come from, and it looks like they live up to their names. I guess they were a bit much for little Gaelion and little Raphtalia."

What?! What was Sadeena implying?!

"You . . . This was your plan, wasn't it?!"

This was bad. Sadeena had obviously intentionally chosen drinks that would be too much for Raphtalia and Gaelion. And now there was a chance that she would make a move on me. Worst-case scenario, I could use Shield Prison and then flee using my portal, maybe.

"Now then. Let's have another drink!"

"No thanks. I'm going home."

"Oh, come on. If you go home, what will happen to little Raphtalia and little Gaelion?"

"I'll take them with me when I use my portal."

"I'm sure you will. But I want to talk with you a bit before you do that."

"Talk? Aren't you planning some kind of rampant debauchery?"

"No, that's not it."

Sadeena cheerfully chugged the remainder of her drink. And then her demeanor changed instantaneously.

"Little Naofumi, I want to know what your true intentions are toward little Raphtalia."

Sadeena completely dropped her usual playful attitude and changed into her demi-human form. She had a dead-serious look in her eyes when she asked.

"You got Raphtalia and Gaelion completely smashed just to ask me that?"

What did Raphtalia really mean to Sadeena anyway? I didn't know what the deal was, but asking Sadeena about it always felt like crossing some kind of line. She never gave me a straightforward answer.

This was something that happened not too long ago.

We were right in the middle of getting the village set up and rebuilding the neighboring town. Having gotten wind of the fact that my most-trusted assistant was a racoon-type demi-human, a whole bunch of demi-humans, racoon-type demi-humans, showed up at the territory.

"Shield Hero, since your most-trusted assistant is a racoon-type demi-human, that makes us practically family. We rallied together and came as quickly as possible to help you with the reconstruction."

When I saw the other racoon-types, I couldn't believe how different they were from Raphtalia. I'm not sure if portly was the right word . . . Basically, they struck me as a bunch of pudgy country bumpkins. They didn't seem very driven. It was more like they figured they could come latch on to me and live an easy life, so I wasn't too keen on the idea of taking them in.

But seeing as they were racoon-types, I also found it really hard to refuse. Any time I met eyes with one of them, they started explaining all the details of how they were related by blood, probably in an attempt to pressure me. That really started getting on my nerves, and I was contemplating just telling them to leave.

That's when Sadeena stepped forward. Unlike her usual cheerful self, she was seething with anger. She pointed her harpoon at them.

"I'm sorry, but any blood ties you might have with little Naofumi's most-trusted assistant are so far separated that you're as good as complete strangers. Don't try to use that as an excuse to win his favor. Understood?"

Sensing her anger, the whole bunch of them were scared stiff.

"Well, if you really want to help out, then I guess you can give us a hand with the reconstruction over at the neighboring town. I'll think about making you an official part of the team later," I told them.

After wrapping up the discussion, I sent them to help with the town's reconstruction. But not long after . . . Yeah, now I remember. I'm pretty sure almost all of them had fled during the night by the time three or so days had passed.

That wasn't the only time Sadeena had acted strangely. Every now and then I would catch her glaring at something in the village, but there was never anybody there. She'd have a wary look in her eyes, as if there was someone hiding or something. But if someone were using concealment magic, I'm sure Raphtalia would have noticed. She never actually mentioned anything, so it was most likely just her imagination.

"Seriously, what's the nature of your relationship with Raphtalia anyway?"

I don't know, but . . . Even I'd been able to work out that finding Raphtalia had been Sadeena's true motivation for buying up the slaves in Zeltoble. Of course, judging by how she interacted with the villagers, securing the slaves was still a big part of it, I'm sure.

"Little Naofumi, little Raphtalia and her parents were what gave my life meaning."

"Gave your life meaning?"

What was her connection to them? That just made things

even more confusing. Back in my world, cultural concepts like chivalry or the way of the samurai had existed in the past. Maybe it was something like that.

"When the first wave occurred here in this world, I wasn't able to protect little Raphtalia's parents. Well the truth is, I had been somewhere far away when it happened, and I couldn't make it back in time. It was carelessness on my part."

There was a hint of regret in Sadeena's whispers. She took another drink. Judging from her demeanor, she definitely didn't seem to be joking. Raphtalia was still out cold. Sadeena tucked her into a simple bed in the cave and then continued where she left off. Sadeena seemed to be serious, so there was no reason for me to be hard on her, even if it was just the two of us.

"But when I finally made it back to the village several days after the wave occurred, nobody was there," she continued.

"I searched and searched. I was sure that they had survived. But I'm a demi-human, so I had to stay away from the shadier side of things in Melromarc. Zeltoble specializes in the slave trade, so I went there and continued my search as a combat slave. I had some big-name connections there, so I figured things would work out if I could save up some money."

"You took quite the detour, huh?"

In reality, Raphtalia had been a dirt-cheap slave. Sadeena may have searched really hard, but she sure ended up a long way off target.

"Searching specifically for a slave named Raphtalia that looked like a racoon was just taking too much time. I did manage to find some of the other village children though."

"Yeah, you were protecting the village slaves, right?"

"Yes. And then when I did finally come across little Raphtalia, I couldn't believe my eyes. I never expected her to be fighting by your side, little Naofumi."

"Talk about a life full of ups and downs. Raphtalia's, that is."

If possible, I wanted Raphtalia to live a comfortable, quiet life once this world had found peace. She'd believed in me, so I wanted her to be happy. That wasn't going to change. Sometimes I just wanted this world to go up in flames, but as long as Raphtalia lived here, I had no qualms about doing my best to make it a peaceful place.

"You said, 'looked like a racoon.' Is Raphtalia not a racoon-type?"

"It's kind of like how I get mistaken for an orca. She's not exactly a racoon, but she's something close."

"I see. Well, Raphtalia is Raphtalia, regardless of her type."

There were lots of animals that were similar, yet different species. Kind of like native and non-native species of the same animal.

"That's what's nice about you. Hey, little Naofumi, if you're not ready to commit to sticking by little Raphtalia until the very end, I'd prefer if you'd just settle for me instead."

"Huh?"

"I'm asking you to be prepared to commit before getting into a relationship with little Raphtalia. If you're not prepared to commit, but you still feel the need to get intimate, then I'd rather you use me to get that out of your system."

Well, I wasn't expecting that.

"Do you think I'm some kind of savage or something?"

Well, I guess I did act like a savage. But I'd rather die than get intimate with a woman. I mean, I trusted Raphtalia. If you asked whether I liked her or not . . . Yeah, I liked her. I was certain about that much. If you told me to tell that to Raphtalia's face, I could. Although I'd prefer not to. But was it in a romantic kind of way? I don't know.

Raphtalia was my trusty sidekick. We were companions that had shared the good times and the bad. At the same time, she was like a daughter to me. In that sense, I considered myself her "father," as Motoyasu liked to call me. As long as this world hadn't found peace, I was sure Raphtalia would remain focused on her mission and wouldn't be interested in things like love and romance. On the other hand, I loved her like a child. Wait a minute, I needed to slow down. I was getting caught up in Sadeena's pace.

When Sadeena said "very end," she probably meant until Raphtalia died, and not just until the waves ended. In manga and games, it wasn't uncommon for the protagonist to settle down in another world. But . . . I wasn't prepared to make that kind of commitment, I don't think. I intended to return to my own world once this one had become peaceful.

Sadeena was probably worried I would try something with Raphtalia, and knowing my personality, that's why she had been teasing me. Her advances seemed like harassment, but by keeping that up she probably figured it would keep me away from Raphtalia. Sadeena was always messing around, but the truth was, she had a knack for calmly observing people's behavior and leading them to act in a certain way. She was the type that would be a real headache if you made an enemy out of her.

She was trying to sound playful, but her eyes were dead serious.

"You must have a good reason to keep pushing the issue."

I wasn't planning on doing anything with Raphtalia, but I wanted to get a better idea of what Sadeena was thinking.

"Oh, alright. I guess I can fill you in just a bit."

Sadeena ran her hands through Raphtalia's hair gently and then began her explanation.

"You might have suspected something like this, but little Raphtalia's father belonged to an important family with a long lineage. I was a miko priestess that served that family."

"Oh? Was this in Siltvelt or Shieldfreeden?"

"Nope. I can't tell you exactly where. I'm already telling you way more than I should."

So it wasn't a demi-human country. And what kind of position was a miko priestess, anyway?

"Little Raphtalia's father didn't want to take over as the head of the family. He eloped with little Raphtalia's mother. I went with them and we left the country."

Hmm . . . So Raphtalia's parents had been selfish. Or not, depending on how you looked at it. I wondered if there was some special reason they had come to Melromarc, seeing as how the country heavily discriminated against demi-humans.

"I lost a lot by leaving, but I gained even more. I don't regret the decision."

"Between her father's lineage and the heroes, which would rank higher?"

"Raphtalia's father would have been more important in the region we came from."

"More than the holy heroes?"

"The legend of the heroes doesn't exist there. Although, there are records of heroes visiting the region. But personally, I think they were just referred to by a different name."

What kind of region was it? And referred to by a different name? Like . . . "holders of the holy weapons," maybe? Either way, I had a feeling I was starting to understand what kind of family Raphtalia had come from. She was the descendant of a family line that was worshipped in some country because it was thought to trace back to the gods or something.

I decided to see if I could reason it out using what I already knew. There was the name and characteristics of the special finishing move that Raphtalia had created herself. And then there was the way Sadeena's demi-human form looked. Both of those had a Japanese feel to them. That reminded me of what the old guy at the weapon shop had said about some place to the east.

"Does the country Raphtalia's father was born in have a policy of isolation?"

Japan was like that a long time ago. It wasn't like that made me special or anything, but being Japanese would make it easier to understand how a country might develop differently due to the effects of such a policy. Also, I'd heard that the country where the Spirit Tortoise had been sealed away had also been closed off. Perhaps there were more isolationist countries than I would have thought.

"Wow, you really are impressive, little Naofumi. That's exactly right. It's been that way since ancient times. There are a lot of countries like that, but ours is one of the most exclusionary of them."

"Are you worried about the country trying something?"

It was an isolationist country in the east. So it was a country kind of like Japan, and Raphtalia was a descendant of an ancient and dignified bloodline there. If they found out about her, they might send someone to try to take her back or something. Maybe that was it.

"That's part of it, but it wouldn't really be an issue if that's all it was. I guess you could say that Raphtalia's happiness is what really concerns me."

"Ugh . . ." Raphtalia moaned.

Sadeena wet a piece of cloth with cool water and placed it on Raphtalia's forehead.

"She'll be waking up soon. Is there anything else you wanted to ask?"

"Why don't you tell Raphtalia any of this?"

"Her father didn't want her to know."

The last thing I wanted was to get dragged into some kind of family feud with Raphtalia's relatives. People could waste time on that kind of thing once the world was at peace. The same went for the whole Church of the Three Heroes mess and the trouble with the nobility. That power struggle stuff was a real pain in the ass.

"Is this going to be a problem?"

"Probably not. They'll probably stay away as long as we don't do anything to upset them—something like you and little Raphtalia getting intimate."

"Do you mean because that would cause internal family issues?"

Sadeena nodded silently. So that was it, after all. Hypothetically, let's say I slept with Raphtalia and she got pregnant. I was worshipped as a god in another country, and

Raphtalia would be pregnant with my child. Those relatives might suspect that Raphtalia was trying to take control of the family, which could prompt them to take action. And Sadeena was worried about that possibility.

"If you decide that you really want to have a child with little Raphtalia, do it after you crush that country and quash those family issues. Promise me."

"Aren't you a bit too worried?"

I couldn't imagine that the country knew everything that was going on. Of course, it never hurt to be careful, but still . . .

"You're probably right. But that country is full of miko priestesses and people that can use unique abilities. You shouldn't underestimate them. Just imagine a bunch of people like me coming to try to kill little Raphtalia."

". . ."

A country full of Sadeenas . . . Why didn't we just have them save the world? Still, Raphtalia was incredibly strong, so it wouldn't be easy to kill her. That didn't mean I was going to do anything irresponsible, of course.

"The truth is, it's really up to you, little Naofumi. I just don't want you to do anything that would make a little girl cry. But I'm an adult, and not a little girl, so I can handle it."

"After all of those excuses, you go there?"

"Oh, stop it! You're making me blush!"

Of course, lineage and all of that was probably an issue

too, but Sadeena really just wanted to ask about my feelings for Raphtalia. That was clear now.

"Ugh . . . Mr. Naofumi?"

Raphtalia regained consciousness and sat up.

"You okay?"

"Umm, yes. I feel oddly refreshed."

I demanded a lot of her. She might have been stressed about things too. In that respect, drinking might not actually be a bad way to blow off some steam.

"That's good," Sadeena said.

"Did anything happen while I was passed out?" Raphtalia asked.

"Nah . . ." I replied.

I was sure Sadeena would rather I didn't tell the truth. There was no need to stir up any trouble. I'd just pretend I hadn't heard any of it.

"Not really. I was just telling Sadeena about how you're like a daughter to me."

"What?!"

Raphtalia shouted out in surprise and her voice cracked. We went back and forth for a bit and she forgot about her initial question.

So I should be prepared to commit if I wanted to pursue a serious relationship with Raphtalia, huh? What a bunch of trouble. I wasn't going to settle down in this world. I didn't intend to, at least.

"Alright then. That's enough drinking. Let's head back and get some sleep," I said.

"Aww . . ."

"He's right, Sadeena. You've had more than enough."

"Hm? Did I fall asleep?"

Gaelion finally woke up.

"Fill me up," he said.

"Oh! I like that attitude, little Gaelion! How about you and I have a drinking contest?"

"That's not a bad idea."

Were these two going to be drinking buddies now? Gaelion was hungover the next day. I guess I'd just have to warn him not to drink too much next time.

Chapter Fifteen: Form is Emptiness

It had been two days since my talk with Sadeena. I'd finished breakfast and was in the middle of training when I heard the clunking sounds of a carriage. A completely unexpected visitor rolled up into the village.

"Hmm? Oh, hey!" I called out.

The old guy from the weapon shop was sitting in the carriage. It looked like he'd grabbed a ride on a carriage transporting ore and other materials.

"Yo! I came to take a look at this village you've been building, kid."

The old guy was looking around at the village.

"You sure have given the place a unique feel, haven't you?"

That was his comment after catching sight of the bioplant field, the camping plant buildings, and the monster stable.

"There's absolutely no denying that," Raphtalia agreed.

I sensed a hint of bitterness in her voice.

"That's just a reflection of Mr. Naofumi! You need to learn to accept that already, Raphtalia!" Atla retorted.

"I'm not so sure about that. But why are you always so eager to pick a fight, Atla?" I asked.

Hearing the old guy's comment and taking a look around,

I couldn't deny that the village was turning out to look pretty strange. The bioplant field and the camping plant buildings were only a couple of the many oddities. The camping plant buildings, in particular, were a real one-of-a-kind. That was undeniable. No matter how you looked at it, the place stuck out among the other towns and villages in Melromarc. I was fully aware that I had some pretty crazy stuff going on there, and having it pointed out by the old guy didn't make me feel any better about it.

"Did you just stop by while you were you out gathering ore or something?"

"There is that, but I have another reason for coming too."

The old guy reached into a bag sitting on the carriage and pulled out an outfit. He handed it to Raphtalia. I immediately understood what it was. Even I knew that my eyes were twinkling as I stared at the outfit.

"Why do you look so excited?!" Raphtalia snapped.

She was standing there holding the clothes with an annoyed look on her face.

"Oh?"

I checked the stats on the miko outfit in Raphtalia's hands.

White Tiger Miko Outfit (crude)
defense up, impact resistance (small), power of the four holy beasts, magic defense processing

Crude? What was that all about? But actually, I hadn't even been able to use my appraisal skill on the outfit before now.

"Hmm, the stats seem a bit low," Raphtalia said.

"Really?"

"Yes."

"Sorry about that. This was the best I could manage," said the old guy.

"Not at all. I think you did a good job, actually," I replied.

"I'm perfectly happy with more normal armor," Raphtalia said.

The old guy had humored my request and supposedly went through a lot of trial-and-error to make the outfit. There weren't very many people in this world looking into how to raise the defenses of cloth, unlike in Kizuna's world. The old guy had incorporated some exotic techniques and managed to pull it off to a certain degree, I guess.

"There's a girl in your village that's good with sewing equipment, right? She gave me a hand, and that made a big difference."

Did he mean S'yne? I didn't recall introducing her to the old guy. But then I remembered she was keeping an eye on me. Her vassal weapon was basically a sewing set. She probably shared some techniques from other worlds that helped the old guy out too.

"I see. Alright, Raphtalia, make sure you wear that from now on, starting today."

"I don't know why you feel so strongly about these clothes."

A big grin crept across my face.

"Because they look so good on you. I'm sure the villagers will agree when they see you in them."

"I didn't want to hear that. Oh, whatever. The stats aren't much different than those of the armor I'm wearing now, so it's not like I'm against wearing them."

"I'm prepared to give my full support to any ongoing research in this area, you know. Is there anything else you might need?"

I nudged the old guy to continue with his miko outfit research and development.

"Mr. Naofumi? Are you listening to me?"

Raphtalia tried to protest. She still had the miko outfit in her hands.

"I hear you. Anyway, go put that on and show the villagers."

"You don't have to sound so pushy."

"I sure wish Mr. Naofumi would buy me clothes. I'm jealous!" Atla exclaimed.

I could feel some kind of intense aura of envy slowly emanating from her body.

"I'll take those if you don't want them," she continued.

"They wouldn't even fit you!" Raphtalia snapped.

"That doesn't matter. I'll wear them anyway and steal Mr. Naofumi's heart."

"What the hell are you even saying?"

Sometimes Atla's enthusiasm was just a bit too much.

"Ugh . . . Fine. Understood. I'll go put it on."

Raphtalia gave up and went to change into the outfit. Several minutes later, she returned with the miko outfit on.

"Oh . . ."

The old guy and all of the villagers were staring at her. She was looking down at the ground and holding her katana sheath in her hands, clearly embarrassed.

"Now that's really something. I see what you mean, kid."

"Wow, Raphtalia! You look even cooler than usual!" Keel exclaimed.

She was staring at Raphtalia too. Right? Right?? I knew it. Raphtalia really did look best in a miko outfit!

"Cool?"

"She means cute, I'm sure. But wow!"

Everyone was staring at Raphtalia in awe, and her face just kept getting redder. Was she really embarrassed? She didn't seem bothered at all when she wore the outfit back in Kizuna's world.

"Now that is a sight for sore eyes," I said.

I felt like a father seeing his precious, young daughter all dressed up in nice clothes for the first time. Okay, maybe that was going a bit too far, but Raphtalia really did look amazingly good in a miko outfit. I'd also seen her in a kimono and a hakama while we were in Kizuna's world, but nothing could beat the miko outfit. It was uncanny. It's like the clothes were made for her. They fit together like pieces of a puzzle. It made the more European-style leather armor she usually wore just look strange on her.

"Well, that settles that. We're sticking with the miko outfit for you, Raphtalia."

"I don't get why you're so set on having it that way, but fine. Understood."

Raphtalia sighed faintly when she replied.

"What else do you have planned today? If you came to ask for the lumos' help, I'd be happy to send them along with you," I told the old guy.

"Oh, yeah? In that case, I guess I'll take you up on your offer," he replied.

And so, with Raphtalia wearing her new miko outfit, we got back to training and taking care of our business for the day. Other than that, Eclair started moaning about her duties as governor and requested my help, so I went over and spent some time in the neighboring town to give her a hand.

The old guy decided to stay the night in the village and agreed to do some maintenance work on the armor that the slaves had been using while he was there. He really was a generous guy. I could never thank him enough.

The sun set and it was almost time for dinner.

"Little Naofumi! I'm back!"

Sadeena had just gotten back to the village. I'd asked her to go do some salvaging in the nearby ocean, along with some fishing to help reinforce our food supplies. She must have made quite the catch, because the basket on her back was packed full of fish.

"I brought you your fish. We're going to have a feast tonight!"

"Yeah, fine. Whatever. For now, I'll just grill—"

I started talking to myself about how I should prepare the fish that Sadeena had caught.

"Oh hey, Sadeena. Welcome ba—"

Before Raphtalia could finish her sentence, Sadeena dropped the basket of fish on the ground with a loud thud.

"Hey, don't drop that there!"

Sadeena completely ignored me and stumbled over to Raphtalia. She reached out and started trying to pull Raphtalia's clothes off.

"Wh . . . what are you doing, Sadeena?!"

"What's the idea, you drunkard?!"

"Little Naofumi! We have to get these clothes off of her immediately!"

"Stop screwing around! Why would she need to get undressed?!"

I'd had that miko outfit made specially just for her. Why did she need to take it off now? Raphtalia and Sadeena were struggling with each other and the slaves started making a commotion.

"Umm, Naofumi, is everything okay? Should we stop them?" Ren asked.

He looked alarmed.

"I guess so. We can't have this screwball undressing Raphtalia in front of everyone. We'll just have to put her down."

I was starting to get angry when I noticed the look of urgency on Sadeena's face.

"Hey, what are you so flustered about? Explain yourself."

"Little Naofumi, don't you remember what I said? About being prepared?"

Huh? The night before last, Sadeena had told me I should be prepared to commit if I wanted to marry Raphtalia—how it would likely cause some kind of family feud or something.

"What about it?"

"It's related to that. We need to get these clothes off of her now!"

"Wh . . . what are you two talking about?!" Raphtalia asked.

She'd been passed out drunk at the time. It made sense that she wouldn't know. But what did Raphtalia wearing a miko outfit have to do with any of that?

"Okay, fine. Raphtalia, go change your clothes. This drunkard is going to keep trying to undress you otherwise."

"U . . . understood."

Raphtalia went to change again. After that, Sadeena finally calmed down. She was staring at the house that Raphtalia had gone inside of to change.

"Seriously, what's going on?"

"Listen, little Naofumi. Do you have any idea what having little Raphtalia wear that outfit means?"

"Hell if I know. It's just a really nice piece of equipment that we brought back from the other world and had repaired."

Sadeena acted like I'd stepped on a land mine, but how should I have known what the problem was? No one had told me anything about something like that! Sadeena covered her face with her hand, like she was getting frustrated. It was unlike her to be visibly irritated like this.

"Okay, little Naofumi, I'm going to explain. Having her wear that outfit has far greater significance than even what we talked about the other day. In *that* country, it signifies a right to the thro—"

All of a sudden, Sadeena took off running. Several seconds later, a column of flames suddenly shot up out of the house that Raphtalia had gone in to change clothes.

"What the hell?!"

"We were too late!"

Sadeena quickly switched to her therianthrope form and began to rapidly recite an incantation.

"Raphtalia!"

Raphtalia leapt out of the crumbling house and brandished her katana. She was still halfway undressed, and her miko outfit was spotted with ash. I heard a metallic sound echo out and something went flying toward Raphtalia! I squinted to get a better look. It looked like a kunai or some kind of iron spike. And then a group of people appeared from out of nowhere and attacked Raphtalia.

"Ugh . . ."

Raphtalia parried and then counterattacked, but her attack was dodged by a hair's breadth.

"Prepare yourself!" the enemy shouted.

Fortunately, Raphtalia was slightly more skilled than her opponents, so she was able to dodge all of their attacks. What kind of weapons were they using? Was that a kodachi? One of the enemies blocked Raphtalia's katana and locked blades with her. Immediately after, another enemy took advantage of the opening, appearing from behind and attacking. But Raphtalia swiftly drew her other katana and blocked the attack. She could dual-wield.

"Brave Blade! Crossing Mists!"

Raphtalia forced a skill off and tried to slice through the enemy, but her katana stopped just short of making contact and sparks shot into the air. Her opponents were pretty strong.

"Haaah!"

"Not so fast!"

Raphtalia used her illusion magic to confuse the attacker and then dodged the attack. She'd only changed her position ever so slightly, so it had appeared really dangerous. The enemies had managed to unleash such a fierce chain of attacks in the mere moments it had taken us to approach.

They must have been some seriously skilled fighters. Raphtalia had a vassal weapon! Levels were capped at 100 in this world. Even if Raphtalia's stats were reduced by the effects of a curse, I was sure she wouldn't be outclassed by someone of that level. She was at least that strong.

"Air Strike Shield! Second Shield! Shooting Star Shield!"

Raphtalia had only been able to focus on protecting herself. I hurried to the front to take over defense.

"Drifa Thunderbolt!"

Sadeena finished her incantation and thunderbolts rained down on the surrounding area, revealing several more enemies that seemed to have been hiding.

What was this? They appeared to be killer whale therianthropes and a rabbit therianthropes. They were wearing what looked like ninja outfits, and they had me, Raphtalia, and Sadeena surrounded.

"Who the hell are these people?" I asked.

Did that mean demi-humans and therianthropes had attacked Raphtalia? Siltvelt and Shieldfreeden were the demi-human countries. But if they'd been from there, I wouldn't have expected them to be this hostile once I showed up.

"Are those enemies?!"

"Oh no! The house is on fire! We restored that house with bubba!"

"Kwa?!"

Ren, Keel, the other slaves, and even the monsters all started to make a lot of noise.

"Fehhh! Mr. Itsuki! Let's join the fight!"

"Okay."

Rishia and Itsuki showed up too, of course.

"What's going on?!"

"What in the world happened here?"

Even Fohl and Atla were surprised by the unexpected state of affairs. The enemy showed no sign of retreating, despite our rapid increase in numbers. They were exchanging glances silently.

"Daughter of the one who abandoned his inheritance of the seat of the Heavenly Emperor! You have made your intentions clear to us! We will do everything in our power to thwart your claim to the seat! Prepare yourself!"

"What?!"

What was that supposed to mean? I looked over at Raphtalia.

"What are you talking about? I have absolutely no idea!" she exclaimed.

"Little Naofumi, little Raphtalia, it's too late. They won't listen to us."

Sadeena narrowed her eyes. She was radiating an aura of murderous intent as she pointed her harpoon at the group of ninja-looking enemies that had suddenly appeared.

What was going on? There were several killer whale therianthropes that looked a lot like Sadeena mixed in among them. I suddenly remembered what Sadeena had said recently. I got a really bad feeling in the pit of my stomach.

"What do you mean?" I asked her.

"Listen, little Naofumi. Those clothes that you had little Raphtalia put on—that you keep calling a miko outfit—are primarily what caused this. You understand, right?"

I had a pretty good idea of what Sadeena was getting at, judging from how she was reacting. I had no idea how in the world that outfit would lead to getting ambushed, but going by what she had told me, I assumed it had something to do with Raphtalia's birth.

"Those clothes have special meaning in little Raphtalia's case."

"I can tell that much. I want to know the reason why."

"Is that a holder of a spirit implement? Permission to draw weapons of judgment granted! And you! Take care of the water dragon's former miko priestess!" shouted one of the enemies.

"Yes, sir!"

There were a bunch of clicking sounds and . . . What were those? The enemies drew strange weapons that were enshrouded in energy resembling pale flame. The enemies readied themselves to attack.

"I guess we don't have time for explanations. We'll just have to fight them off for now," I said.

The group of killer whales that looked like Sadeena sprang into action. Before Sadeena could even move, they lunged at her at full speed and thrust their staffs at her, sending her flying through the air. The thrusts must have been incredibly powerful, because Sadeena was thrown high into the air, toward the cliff. The enemies leapt at her and latched on to her body in what appeared to be a suicide attack. They all went tumbling together over the cliff and down into the ocean.

"Sadeena!" Raphtalia screamed.

As if in response to her screams, the enemies raised their weapons high into the air.

"Haaaaah!"

The first attacker swung a maul, and I stepped forward to block it. He was really quick. Almost as quick as Sadeena was when we fought her in Zeltoble, after she'd become serious. I needed to watch out for defense rating attacks and defense ignoring attacks. But I didn't know if the enemy could use either, so I decided to block the attack with Shooting Star Shield. There was a loud cracking sound, and the maul smashed through the barrier as easy as if it had been the crisp outer layer of a chocolate-dipped cone.

Was this a joke? Could it really be possible to destroy my Shooting Star Shield so effortlessly? I could have understood if it had been the Demon Dragon or another hero, but these were just normal people, as far as I could tell. Something seemed a bit different about the way it had been destroyed too. I wasn't sure how to describe it. It had just kind of dissolved, like the barrier had been nullified.

"Ugh!"

I blocked the enemy's sideways swing with my shield, and I felt the massive impact pass through the shield and into my arm.

I hadn't taken any damage. It hadn't been a defense rating or defense ignoring attack. And yet it had easily smashed through my Shooting Star Shield. On top of that, I had the Demon Dragon Shield equipped and the counterattack effect hadn't activated. The accessory I had attached to my shield recently didn't react either. None of my effects were functioning.

"Mr. Naofumi!"

Another enemy attacked Raphtalia behind me. Damn it!

"Dritte Shield!"

I summoned my third shield to protect her.

"It's no use."

The enemy that had attacked Raphtalia was using a

sword-breaker dagger. As expected, the enemy sliced through the shield that I had summoned with ease.

I had learned the Way of the Dragon Vein, and I could feel that I was becoming more and more sensitive toward magic recently. Surely I would be able to tell whether my stats had been reduced by magic. I took a quick look at my stats, just to make sure. There didn't seem to be any kind of debuff magic at play. Did that mean the enemy had surpassed my defense with pure brute force? But our stats were higher than theirs.

"We have to protect bubba!"

"Wait! Be careful!" I shouted.

Keel and the others paid no heed to my warning and rushed into the fray. Was I going to end up with dead villagers on my hands?! The thought flashed across my mind, but they were actually coordinating and maneuvering rather well. Their guard was tight. In that case, I would just cast Zweite Aura to reduce the damage they may take.

There seemed to be some highly skilled fighters mixed in among the enemies, but we had them outnumbered and they seemed to be struggling. But there was a different problem. Keel and the others were fighting back with weapons that had no edge.

"Naofumi! Ugh . . ."

Ren, Rishia, and Itsuki tried to join us, but the enemies blocked their path.

"Ren! Or Itsuki! Give us some backup!"

"Understood!"

"Naofumi, do your best to withstand this!"

Ren and Itsuki both fired off their skills.

"Hundred Swords!"

"Arrow Rain!"

When they did, I shoved the enemies away and held my shield up into the air.

"Shooting Star Shield!"

I generated a barrier and buckled down to protect Raphtalia and the others from Ren's and Itsuki's backup attacks.

"Ugh . . ."

The enemies that had been surrounding me groaned, and then went on to bat Ren's and Itsuki's skills out of the air with their weapons. Just what the hell were those weapons?! What was with these enemies?! Bastards!

"Why are you attacking us?!" Ren screamed angrily.

He was slicing at the enemies, but his attacks were too weak. No. His stats were clearly higher, because he did seem to be overpowering them slightly. But it was like the enemies were wearing chainmail or something. Even if Ren's sword made contact, it was like he couldn't surpass their defense.

"What's with these guys?!"

"Lea———Spider Net!"

S'yne suddenly appeared and cast her spiderweb of thread

over the area. The enemies were caught off guard by the surprise attack and got tangled up in the thread, slowing their movements. That would prove to be a mistake.

"Here I go! Brave Blade! Crossing Mists!"

"Hiyaaa!"

"Let's do this, Mr. Itsuki!"

"Okay."

All of our best fighters took advantage of the brief opening and attacked.

"Ugh . . . But we will not back down!" shouted one of the enemies.

"Their armor is ridiculously tough!"

"Yes."

Raphtalia, Ren, and Itsuki just barely managed to cut through the enemies' armor and chainmail, but none of them had even come close to causing a fatal wound.

The enemies' skilled coordination and polished movements seemed almost supernatural, and they were what made their attacks so efficient. Our stats might have been higher than theirs, but they outdid us when it came to technique.

"Ugh . . ."

"Request for permission to employ the sakura stones of destiny!" yelled one of the fighters.

"We didn't bring any for this operation! Be prepared to die an honorable death if you must!" replied another.

"Yes, sir!"

It sounded like they had another secret weapon. But now wasn't the time to worry about that!

"You're not welcome here!" Atla exclaimed.

She caught one of the enemies off guard and punched him in the chest.

"Ugh!"

Huh? Atla's attack destroyed the enemy's armor. But Ren and Itsuki were complaining about being unable to breach the enemies' defenses. Raphtalia's, Ren's, and Itsuki's attacks hadn't been very effective. And my skill had been destroyed effortlessly. What was the common denominator?

Was it that we were all heroes?

But this wasn't the time for pondering. We needed to do something and we needed to do it quick. Our enemies were incredibly skillful. S'yne's web of threads had already been cut to pieces and rendered ineffective. Was there no way to finish this quickly?

"Raphtalia!"

It was sink or swim! I looked at Raphtalia and signaled with my eyes for her to begin focusing her mind. She nodded. I turned my back to her and began to recite an incantation while continuing to guard against the attacks of the enemies in front of us.

We'd just have to play it by ear and hope this worked. We were going to use illusion magic—Raphtalia's specialty—to try to confuse the enemies. The puzzle pieces appeared, floating, in front of my eyes.

"Can you do this, Raphtalia?"

"I'll try my best!"

The spell I'd cast as the base for our magic wasn't an aura spell. It was a guard spell. It was a type of support magic that I'd learned a long time ago, but I stopped using it once I learned the aura spells. Being that it was her first time casting cooperative magic, Raphtalia seemed slightly unsure of herself. But she must have caught on faster than I had, because it was going pretty well for a couple of amateurs.

"Power of two, lend your strength to confuse the enemy with an illusion! Re-spin the threads of fate, and turn their defeat into a victory!"

Nice! The incantation was going well. There was something about it. It felt like we were able to combine our power more quickly than when I cast cooperative magic with Sadeena. Of course, the fact that I'd cast such a low-level spell probably had something to do with it. Whatever, we had to try!

I continued blocking the enemies' attacks while we were reciting the incantation. All of the training I had done with Atla and Raphtalia lately was paying off now. Atla's vicious attacks were driven by instinct. These enemies were skilled, but their movements were formulaic, which made them easy to deal with.

We finished fitting the puzzle pieces together to form the magic.

"*Dragon Vein! Hear our petition and grant it! As the source of your power, we implore you! Let the true way be revealed once more! Show our enemies an illusion to confuse them!*"

"Form is Emptiness!"

The target icon popped up on my screen. The spell was set to cast on everyone that I recognized as an enemy. Without hesitation, I finalized the incantation and cast the spell. There was a loud pop, and the magic that Raphtalia and I had cast took its effect on every single enemy there!

"Haaaa!"

The enemies' fierce attacks began to miss us, and they began moving in all of the wrong directions. It was hard to tell, but it seemed like our illusions were putting up a good fight.

"Wh . . . what happened?!"

"We cast some cooperative magic. These bastards are going to be full of holes for a bit!"

"It seems that we succeeded in creating sensory confusion with the illusions. But be careful! I'm sure you realize this, but attacking them will cancel the effect. They'll figure out what's going on soon!"

"Then what should we do?!"

"The effect won't last long. In that case . . ."

Raphtalia took a stance that I'd seen her use before.

"It would seem they have some kind of powerful resistance against our weapon skills. I'm sure that Mr. Naofumi and the other heroes have noticed," she said.

"Yeah."

"We need your strength too, Ren and Itsuki. We need to make the absolute most of this chance!"

"Got it!"

"Okay."

"Fehhh . . ."

"Don't waste this opportunity," I told them.

I started casting my aura on as many of us as I could, starting with the strongest fighters. It probably took less than a minute. Raphtalia finished recharging her magic power and gave everyone the signal to attack.

"Shooting Star Sword!"

"Eagle Piercing Shot!"

Ren and Itsuki led the attack, and everyone followed up with their biggest skills and most powerful techniques. Atla delivered a heavy blow to her opponent's chest with her fist. But the enemy immediately took a defensive stance, perhaps because they sensed Atla's hostility, or just as a result of combat experience.

"Here I go! Hiyaaaaa!"

The blade of Raphtalia's katana began to glow and she unleashed something that wasn't a weapon skill. It was an attack

that would extend across the whole area.

"Eight Trigrams Blade of Destiny!"

It was a quick-draw attack with incredible momentum, but everyone must have known it was coming, because we all crouched down and dodged the attack. A trail of light shot out and directly into almost all of the enemies who had been standing there confused. A yin-yang pattern appeared in the air briefly, and then the enemies were all sent flying through the air.

"Gaaaahhhh!"

The surprise attack incapacitated all of the enemies at once.

"An attack that combines magic power and life force, I see. As to be expected of the one that calls herself Mr. Naofumi's sword. But I won't lose to you!"

After adding her commentary, Atla climbed up onto one of the fallen enemies and threw her arms into the air to signal our victory. It must have been around that same time. Several massive lightning bolts rained down near the shore and Sadeena burst up out of the water.

"Now, now. If you think that's all it takes to stop me, you're gravely mistaken."

"These people were super strong!"

Keel was poking one of the fallen enemies excitedly with the sheath of her short sword.

"Oh? Did you protect everyone, little Naofumi?"

"I guess you could say that. Actually, it was Raphtalia that finished them off."

"Yeah! That was amazing."

"Yes. By the way, our weapons and skills seemed rather ineffective against these people. Are they useless?" asked Itsuki.

He was still behaving as indecisively as ever.

"It'd be nice if we could get one of them to talk," I said.

I kicked one of the fallen enemies over onto his back. His eyes snapped open and he started to get up, but I stomped him back down to the ground and pinned him there with my foot.

"You realize the fight is over, right? Now it's time to make you talk!"

"Ha! We won't tell you anything!"

As soon as he finished speaking, light began to leak out of his body and the bodies of all of the other surrounding enemies.

"Daughter of the one who abandoned his inheritance of the seat of the Heavenly Emperor! We have noted your declaration of war. Messengers have already been sent to inform our people. Our assassins will never stop coming for you. Your days of peace and quiet are over! Hahahaha!"

"Little Naofumi!"

"Everyone, get back!"

"Glory to the Heavenly Emperor!"

I gave the order and we all moved away from the fallen enemies. As we did, the enemies' bodies exploded and went flying into the air.

"They blow themselves up as soon as they lose? What the hell?"

And talk about grotesque. There were corpses all over the place and it reeked of blood. It smelled like blasting powder too. Who the hell was going to clean this up?! Damn it! And to top it all off, now some of our buildings were on fire.

"Anyway, hurry up and put out those fires! Do what you can to minimize the damage!"

The battle was over. We went about putting out the fires and then regrouped later.

Fortunately, we'd managed to put out all of the fires quickly. After all, the camping plant was a plant, and it didn't burn very well. Even if the camping plant buildings were destroyed, replacing them would be simple. I was thinking about how great the plants were when . . .

"This . . . This weapon is . . ."

The old guy from the weapon shop was at a loss for words. He was looking at one of the weapons that the enemies had been using. It had been broken by the suicide-bomb blast.

"What is it?"

"Umm, never mind. It's nothing."

"You sure?"

He was acting strange. But he wasn't going to talk, so I didn't push the issue.

"Sorry you got caught up in a mess like this on the night you finally came to see the village."

The old guy had put up a good fight of his own a short distance from where we had been. But he deserved an apology more than my gratitude.

"No worries. By the way, kid, you mind if I hold on to this weapon and do some poking around?"

"Huh? Oh, sure. Those weapons had some strange abilities, so it'd be great if you could find anything out."

They had been uncannily effective against us heroes. It'd be great if the old guy could study the weapon and figure out why. I couldn't help but get my hopes up.

"Okay, Sadeena. Will you explain now?"

"I guess I should. We got interrupted when I tried to explain earlier. It doesn't look like I'm going to be able to keep it a secret anymore either."

Sadeena was back in her demi-human form now. She shrugged with resignation and began to explain.

"I was keeping this secret until now, little Raphtalia. But in a certain country, you are the equivalent of what would be royal family in Melromarc."

"Huh?!"

Raphtalia pointed at herself with a look of surprise on her face.

"Is that right? And she's one of Naofumi's party members," Ren mumbled.

"What a surprise. It's a surprise, right? Rishia?" Itsuki asked.

"Yes, it is, Mr. Itsuki."

Everyone around us started whispering among themselves.

"It's nothing to be surprised about," Atla said.

What did she mean? Had she sensed some kind of hint of nobility in Raphtalia or something?

"Raphtalia is an obstacle keeping me from having Mr. Naofumi all to myself. Nothing about that has changed."

Several people shook their heads in disbelief. I did the same.

"You're unshakeable," I said.

Now that I thought about it, Fohl and Atla were related to Trash, and they had blood ties to the former leader of Siltvelt. They were basically royalty too.

"Back to what we were talking about. So what does a miko outfit have to do with any of that?" I asked.

Sadeena had a troubled look on her face. She was staring at Raphtalia, who was still wearing the miko outfit. After several moments, she ran her fingers through her hair and looked over at me.

"Well, those people we just fought mentioned the Heavenly Emperor, right? Think of him as the king."

"Okay, got it."

"Those clothes that you call a miko outfit, in the country Raphtalia's parents were from—Q'ten Lo—that's an outfit that only the Heavenly Empress is allowed to wear."

Oh, so that was it. Ren, Itsuki, Rishia, Atla, Fohl, and pretty much everyone else there all seemed to finally start to understand.

"In other words, even from a lineage perspective, it's only natural that the miko outfit would look so ridiculously good on her. And wearing it would signify that she's the country's ruler," I said.

"That's right."

"And Raphtalia's father didn't want to become king, so he abandoned his royal status, eloped, and came to Melromarc," I continued.

Sadeena kept nodding.

"So the way they see it, Raphtalia is a subordinate of the Shield Hero, also known as the god of the demi-humans and she's off in some remote region wearing their royal garb. Clearly she intends to take the throne. That's a declaration of war. She must be killed. Does that pretty much sum it up?"

"Little Naofumi, you sure are sharp. I'm impressed!"

"It's blatantly obvious! And once the message gets back to the country, they're going to just keep sending assassins after Raphtalia!" I barked.

Come on! Why did I always have to be inundated with such annoying problems?! Just when I'd finally managed to get Ren, Itsuki, and Motoyasu to implement the power-up methods!

Well, Motoyasu was missing, but still . . . I wanted to hurry up and take care of the heroes' curse effects and meet up with the seven star heroes, but then this happens! Give me a break already!

"I figured it wouldn't be a problem as long as we didn't provoke them. I never imagined you would have Raphtalia dress up in that outfit."

Ugh . . . Why did things have to turn out like this? I'd just wanted to enjoy the sight of my cute little daughter dressed up all nice! Damn it!

"Sadeena, I noticed you staring at empty spots around the village every now and then before. That was because you could sense them hiding there, wasn't it?"

"Yeah, it was. They use their own unique concealment techniques that are difficult to detect, even for me."

"How long had they been keeping watch?"

There was a slightly grim look in her eyes when she answered.

"Ever since little Raphtalia's parents left the country."

"Oh, really?"

In other words, that meant that the enemies we'd just fought had watched the village come under attack during the wave. They watched it get destroyed, and they watched Raphtalia's parents die. The stood by and watched as Raphtalia almost died, and they watched her suffer as a slave. All that time, they stood by watching, silently, and never even tried to help.

Basically, they had absolutely no interest in anything other than their royal family issues. They didn't care if Raphtalia was distressed over the loss of her parents. They didn't care if she ended up a slave and got whipped. And they didn't care about any of the countless hardships she'd been through thanks to me.

To hell with the Heavenly Emperor! They sure had a lot of nerve going on about their emperor when they were happy to just completely ignore his blood relatives. The fact that they had been keeping an eye on us this whole time just made me feel sick!

"Muhaha . . . muuuuhahahaha!"

I'd been pushed over the line.

"Mr. . . . Naofumi? Umm . . ."

"They have a lot of nerve. If they want to come invade my place and try to kill Raphtalia, then I'll just have to make them pay. Sadeena, you told me I would need to be prepared to crush a country, right? Well, why not? I'll do just that. I'm going to go to that country and I'm going to crush it with my own two hands!"

"Oh my!"

Why the hell was she looking at me like she was spellbound or something?

"You're really going to?" asked Ren.

I nodded emphatically.

"I am. I absolutely hate trash like that. You understand that, right?"

"Yeah. I guess. If they're going to fire at us, then we'll fire right back. I can't imagine anything good coming from ignoring the issue."

"The only reason any of this happened is because you had Raphtalia wear that miko—hmrgm!"

I glared over at Itsuki and Raphtalia quickly covered his mouth with her hand. Hmph. I had a clear target for my anger for the time being, so I'd let that slide. In return, I expected him to get stronger so that he could help me make those bastards pay.

I looked over at Raphtalia. She was slouching and looked disappointed.

"You against this?" I asked her.

"No. I don't think we have a choice if they're just going to keep coming. It's just . . . I'm sorry."

"Don't be. If this is the obstacle standing in the way of me being able to dress you in that miko outfit, then overcoming it is the only choice. If we can't go around the obstacle, then we'll just smash right through it at full speed!"

That's right. If those bastards were going to attack the village I'd built, then fighting back was my only choice. This was a battle that couldn't be avoided. I wasn't going to sit around, scared, waiting for the enemy to come to us. I'd take the fight to them! No, fight wouldn't do it justice. This was going to be all-out nuclear warfare!

"Now that that's decided, let's get straight to work. Sadeena, tell us the enemy's location."

"Sure thing!"

And so I made up my mind to invade Q'ten Lo, the isolationist country with ties to Raphtalia's birth.

The Rising of the Shield Hero Vol. 12
© Aneko Yusagi 2015
First published by KADOKAWA in 2015 in Japan.
English translation rights arranged by One Peace Books
under the license from KADOKAWA CORPORATION, Japan.

ISBN: 978-1-944937-95-9

Written by Aneko Yusagi
Translated by Nathan Takase
Character Design by Minami Seira
English Edition Published by One Peace Books 2018

Printed in Canada

5 6 7 8 9 10

One Peace Books
43-32 22nd Street STE 204 Long Island City New York 11101
www.onepeacebooks.com